2

THE JOURNEY PRIZE ANTHOLOGY

The Best
Short Fiction from
Canada's Literary Journals

McClelland & Stewart

THE
JOURNEY PRIZE
ANTHOLOGY

The winner of the $10,000 Journey Prize for 1989 was:

Holley Rubinsky (of Toronto, Ont. and Kaslo, B.C.)
for her story "Rapid Transits."

THE
JOURNEY PRIZE
ANTHOLOGY

The Best
Short Fiction from
Canada's Literary Journals

Canadian Cataloguing in Publication Data
Main entry under title:

The Journey prize anthology

SBN 0-7710-4431-3

1. Short stories, Canadian (English).*
2. Canadian fiction (English) – 20th century.*
PS8329.J68 1990 RR C813†.5408 RR C90-094226–6
PR9197.32.J68 1990

Printed and bound in Canada

Design: T.M. Craan

McClelland & Stewart Inc.
The Canadian Publishers
481 University Avenue
Toronto, Ontario M5G 2E9

Dear Reader:

In the spring of 1988, final arrangements were concluded with James A. Michener for his novel, *Journey*, to be published by McCelland & Stewart in Canada. At that time, Mr. Michener made it clear that he did not wish to draw royalties from the Canadian edition. Rather, he wanted these funds to remain in Canada and be used in support of talented writers in the early stages of their careers. This generous donation has gone into the creation of the $10,000 Journey Prize, to be awarded annually to an individual writer.

As a statement of our own support for new writers, and in celebration of the craft of writing itself, McClelland & Stewart makes its own commitment by publishing annually THE JOURNEY PRIZE ANTHOLOGY. We invite editors of literary journals across Canada to participate in the publication of this anthology by submitting to us what they consider to be the best piece or pieces published in their journals in the previous year, by new writers or by writers whose publishing activities have not given them the national profile they deserve.

This year, the more than seventy submissions were read and selected for the anthology – without benefit of author or journal names – by an editorial board headed by the acclaimed novelist and short story writer, Leon Rooke.

The aim of THE JOURNEY PRIZE ANTHOLOGY is to support deserving writers by giving their work the widest possible exposure, and to provide for a national reading audience something of the range and diversity of what is being written across the country and published in Canada's literary journals.

In addition, the authors whose pieces have been selected to appear in these pages are contenders for James A. Michener's $10,000 Journey Prize, which will be awarded for the second time in May 1990. In recognition of the vital editorial role journals play in discovering and promoting new writers, McClelland & Stewart makes its own award of $2,000 to the journal which has submitted the winning piece.

I am pleased that McClelland & Stewart has the opportunity of joining with James A. Michener to further our mutual desire to give support and encouragement to new and talented writers.

Sincerely,

Avie Bennett
Chairman & President

CONTENTS

K.D. MILLER

Sunrise Till Dark

Aunt Ella was fire-marked, from her hairline all the way down. One side of her face was magenta, and one arm and one leg. I was told that it was not fire but birth that had somehow marked her. Yet the magenta skin looked rougher than the rest, and I always imagined that it would be fiery to my touch.

She and her brother, Uncle George, who was two years younger and was not fire-marked, sipped their soup in unison. I watched them: the same slow raising of the spoon to the lips, the same shuddering sip, the same slow lowering of the spoon back into the bowl.

I was told that they were my father's aunt and uncle, but I did not quite believe it. My father, I thought, was too big to have aunts and uncles. He even seemed to agree, calling them plain "Ella" and "George." And they themselves were surely too old to be brother and sister.

They did not act like brother and sister. Uncle George had not, as my brother had done, drawn a skull-and-crossbones with black crayon on white paper and hung it in his bedroom doorway to keep Aunt Ella out. Nor did she ever sneak into his room, wait there until she heard him coming, then duck past him, screeching.

"Are you guys married?" I asked them once when we were visiting. The second the words were out in the air where I could not pull them back in, I knew I had made another mistake. My father laughed too loud, my mother grew red in the face, and my brother began to smile his slow, superior smile.

It was a good day for my brother. He had already caught me taking a second licorice allsort from the covered china dish on the table in the hallway. Aunt Ella always uncovered the dish for us when we came to visit. We were under strict prior instruction from our mother to take just one.

I would study the allsorts, trying to choose. Don't take one of the ordinary little square sandwiches, I would always tell myself. Take one of the wagon-wheels rimmed in coconut, or one of the soft beaded cushions, or one of the white logs covered with licorice bark you can skin off with your teeth. At last, pushed by my mother's "For heaven's sake, just *take* one!" my hand would jump into the dish, and my fingers close on one of the ordinary square sandwiches.

But on this day, I could not get the black-and-white skinnable logs out of my mind. When I thought no one was looking, I sneaked back down the hall. I lifted the china lid and replaced it miraculously without a clink. Then I peeled the little log I had taken, chewed the licorice and popped the white sugar cylinder into the other side of my sweetening mouth.

That was when I heard my brother breathing behind me. I turned around and saw his slow smile already starting. "Are you going to tell?" He turned his back. "Are you going to tell?" He walked slowly toward the kitchen, where the grown-ups were. "Are you going to tell?"

Of course he was going to tell. But in his own time. He would wait until we were all home having supper, just before dessert. Then he would open his lips, just like the people in Sunday School stories, and would speak. And lo, our mother would pause with a bowl of butterscotch pudding in her hand, and would turn on me her wrothful eye.

So it was a good day for my brother. I was still trying to decide which was worse – calling Aunt Ella and Uncle George "you guys" or asking them if they were married – when I saw them looking at me. Their twin pairs of blue eyes were very round and young for the moment they were on me, then quickly hooded, bent back down to their soup.

*   *   *

There was something quietly muttering in a pot on a back burner of Aunt Ella's stove. I stroked each porcelain knob lightly with my finger, waiting for her to tell me not to touch. She did not.

I was being left with Aunt Ella and Uncle George that afternoon while my parents and brother went on some errand for which I was too young, or too small, or too much trouble. "Don't be any trouble," my mother had said. And, without really understanding what trouble was, I had promised not to be it.

Aunt Ella's stove kept fooling me into thinking it might be fun. Big and old as it was, there was something toy-like about all its knobs and gauges. "We haven't any toys here," Aunt Ella said quietly, as if reading my thoughts. She had turned from the kitchen sink she was scrubbing. "Not very exciting, George and me, for a little girl." I pointed to the can of Dutch Cleanser in her hand. "We have that in our kitchen." She looked at it, smiled and said, "Well, yes, I guess just about everybody does." She had a gold tooth on the side.

I came to the sink to watch, standing on tiptoe, mashing my lips against the edge. The white powder turned into a grey paste as Aunt Ella scrubbed the bottom and sides of the sink with a blue cloth. My mother always did this quickly, swiping at it, "lick and a promise," as she said, ending with a short blast of water from the tap. But Aunt Ella loved the stains she was scrubbing out. And she ran the water gently afterward, swishing it in little waves with her cloth, rinsing away every speck of cleanser, then rinsing the cloth itself and hanging it up.

"There. Isn't that lovely?" she said shyly. And it was lovely, the whiteness of it, the gleaming.

"Now I make tea for George. He sits in the sunroom in the afternoon and reads his paper." I did not know about tea. My parents drank instant coffee. Aunt Ella gave me a tea bag to look at while we waited for the kettle to whistle. I liked the soft paperiness of it, the whispery sound it made, and the way its dim contents shifted when I turned it.

I decided that the afternoon in this house was longer than the afternoon in my own, and that the same things happened here in the same order every day. This was a comforting thought. I thought it over and over while the kettle whistled and Aunt Ella poured the boiling water glugging into the teapot.

In my own house, I never knew what was going to happen. My brother went off to cub camp, then came home, then went somewhere else. My parents took apart a room of the house, put it back together in some new and strange way, then started in on another room. There was always somewhere that was swathed in plastic or smelled of sawdust. Every other month, I had to go to a store full of shoes where a man measured my feet. "You're growing *so* fast!" my mother always said, shaking her head, opening her purse.

But nothing changed here. In spite of what the pictures in the hallway said.

"That's George," Aunt Ella told me, pointing a magenta finger at an old brown photograph. We were waiting for the tea to steep. She had explained to me what "steep" was. The photograph she pointed to was of a very feminine baby, beruffled and beribboned.

"That's not Uncle George!" I crowed. "That's you!"

"Oh no it isn't, child. No. Surely you can see that it isn't me." I looked and looked. Then it hit me. The baby's face was unmarked. "I forgot," I said, flushing. She put a hand on my shoulder.

There were so many old pictures of Uncle George, in short pants, long pants, a cap, a straw boater. Pictures that changed in tint from brown-and-beige to black-and-white. "Where are the pictures of you?" I asked. She did not answer. I asked again. A little briskly, she said, "Well, they didn't. My parents didn't, you see. They didn't think it fitting."

I tried to imagine never having to have my picture taken. I decided I wouldn't mind. But perhaps Aunt Ella minded, for she said, almost defiantly, "There is *one* of me." She pointed, this time with the white hand, to a small, cracked photograph in a pewter frame. It was of a young woman in a long-sleeved white dress pulled tight in front and bustled out the back. She had on a white flowered hat that kept her face in shadow.

"George took that one." Aunt Ella said, shy again. "I was twenty. I remember that day. We were all set to go out hunting eggs."

"Easter eggs?" I asked hopefully.

*   *   *

The tiny blown shell was impossibly light in my hand. A breath would roll it off my palm onto the hardwood.

We had brought Uncle George his tea in the sunroom, and Aunt Ella had said, "Lady here to see some eggs, George."

They were kept in labelled shoeboxes, bedded down in cotton batting. Robin's eggs like drops of sky. Speckled eggs – the speckles blurred, as if dabbed onto the still-wet shells with a watercolour brush.

"We'd go off, Ella and me, whenever we could get away together," Uncle George was saying. "We'd take a blanket and pack a picnic lunch – "

"What do you mean, 'we'?" Something girlish and giggly in Aunt Ella's voice made me look up at her. "I'm the one who packed the lunches. You never so much as made a sandwich!"

"Oh?" Uncle George shot back. "And who carried the heavy basket, Miss, and helped you over the fences, and swatted bees away from you?" There was a laugh hidden in his voice too.

"We'd be out sometimes sunrise till dark," he went on more quietly. "Some days the sun would be so hot even the bees would be heavy and slow with it. So we'd leave the blanket spread after lunch and just sleep. Sleep for hours some days. I remember us waking up once when the day had cooled and the dark was just beginning to fall."

They were quiet for a long time. I began to think they had forgotten I was there. I reached and picked up a grey-and-brown speckled egg.

"You like that one?" Uncle George asked. I nodded. "Hen that laid that one," he said (he had already explained that all lady birds were "hens"), "knew a pretty good trick. And we saw her do it, didn't we, Ella."

"We did. I remember."

"She'd hidden her nest pretty well, way back deep in the shadows. But as soon as we got near it, she came right out of hiding and pretended to have a broken wing. Flopped around on the ground to lure us toward herself. And once we were a safe distance from the nest, she took off. Flew straight up and away into the sunshine."

"Who showed her how to do that?" I asked.

"Oh, she just seemed to know, all by herself."

"Perhaps God taught her, George," Aunt Ella prompted gently, cutting her eyes in my direction.

"Well, yes, come to think of it, I guess that's what happened."

I decided that no matter how she had learned it, it was a good thing to know. So much better than knowing how to tell time, which was my current assignment at home.

I yawned. The sun in the room was making me drowsy. Aunt Ella sat down in a chair and pulled me up onto her lap. I leaned back against her breasts, my eyelids heavy. Her hands were clasped in front of me, magenta over white. I reached a finger and touched the magenta skin. It did not shudder or flinch. Then I touched the white skin. There was no difference in temperature.

Suddenly I pulled my finger back. "Am I being trouble?" I asked. Uncle George grinned at his sister. His teeth were as white as his hair, but he hadn't any gold ones. "No," Aunt Ella said. "You're not."

Music was coming in the window – tinkly, one-note-at-a-time bell music. "Carillon," Uncle George said, checking his watch. "We hear it every afternoon. Comes from over there." He pointed out the window to a steeple poking up above the trees.

"Sh-sh-sh-sh-sh!" Aunt Ella had stiffened. I twisted and looked up at her face. Her chin bobbed with each note, and her eyes yearned. Uncle George was leaning forward in his chair now, his good ear cocked to the window. Almost in unison, they said, "Blessed Assurance." Then, in a high, shaky voice, Aunt Ella began to sing the hymn, in time with the picked-out notes. I could feel the singing in her body, and could hear the soft minor note of her digesting lunch.

I fell asleep. Not a deep sleep, for as I was dropping off, I remembered something that puzzled me and kept me floating near the surface. I remembered my father telling my mother that as soon as they were grown up, George and Ella quit going to church. Quit altogether. Never went back.

*   *   *

When the noise of my returning family woke me, it was as if all three of us had been asleep. Aunt Ella kept hold of me, her quickening breath the only sign that she had heard my mother's "Hello? Folks? We're back!"

I had a strange, half-asleep thought – that my parents and brother were a dream from which I had almost awakened. That this was where I really lived.

Aunt Ella still held me. At last Uncle George caught her eye. She unclasped her hands as he began struggling up out of his chair.

I thought suddenly of the eggs, and was afraid for them. Afraid of my mother's quick impatience, my father's big voice, my brother's cool, weighing eyes.

But the eggs were gone. Uncle George must have put them away while I slept. Or perhaps I dreamed them.

*   *   *

"Did you say thank you to Aunt Ella and Uncle George?" my mother asked me as we were going down the porch steps on our way to the car. I was forever forgetting to say these two words that were for some reason so important, forever disappointing her. The time would come, very soon, when I would say an automatic "thank you" to every adult I encountered.

I did not answer my mother. "You *didn't* say thank you, did you?" she sighed. She could always tell every single thing I had done or had not done, just by looking at my face. "All right then, we'll wait for you in the car. March back inside and do it."

But that house was for tiptoeing, not marching. I made no sound as I went down the long hall, hardly glancing at the covered dish of licorice allsorts. I stopped near the entrance to the sunroom, where they both still were. They did not see me.

Aunt Ella was standing behind Uncle George's chair, arms circling his neck, cheek resting on his white head. He took one of her hands in his and kissed the fingers. Then he turned it over and gave the palm a long, slow kiss. She slid the fingers of her other hand inside his shirt collar. Very slowly, in widening circles, she began to caress his neck and shoulder.

I held my breath. Then I began to back soundlessly away from the door to the sunroom. I knew only that I had found something not meant to be found, and that the tiniest noise from me would somehow shatter it. When I was halfway down the hall, I turned and ran the rest of the way on tiptoe.

In the car, my mother looked at my flushed face and said, "What? What is it?"

"Nothing." I ducked my head. Now my brother's eyes were on me too. I could feel my cheeks getting hotter.

My father was about to turn the key and start the car. My mother put a hand on his forearm to stop him. "Now come on," she said. "Something happened in there. Did you break something? Were you any trouble for Aunt Ella and Uncle George?"

"No!" I squeaked miserably.

"Well," my mother said, pulling the button up on her door, "I'm going back in there and ask them." Her hand was on the door handle.

"I *did* do something!" I blurted. My mother turned and looked at me. Her hand was still on the door handle. "All right," she said evenly, "you'd better tell me what."

"I took another licorice allsort!" I wailed. "I took one of the little logs! And I ate it!"

Slowly, my mother raised her hand from the door handle and pressed the button back down. She caught my father's eye, and for a moment the two of them looked like they were trying not to laugh.

Then, as my father started the car and my mother took a deep breath, revving up for the requisite talking-to, I began to feel light. I felt lighter and lighter all the time I watched my mother's mouth move. And soon I was so light that if there had been no top on the car, I would have been flying.

RICK HILLIS

Limbo River

The bus trip took so long we felt like bugs trapped in a jar. It didn't seem like we were getting anywhere. The windows always framed the same rigid wall of mountains, and the same highway unscrolled blackly before us like a river. I slept a lot. My mother awoke me as we passed Frank Slide, the horizon ruined by chunks of rock the size of houses.

"In the middle of the night," she whispered to me, "a mountain collapsed and buried the town that was here. There was only one survivor, a baby girl. Nobody knew anything about her, so they called her Frankie."

I pictured a mountain splintering like a rotten molar. Rain was slanting into my window, making the same tinny sound as it had on the roof of our trailer back in Chilliwack. I pictured saucepans in the aisle catching the *plink plink* of falling rain.

"Nobody knew anything about her," my mother said. "Think about that. Total freedom!"

The first thing we set eyes on when the taxi dropped us off in front of the Alamo Apartments was Marcel. He was sitting on one of three kitchen chairs set out on the lawn.

The chair legs had been pounded into the ground like tent pegs so they wouldn't move, and the grass beneath them sprang up nearly to the seats. Even though it was about seventy-five degrees out, he had on a stained canvas parka with pockets huge enough to hide his beer bottle in.

My mother pretended to survey the area. There was a park across the street with a metal sculpture in it that looked like an axle of an overturned tricycle, the wheel on top poking the sky like a halo. On the far shore of the park was a river that glistened like foil. The heads of some kids bobbed offshore and water-skiers slalomed around them, peeling off strips of brightness.

When it became clear Marcel wasn't going to help her with the two boxes of belongings she was carrying, my mother put them down on the sidewalk and lit a cigarette. She usually hated drinkers, but she chain-smoked.

Marcel said, "I don't blame them kids for playing hookey from school." He was looking out at the river. "School's just another prison."

Mom said flatly, "Kids belong in school."

"Why isn't he then?" Marcel was pointing at me.

"Good Lord, we just got off the bus." My mother looked down at Marcel. "You're one to talk, why aren't you at work anyway? You sick? Is that why you got that big heavy coat on?"

"I'm on welfare. This coat isn't as warm as it looks."

My mother raised her chin as if about to sneeze, then patted down her skirt. "Unfortunately we are on welfare ourselves, but not for long. I think it damages the human spirit."

"It does, but it beats working."

"Work is what makes the world go around!"

"Work is prison," Marcel said. "Give me welfare or give me death."

My mother's lips got hard as two bones. "Is that alcohol you're drinking out here in public?"

She knew darn well it was; she'd served enough beer in her day. But she was fed up, I could see it. This man sitting on a kitchen chair on a lawn drinking beer in the middle of the afternoon was my original Dad all over again. He had my numerous "uncles" written all over him too. My mother had earned an aesthetician's diploma from Beauty School, and wanted to make a fresh start away from these people. Problem was the only type of person who lived in the places we could afford were the Marcels of the world, and until Mom got a job – or until I got old enough to quit school and get one – we were stuck here.

"Is it?" she said again.

"Why do you ask?" Marcel peered into the neck of his beer bottle like it was a microscope. "You want a sip?"

"*Oh!*" Mom staggered inside with her boxes and Marcel said to me, "Who was that masked man?"

"My mother."

"Thank goodness, for a minute there I thought she was mine."

Marcel swore he'd never done anything wrong in his life-time. The reason he wound up in jail in the first place was only for drunk driving.

"When a fist gets twined around your heart," he said, "you drink for to get free. Someday you'll know what I'm talking about. Anyway when I drank, I just drove for to get free faster."

Crimped over street signs, squealed around corners up onto two wheels, got into fender-benders. Got his licence taken away four times in six months.

"Then I went and nosed my car into a creek and couldn't get free of it because of the weight of the water. When the cops winched me out the next morning and made me blow – even though I hadn't had a drink for about ten hours – I *still* buried the needle."

The pen was located out by where the blue vein of river wound through scrub prairie land. During exercise period, Marcel would hook his fingers through the chain-link, look out over the river. It wasn't fair he was in here for just burning tire marks into lawns, et cetera, was it? Gusts of wind blew in off the river, pasted the hair to his head. It blew like guilt through the bones of his body and the guards could tell he was shaking it rough, so they told an old con named Pope to go talk to him.

"Now Pope," Marcel told me a few days after we'd moved into the Alamo, "was a recidivist criminal. B&Es, paperhanger, shanked a guard once . . . he'll die inside, but he's a smart cookie. What he told me was to buck up and be a man.

"I said, 'I didn't do nothing wrong though. I don't even belong here!'

"'You and me both, pal,' he said. 'You been reading my mail.'"

We were sitting on the chairs pounded into the lawn, watching the river. Marcel said he liked to watch it because every day was a different river. The current worked like a knife. Ghostly sandbars rose out of the water, and each night the current would rearrange them, carve them away or sometimes build on long spines of silt. One of my uncles said the same about the ocean once. Every day was brand new, always a new corpse washed up on shore.

"Here's what the Pope really told me," Marcel said, "and I pass it on to you, Sean, for your wisdom bank: 'Deny it if you want to, but society don't like you no more and has kicked you out. That's why you're here. And you might as well roll with the punches because this place is going to chew you up before it spits you back onto the street. Take my advice and look around. These ain't the first walls you've been inside, pal, and if you listen close you'll hear chains every day of your life. Get smart, roll with the flow.' I'll never forget him telling me that."

My mom didn't like me hanging around with Marcel, but what else was there to do? Most of the other tenants were at the bar by the time I got home from school, and we didn't have a TV. For a while I swam in the river with the other kids, but then Mom found out they were Métis and forbade it.

"Why?" I asked.

"Ringworm, rickets, head lice, scabies is why."

So it was me and Marcel. He told me "Limbo is good for the body and what's good for the body is good for the soul." Same went for Smokey sausages, Player's sailor-cut cigarettes, whisky, beer, and wine. He said, "In the old days when limbo was big and competitions were held all across the country, and the prizes were booze, nobody bought liquor when Marcel Gebege was in town." And he limboed for me once. Put a yardstick across the mouths of two forty-ounce whisky bottles and crab-walked under it, spread his feet wide and hopped through on the bolts of his ankles. I was only eight at the time, and could bend like a pipe cleaner, but I couldn't get as low as Marcel. He got snake-belly low.

He told me how a cell is a bowl about the size of an empty head. That's how teeny his thinking got in jail. He said, "In jail I learned time is slow and quiet as a bowl of water. If you look, you can see things."

"For instance, I sense your mom doesn't really like me, does she?" he asked.

"Not really."

"That's okay. Most people don't. Do you like me, Sean?"

"Yes."

"I thought you would. You remind me of myself at your age. A bit of a loner."

The real reason Marcel drank at home was because he was having an affair with the woman who lived across the hall from him, Rhonda Bighead. I already knew plenty about affairs and hanky-panky, so it didn't take long to figure it out. When Rhonda's old man would go to the bar, Marcel would peel his rear end off his kitchen chair and go inside.

"Excuse me, I think I'll repair to my place for a nap."

Rhonda's old man was known as FBI for Fricking Big Indian. He had arm muscles like baloney rolls and all his teeth were punched out from bar fights.

Mom was furious when she learned about Marcel and Rhonda. She was having a lot of trouble finding a job as an aesthetician and was smoking more than ever, which costs money.

"That bitch is using him!" she cried at me one night. Mom had gone down to the laundry room and saw Marcel's phone cord snaking out from under his door, across the hall carpet, disappearing under Rhonda's.

"She's just after him for his phone!" Mom insisted. I think she was jealous for not getting the idea first. Plus Marcel wasn't a bad catch. He was about fifty-five but he looked forty. He seemed quite healthy for drinking all the time.

We didn't have a phone ourselves because we couldn't afford the deposit yet, and this made it hard for Mom to fill out applications for work. Another thing was, we didn't know anybody, and sometimes we felt stranded in a city of silence without a phone. It made Mom's blood boil to think of that slut Rhonda Bighead having a heart to heart with somebody on Marcel's nickel when we didn't have a soul to call up; no phone to call on even if we did.

The river started to drop. In some places it looked more like a highway than a river. Marcel told me when the ice goes off a river, it breaks like somebody standing behind a hill with a hand-gun.

"One of the weirdest times of my life was when I crossed a river with the ice breaking. I was about your age or a little older, leaping floe to floe, ice all around me like dirty chips of glass. I could have gone under at any time, the ice would have closed over me and I would have drowned. But I'm lucky that way. I just keep pulling up aces. What's the worst thing that happened to you so far?"

I had taken money from my mom's purse and had shop-lifted. Or what did he mean? I thought of the time I got pushed out of a big cotton tree – me laying on the ground like an upside-down kite, breath locked inside my chest like my heart was trying to break out, and cotton blowing down the street like snow.

"Too many to pick from, huh?" Marcel said. "Well, let me tell you about the lowest I ever got. You got a minute?"

"Yes."

"Okay, listen and you might learn something. This was 1982 up in Fort Steel where I was working at the time – last job I ever had. Anyway one night I get this phone call. Come to Regina right away. Your daughter's been scalded. She was about two or three years old at the time. She'd be about your age now, I guess. Anyway, her mother'd put her in the tub to sleep and somehow my girl turned on a tap and scalded herself and drowned –"

He looked at me and wiped his mouth.

"– What was I supposed to do? I took all my hard-earned money and went to the airport to fly back for the funeral. But the bitch in the ticket cage says there ain't no seats left. I said, 'Lookit, my daughter just got scalded to death and I need to get back for the funeral *tomorrow!*' 'Don't raise your voice to me,' she said. Anyways, so I go into the little lounge they got there at the airport, and I'm telling the bartender about the fix I'm in when this lady at the bar – real good-looking, too, kind of looked like your mom – says I can have *her* ticket.

"About two minutes later an announcement comes over the loudspeaker: SEATS AVAILABLE ON FLIGHT TO REGINA, SEATS AVAILABLE. So I thank the woman and go get a ticket. Well I'll be damned if when I get on the plane we aren't on the same flight together, me and this woman. So, I buy her a few drinks and when we land in Regina we go to a bar. We're not there half an hour when two cops come in looking for me. It turns out I got a warrant out on me for not paying alimony, so they take me downtown and lock me up. 'My daughter died,' I kept telling them. 'I came all the way from Fort Steel for the funeral!' Next morning I'm up before the judge. Hung over, tongue thick as a steak, I say, 'Your Honour, Sir, I am a few months behind in alimony – true – but I have come for my daughter's funeral and I have money to cover the alimony . . .' The judge looks at me for a minute. Then he says, 'RELEASE THIS MAN. He should NEVER have spent the night in jail. Take him out this instant, and when he hits the front doors: IMMEDIATE RELEASE!'"

"Immediate release," I repeated dumbly. I kept wondering about the baby girl. Did she turn on the taps with her toes, or what?

"That's the kind of guy I am," Marcel said. "Lucky. You never know what's going to happen to you down the road, but if you have faith in the deck you'll pull up aces. That's what I know. Like that woman and me ending up on the same flight or that judge giving those cops hell in front of me . . ."

One night after school, I was in the laundry room fold-
ing shirts when I heard Rhonda Bighead's old man booming through the wall.

"What do you care?" I heard Rhonda yell. "Marcel is
both our friend!"

I pressed my ear against the wall. Furniture slid across
the floor, dishes were shattering. I thought I recognized the
sound of somebody being thrown around the way I'd witnessed mom thrown around and slapped, and the way she
had thrown around and slapped me for doing things that
bugged her. Nobody really wants to hurt anybody, but
sometimes talk doesn't say anything.

There was a scream, then nothing.

I ran upstairs to get my mom, but I knew she wouldn't be
home. I sat for a minute in the apartment, then went downstairs and knocked on Rhonda's door.

"What do you want?" FBI barked through the door.

"This is Sean from upstairs?"

"You better come in here, man."

Rhonda's arm had been opened up with a butcher knife.
Also her back from when she must have tried to get out the
door. I'd seen my mom open the utensils drawer and rattle
her hand around in there to back my uncle off once, but I
doubt she would have used a knife or fork on him. Rhonda
was laying on her side on the floor, her eyes trying to stay
shut like someone woken up who wants to get back to sleep.
I started to back out the door, but Rhonda's old man said,
"Close the door and come in here."

He was sitting on the couch staring off into space.

"Call Yellow Cab." He pointed at Marcel's phone sitting
on the carpet just inside the door.

They were piling into the cab to take Rhonda to the
hospital when two police cruisers closed in in front of the

Alamo Apartments, sirens screaming. The cops cuffed FBI, pushed him by the head into the back seat.

An ambulance blinked up and one of the attendants got out and snapped down the legs on a gurney. "Where's the victim at?"

I looked at Rhonda's old man in the rear of the cruiser, a black shape swimming back and forth across the dark blue cage, slamming his fists into the windows and wire mesh.

One of the cops said, "Which one? The victim of circumstance and history or the one he shanked?"

Rhonda wheeled around. "Don't talk about my baby like that, you *pig*!"

Marcel immersed himself in booze. He drank like a man taking off his clothes and getting into a pool of water. Floating the way a heart floats in a chest. That's how depressed he was.

"I draw the line at raping a woman," he said to me. "I wouldn't stoop low enough to be a skinner, but nothing's worse than not having a honey. Rhonda's cut me off, but I still let her use my phone. What the hell. Know what I mean, Sean?"

"Kind of, I guess."

"Well if you don't, you will soon enough. You know what I just noticed about you?" Marcel said. "You're kind of quiet the way I was when I was a kid."

I never *felt* quiet. I just thought nobody ever listened to me.

"I'll tell you something you probably won't believe, but when I was your age – and this is just between you and me, okay? – I had a club-foot that since has been repaired by surgery. Would you believe I spent every recess of my school life over by the playground fence, looking out at the street so I wouldn't get a soccer ball bounced off my face?"

"Really?"

"Absolutely." He patted his chest with the palms of his hands. "And look at me now. The sky's the limit. You'll see."

A few nights later I was entertaining myself by tightrope-walking the rim of the fence that separated the Alamo from the chrome and glass condominium next door when Mom clicked up the sidewalk in her high-heeled shoes. She brushed off the seat of the kitchen chair next to Marcel and sat down on it.

"You'll be pleased to know, Sean, that I begin work tomorrow at Beauty City."

"Congratulations, Anita," Marcel said. "That calls for a toast." He hoisted his beer bottle into the air.

"Thank you, Mister Gebege." Mom took out a cigarette and Marcel held his lighter under it. "I see you are still supporting the breweries."

"Listen, I drink, but I control it, it don't control me."

"You don't have to explain. I know," Mom said. "I spent too many years working in the bar industry not to. They might start out in control but in the end they live their life in the bottle."

"I drink for to get free," Marcel said.

"I'm teasing you," Mom said, smiling, blowing smoke out of her nostrils.

Somehow at that moment I knew I was in for another uncle. Which meant I would be losing both my mother and only friend in one fell swoop, but at least we'd have a phone to use now. I watched Marcel take a beer from his pocket and Mom fall off the wagon.

"Don't look at me like that, Sean, I'm just celebrating," she said to me. "Can't I do that?"

I looked away, up at the flat purple streak above the river, and underneath it to the Métis kids yelling at each other, slapping around in the water. Then I looked down at the huge denim patches on the knees of my pants and the oversized Sally Ann runners on my feet. That's the sorriest I ever felt for myself in my life.

Every day a different river. The water level kept dropping until the white foam that used to gush and splash over the dam downriver shrunk to a thin trickle like an overflowing sink. The skiers and Métis kids moved upriver where the current still gouged the channel deep. In front of the Alamo Apartments, sandbars started to sprout grass. Between them, tucked like blue stones, were tear-shaped pools.

A couple of days after Mom started making me call Marcel "Uncle Marcel," he presented me with a bike, an expensive BMX. It wasn't new, but it was the best present I ever got. He'd found it in the river and used a solution to clean off the rust.

He said he was crossing the bridge on his way to the Shamrock bar when he caught something glittering in one of the pools. He couldn't believe it was a bicycle, the chrome rims glinting like a pair of eyeglasses.

Maybe somebody stole it and threw it off the bridge when the water was high. Or it happened during winter and had spent months on the ice covered in snow. Maybe even some poor lost soul rode onto the ice and fell through. That kind of thing really happened though you wouldn't believe it would. People just were swept away sometimes by the current. They just disappeared. In winter the Mounties didn't even bother to look until spring when they could drag the river. By then the victims were misshapen balloons hung up in debris, after spending all winter locked in their frozen bodies under the skin of ice.

Anyway, that night after he spotted the bike, on his way home from the bar Marcel went down to the river, stumbled across the sandbars to the pool, through the shallow trickles of water. He stripped off his shirt and shoes, hopped for what felt like an eternity on one foot (ankle hooked in pant cuff), got down to his gochees, and slipped into the pool.

He said he was floating on the surface, looking down at the round lenses of the wheels when he saw something invisible from the bridge – blue shapes darting, flashing in the blackness.

"Fish. Maybe half a dozen of them," he told Mom and me. "Big bottom-feeders – carp or suckers. Maybe even sturgeon – "

I pictured shadowy blade shapes hovering above the bicycle, facing into the current.

"The river's drying up," Mom said as Marcel oiled the chain of my BMX. "The flow between those pools is so shallow now – how are they supposed to get out?"

"They *aren't*," Marcel said. "That's the whole idea. It's just nature's way. It's too late and now they're locked in. You can't even put them out of their misery because it's illegal to fish by the dam."

The Métis kids came up out of the river to ride the bike. They couldn't do it any better than me even though they were older, maybe even eleven or twelve. I guess they never ridden a bike before either. They wobbled up and down the street in front of the Alamo, weaving in and out of traffic until my mom put her foot down.

I was alone when Rhonda's old man came to the door, slapping the fat end of a baseball bat into the palm of his hand. Rhonda wouldn't press charges, so he was on the street, free.

"Where's Marcel, and no bullshit, okay? I got nothing against you, man, but I know your old lady's got a key to his place, and if you don't let me into it I'm going to have to club you." Even though I was only eight, he waved the bat in my face. I doubt he would have done anything to me, but I let him into Marcel's anyway. For a lot of reasons it seemed like the right thing to do.

Marcel wasn't in his apartment so FBI commenced to smash things up. Caved in the aquarium so water gushed onto the carpet, then ground his heels on the little fish who flipped around on the floor. Punched a few holes in the gyprock. Brought the bat down over the top of the TV so the tube exploded in a galaxy of glass across the carpet. He placed a few long-distance calls on the telephone, then hung up and splintered it with the bat. Then he tucked Marcel's toaster oven under his arm and left.

Marcel was sitting on our couch shaking when I got back upstairs.

"Did he at least leave me one beer?"

"He wanted to break your legs."

"I know. Fortunately some queers moved in down the hall and I was over there bouncing them off the walls. It was just dumb luck he didn't find me. You ever throttle a queer before?"

"No."

"Don't worry. Your day will come."

One of the Métis kids drowned in the river. The paper said they were swimming single file out to a sandbar where the water-skiers partied (they would do anything for a chance to ski or even ride in the boat), and one of them went down as if a weight was attached to his ankles.

One of the older boys cut fast strokes to the spot where he went under. He dove and dove, surfacing to fill his lungs, shaking his head. A grainy photo had the spray from his hair making a white flower of froth of the water.

I ran out onto the bridge when I saw the flashing Rescue van. Uniformed men lined the black bridge, heads hooked over the edge. The Mounties launched a small boat, dragged a grappling hook back and forth across the river. The water-skiers spiralled the little sandbar in their boat and a boy not much older than me sat on the prow, stabbing a paddle into the water.

The boy who dove was collapsed on the bar, hands clutching the sand, legs in the water.

The morning after the drowning I went downstairs to go to school and found my BMX missing. I couldn't believe it. I thought I must have left it somewhere else, but I knew I hadn't, and my next thought was those fucking Métis had stolen it. All day in school I steamed. I almost totally forgot about the drowning. How could those ringworm-headed, hookey-playing sonofabitches steal my bike after I let them use it?

I got home to find Uncle Marcel sitting on one of the chairs. By now the grass was so long underneath it, it draped over his lap like a Luau skirt. He was drunk out of his mind.

"I have to show you something," he said, pulling a black vinyl box the size of a pencil case out of the big pocket of his parka. "I bought it for your mom." He snapped open the lid. A heavy gold chain with a locket at the bottom lay on a velvet pad. "Secondhand," Uncle Marcel said, "but it still cost forty bucks." He took the chain out and tried to hand it to me. "Just feel the weight of it."

"You stole my bike," I said. The idea just flashed in my mind. "Didn't you?"

"Hey you hold on!" He put the chain back in his pocket. "I didn't *steal anything*."

I glared at him.

"I didn't steal *anything*. It was my bike," Uncle Marcel said. "I found it and I let you use it and then I took it back. Actually I found the original owner and gave it back to him."

"*Indian giver*," I cried. I couldn't help it. I was wracked with huge gulping sobs. I thought I was going to drown from lack of air.

When Mom came home, she stormed into my room, wearing the chain.

"I told you to keep that damn bike locked!" I smelled booze on her breath. "If you don't look after your things you don't deserve them!"

"*I did lock it!* Marcel stole it!"

"Shut your dirty lying mouth!" my mom screamed at me. "He got that money from a Scratch & Win!"

Though it wasn't mentioned in so many words, I'm sure it was due to the bike episode, to smooth things over, that we went to the fair. I'd never seen a circus, zoo, marine world, or wax museum, much less a fair, and though I hated the idea of being bribed into being nice and civil again, I really wanted to go. Mom and Marcel had bought an old clunker of a car and this was our first trip in it, about a hundred and fifty miles to where the fair was set up in Regina.

As we were pulling away, Rhonda Bighead and her old man were reeling through the park on the way home from the bar. Rhonda's gashes healed nicely and she was holding a bouquet of white flowers her old man had ripped out of a bed in the park. When they got to the red scab of flowers at the base of the buried axle sculpture (supposedly a tree, I learned), he bent like a hero at the waist, tore out a handful and presented them to her.

Rhonda hugged the flowers, roots dripping dirt. She staggered a few steps backwards and fell over. Her old man tried to pick her up, but pitched on top of her, at which point she started swearing and slapping him on the head. Marcel spewed some beer out of his mouth and nostrils, and my mom eyed him.

"I don't mind you drinking, but drinking and driving don't mix, Marcel Gebege!"

Marcel honked the horn as we passed and both Rhonda and her old man turned, cursing us, throwing flowers.

The clunker had a shot transmission, so we had to stop about every thirty miles for Marcel to add fluid. This was synchronized perfectly with his need to stop and water the ditch. We'd been on the road about an hour when the motor started to rattle. Then the car started shaking and the motor really roared under the hood.

Nobody said anything as Marcel slowed to fifteen miles an hour and squeezed over to the shoulder. Vehicles shot past, clots of mud dropping off, exploding against the blacktop, peppering our windshield.

"I should have guessed," Marcel said finally without looking at anyone, "the motor's going to blow. Story of my life. One step forward, two back. On the bright side," he said a few miles and about half an hour later, "we aren't burning much gas at this speed." He tapped the gas gauge which read Full.

The needle bounced back to Empty and then fell off, a red toothpick behind the glass.

Mom groaned. "What next?" she said.

"Who could have predicted something like this would happen?" Marcel said half to himself.

"Me," said Mom. "*I* could have, but you talked me into believing you. When am I going to learn, Sean?"

"Don't worry, Sean," Uncle Marcel said, "we'll get you there even if we have to walk."

"I'm not walking anywhere," Mom muttered.

We pulled into a service station outside a town called Stalwart. It was nearly dusk already. We'd been on the road since lunch. Everywhere looked like the moon to me. That's how far away the fair seemed too.

A German shepherd dog ran out of the garage and dove at the front of the car, whining and jumping back. The grease monkey, a kid of about fifteen, came out wiping his hands on a red rag splotched with grease. He stopped, crossed his arms and shook his head back and forth.

"You got problems," he said. "King! Go lay down." The dog reared up and barked at him, then dropped back out of sight, whining. The kid walked over to the dog and said, "Oh, hell." He pulled a bird we must have hit out of the grill, the feathers of one wing were bent back like teeth on a pink comb. He threw it into some weeds and the dog chased after it, barking.

Marcel was resting his forehead on the steering wheel.

"When you say blow," Mom said to him, "what exactly do you mean?"

I was glad she asked. I had a picture in my mind of the three of us, legless, draped over the open doors, everything on fire.

Marcel lifted his head and looked at her. Then he looked at me in the backseat and grinned like nothing was wrong. "It just quits running," he said. "Nothing to worry about. Hey," he said to the grease monkey who was stretching over the gas hose, "how far do you think we'll make it before she goes?" The dog was playing with the bird, flinging it into the air, catching it.

"You never know with these old beaters." The kid adjusted his brimless cloth cap. "Sometimes they last forever. Sometimes they don't make it off the lot."

We gassed up and clattered back onto the highway. It was already quite dark and the pavement glistened ahead of us like ice on a frozen river. For hours, it seemed, I could see the yellow Ferris wheel lights shining in the sky, and despite everything I got so excited I thought I could smell foot-longs, corn dogs, candy apples, cotton candy, over the burnt stench of the oil and cigarette smoke in the car.

It was a bottom-of-the-barrel fair. Workers all tattooed up like a bad face; rides greasy, probably suffering from metal fatigue. The foot-longs were about the size of your thumb and cost two bucks a throw. But so what? It was a fair! And the night was swept along in a blur of light and colour, odour, sound.

Mom and Marcel riding The Death Trap, a bench chained to a giant arm that whirled around in the air like a propeller. Me, flopping a rubber frog onto a lily pad with a huge tongue depressor, winning a fly in a cube of clear plastic. Marcel limboing under a wooden rod set upon bowling pins – passing through like he was kneeling on air – winning a stuffed snake he gave to Mom. Mom winning a plaster seagull for stumping The Guesser on what exactly she did at Beauty City.

At about midnight Marcel took me onto the Zipper.

It was a mesh cage that spun and orbited around a greasy hub like a planet around a star. There were broken bolts and nuts in the popcorn and cigarette butts scattered around the base, but we didn't care. "We're here for a good time, not a long time," Marcel laughed. And as he said this our cage jerked, lifted us into the night sky and we spun upside-down and Marcel's change flew out of his pockets, whizzed past our ears like shrapnel. My heart tore free of my chest and I felt it in my mouth. We dove towards the ground, but at the last minute were scooped up, swirling through the blackness, me and Marcel, screaming at the stars between our shoes.

ANDRÉ ALEXIS

Despair: Five Stories of Ottawa

1.

There was a man named Martin Bjornson who lived, precisely, at 128 MacLaren. He lived with his mother, whom he knew as Mrs. Bjornson, and a fifty-year-old parakeet named Knut. The parakeet had learned to cough and spit like a tubercular old man, sounding much as Martin's father Frederic had sounded, but it was otherwise unremarkable.

One night, while the Bjornsons were at home playing a game of two-handed whist, Knut coughed, spit up, and then said, quite distinctly it seemed to Martin, "Jesus, Maria, my corns are killing me." These were Knut's first and last words. After pronouncing them, he keeled over on his perch and died. The Bjornsons were as surprised by Knut's unexpected revelation as they were by the sudden death which followed it. It took them quite some time to finish their game of whist (won by Mrs. Bjornson with a flourish of trump). When they had finished, and when he discovered that his mother was not named Maria, Martin said:

– Did you understand what Knut meant, Mother?

– Did Knut speak? asked Mrs. Bjornson.

– Yes, he did, said Martin.

And he resolved to get to the bottom of the matter.

The day after Knut's demise, Martin began to wander about the streets of the city repeating aloud the parakeet's final words – "Jesus, Maria, my corns are killing me" – in the hope that anyone who recognized the phrase might unveil its mystery to him. The results were at first unpromising. After a week of wandering, the only people to speak to him were a panhandler named Morris and a dental assistant named Antoinette Lachapelle. Finally, Martin was heard by a pharmacist named Mario Prater who understood him to be saying "Jeez, Mario, my corns are hurting me." Mr. Prater, suppressing his disdain at such a blunt request for help, answered that adhesive pads were available for any foot. What he said was:

– You know, foot pads could help you there.

Which Martin mistook for a reference to a "Mr. Paz."

– Paz? Martin asked.

– Yes, answered Dr. Prater.

Martin thanked the pharmacist by pressing six or seven quarters into the palm of his hand and mentioning that, given enough notice, he and his mother would be pleased to have him dine with them.

– Smorgasbord! Martin cried as he walked away.

Now, despite the cheerfully given invitation, this encounter was an unhappy one for the pharmacist and proved to be a tragic one for the Bjornsons. It was unhappy for the pharmacist because he felt ambiguous at being seen to take spare change from a passerby. (He let the coins drop into his pocket, straightened his bow tie, and whistled as he walked away.) It was an unlucky exchange for Martin because although his mother did not know any "Paz," she had known a Mr. Prinz. (This particular *Prinz* had seduced her before her marriage to Mr. Bjornson, when she had been a girl in Carleton Place.) And when her son told her that Mr. Paz had had something to do with "Maria's corns,"

she understood him to say that "Mr. Prinz" had had something to do with them. Her heart began to palpitate. She
had trouble breathing, and then she gave up the ghost. (She
had kept her first name from Martin precisely because she
feared he might one day discover her connection to Mr.
Prinz, his biological father.)

Mrs. Bjornson's death left Martin without father, mother,
or family pet. In the face of such loss, it took real determi-
nation to carry on his search for the meaning of Knut's last
words. But, after burying his mother in the clay behind
their home, Martin carried on.

Mr. Paz, the only F. Paz in Ottawa, lived in the West End,
behind the Merivale Shopping Centre. He was a blessed
man, devout and careful. He remembered all of his sins as
thought he had just committed them, and he suffered for
them. So, when he saw Martin coming up his driveway, he
thought he recognized the son of the only woman with
whom he had committed fornication, a sin that was just
then on his mind, and he rushed out to face him.

– I know what you're going to say, said Mr. Paz, and I'm
not completely innocent, but your mother, you know, your
mother wasn't always . . . honest. . . .

– What do you mean? Martin asked.

– She was a good woman, but she was just a little bit of a
liar, said Mr. Paz humbly.

– Make that clear, Martin said.

– I'm afraid she told me she wasn't married when we met,
said Mr. Paz. And she mentioned that she had a parrot that
could recite Leviticus backwards and forwards. . . .

– I didn't even know Knut could speak, Martin said.

– Knut? asked Mr. Paz. Was that the parrot? It couldn't say
a word. She said that to seduce me, don't you know . . .

Martin struck Mr. Paz with his fist and left him lying on
the ground. Mr. Paz lay on the green grass with his arms

out, like a man crucified. Soon Mr. Paz's body rose from the lawn; his body rose. It ascended. It floated above the houses in Merivale. It sailed over the thousands of freshly tarred roofs. It passed by tall buildings and from the ground it appeared to be a cross or a starfish, and then a speck in the sunlight.

Martin returned to his home angry and discouraged. He did not know that Mr. Paz was dead, and that he had been the cause of his death. That night he kept his mother company, sitting by her grave. It was a summer evening and there was a slight, warm wind. The wind reminded Martin of silence, and the silence reminded him of Mrs. Bjornson. And he thought of the mysterious ways by which death enters the world.

2.

At precisely 128 Beausoleil, there lived a Russian translator named Leo Chung. He lived alone in a small apartment on the 11th floor. He had few possessions, and what furniture there was had been passed over by the thieves who regularly entered and stole from the apartments in the building. It was well known that 128 was not a good address.

On a Saturday, Mr. Chung was laundering his shirt and tie in the building's basement laundry. He could hear the noise of people congregating in the meeting room beside him, and when it grew particularly noisy he looked in.

In the meeting room, tenants from all over the building sat in fold-out chairs before a large block of clear ice which stood beside a desk at the far end of the room. The building's superintendent stood up upon the desk. In the ice was the body of a certain Alfred Paradis, Mr. Chung's neighbour on the 11th floor. Mr. Paradis' face was blue as powdered bleach. The superintendent was addressing the crowd.

– . . . once again, he said, I'd like to thank you men for your good work. We'll never know, like Mrs. Korzinski said the other day, why Paradis here stole our things, but by golly we got him . . . as I was saying to myself the other day: here's a man with so much stolen furniture in his place you couldn't get anywhere without climbing . . .

– Are you going to bury him? Mr. Chung asked from his end of the room.

– He doesn't deserve it! someone shouted.

– C'était un monstre, said the widow Paradis.

– He'd be expensive to put under, said the superintendent.

– I'll pay, Mr. Chung said.

There was an anti-Oriental silence.

– Well, said Mrs. Paradis, si c'est lui qui va payer I don't care . . . (Mrs. Paradis thought: he was good to the kids. But, though the kids had climbed happily over the side tables, armchairs, and love-seats to get at the bathroom, she couldn't count the number of times she had almost lost it on the furniture.)

– We bury him then, said the superintendent.
And he rapped on the block of ice with his gavel.

Almost two weeks later, Mr. Chung lay in bed, asleep. He was woken by the sound of dry coughing. When he turned on his night lamp, he found he was almost face to face with Alfred Paradis who sat in the chair beside his bed, and whose face was as baby blue as the last time Mr. Chung had seen it.

– Did I wake you? Mr. Paradis asked.

– Yes, Mr. Chung said.

– No problem, said Mr. Paradis. I just wanted to thank you. Hard to thank a man when he's asleep. . . .

– Of course, said Mr. Chung.

– It was good what you did, getting me a real burial, said Mr. Paradis.

Mr. Paradis scratched himself.

– I'll tell you, said Mr. Paradis. Death doesn't cure psoriasis. I still scratch like a dog.

– Is there anything else? Mr. Chung asked.

– Yes, said Mr. Paradis. I give you three wishes, you know.

– Fine, said Mr. Chung. I'll think about it.

– Take your time, Mr. Paradis said.

Throughout the night, Mr. Paradis did indeed scratch like a dog. It sounded like the shaking of a bag full of leaves, and it kept Mr. Chung on the edge of sleep for hours. In the morning, Mr. Paradis sat at Mr. Chung's kitchen table blinking vigorously.

– You drink coffee? he asked.

– Yes, said Mr. Chung.

– Let me have some. It's not instant is it? said Mr. Paradis. Darned little brown things that melt in water. How do you know that's coffee? Could be cockroach dung for all you know . . . so, do you have any wishes?

– I don't want anything, said Mr. Chung.

– Go on, said Mr. Paradis.

– World peace, said Mr. Chung.

– Make it something do-able, said Mr. Paradis. You must be some kind of intellectual.

– Money, then, Mr. Chung said.

– I can do that, said Mr. Paradis. I can get you money, but large amounts I'll have to steal.

– A raise then, said Mr. Chung.

– Three wishes and you want a raise? If it was me, I would go for good furniture, but a raise I can get you. You got a raise.

– A car, said Mr. Chung.

– Buy it with the raise, said Mr. Paradis.

– There's nothing else, said Mr. Chung.

– A new couch? A dining-room set? Something Moroccan?

– Whatever, said Mr. Chung.

When Mr. Chung returned from work that night, his small apartment was lavishly decorated, filled with French furniture from the reign of one of the later Louis. There was scarcely room in which to manoeuvre. Mr. Paradis sat blinking in a red velvet Louis XVI love-seat.

– Did you steal this? Mr. Chung asked.

– No chance, said Mr. Paradis. And seeing how well set up you are, what do you need me for, eh?

– Yes, said Mr. Chung.

– Good furniture at a good price, said Mr. Paradis. That's what Heaven's about.

Mr. Paradis began to fade away, scratching himself here and there as he went. The sound of dry leaves remained even after he was gone, and the apartment smelled of wet earth, a smell which hung about for days as there were no windows that could be opened.

Later that night, when Mr. Paradis had disappeared for good, Mr. Chung gathered the lace antimacassars that were draped on the furniture and threw them down the garbage chute. Then, two hours before dawn, when he was certain he would not be seen, he cleared out every piece of furniture Mr. Paradis had left behind and put them in front of the apartment building for the garbage collectors. From that moment, he felt reassured that his life would continue in peace until his death. And it did.

3.

In 1987 Mr. André Bennett of 128 Gloucester invented, or rather discovered a solution to world hunger. He bred a plant which passes through the body as food does, but which, when defecated, reverted to its original colour, shape, and consistency and could thus be replanted and harvested time and again. This was, to the majority of Ottawans, an interesting but unpalatable discovery. Very few could see how, without expert promotion, one might get the poor and starving to eat what they had just expelled.

The plant itself was much like a Canadian thistle, with smaller but more profuse spikes and a flower that was bright red against its lime-green stalk. It was lovely to behold, like something from a harsh world, but it had not been tested. It had never been given to human beings, though it had sustained a colony of rats for a year before Mr. Bennett made his discovery public.

As might be expected, Mr. Bennett's discovery attracted the attention of men of ambition throughout the city. And the first to promise him significant gain was Reed Marshall. Mr. Bennett surrendered his fate and the fate of his plant to Mr. Marshall's care forthwith.

Mr. Marshall had political ambition, and his first act was to announce his candidacy for the office of Mayor. His platform was "an end to hunger in the valley." With the help of his brother Frederic, the owner of a local radio station, he quickly disseminated his ideas throughout the city. His first task was to end hunger in Ottawa, and through a radio contest the seven poorest families in town were discovered and given the privilege of being the first to eat what was now called "Bennett's Flower."

Food Day, as it was promoted, was a hot afternoon in July. A spruce rostrum was built in Minto Park, and it was just wide enough to accommodate the ninety members of the city's seven poorest families. Mr. Marshall spoke to the small crowd gathered in the park. He spoke into a microphone set before the rostrum. Several young boys pulled at the black electric wires that lay twisted on the pavement. At the end of his speech, he presented Mr. Bennett to the crowd, and Mr. Bennett pulled the long, lime-green stalks from a plastic bag and handed them to the people on the rostrum. Thus, it was the Andrés, McKenzies, O'Briens, Lafleurs, Chaputs, Laflèches, and St Pierres who discovered that the plant did not grow *after* it had been consumed and defecated but *while* it was being digested. The plants grew in their stomachs, up through their esophagi and out of their mouths. The plants also grew downward into their intestines and out of their anuses.

Besides causing extreme discomfort, the growth of Bennett's Flower was phenomenal. Every hour, the family members had to bite off the tops of the plants as they grew from their mouths, and cut off with secateurs the growth from their nether extremities. This meant they could not sleep, and when they did, as the children did, their agony was doubled. The spikes along the stalk were, of course, a continual discomfort.

There was nothing to be done for any of them.

It was certain proof of Mr. Marshall's talent as a politician, however, that, acting quickly, he turned the disaster and suffering of the poor to his own advantage. He personally saw to it that Mr. Bennett was reprimanded for his shoddy scientific methods. But, he also spearheaded a campaign to ensure that funds be put aside for Bennett to continue his research on the plants, with a view to the discovery of a herbicide which might assuage the humans from whom Bennett's Flower continued to grow.

– This research, he said, will surely be of comfort to the poor.

And, it might have been, were it not that every member of the seven families died of starvation long before any balm was concocted. Still, it was ennobling to see the thin and naked poor, the Andrés, McKenzies, O'Briens, Lafleurs, Chaputs, Laflèches, and St Pierres, snipping or trying to snip the plants from the mouths of their children, as they continued to do until their own last breaths.

4.

Nothing would give up life:
Even the dirt kept breathing a small breath.
> – Theodore Roethke

When the cemetery on Montreal Road was dug up to make room for the dead, there was a general outcry. A committee was formed to ensure that the bones and relics of our ancestors were treated with respect. To their dismay, they discovered that the cemetery was infested by an until then unknown breed of worm. The worms were lily-white, not more than an inch long, and narrow as pins. At their extremities, the worms had minute, bright-red spots. And, when they were touched or exposed to the light, they emitted short, sharp cries. The gravediggers, or Thanatory Engineers as they preferred, could not dig up a spadeful of earth without exhuming thousands of them. They made the wet earth look like contaminated faeces.

Shortly after they were discovered, the committee chairman, a distant relative of a distinguished corpse, Mr. Alan Thomas of 128 Wurtemburg, picked up one of the worms with his wife's tweezers and put it in a glass vial he had brought for the purpose. He took it home to study. He put the vial down on the low, glass-topped table in his family room, and it was here that his five-year-old son Edward discovered it. Edward opened the vial and swallowed the worm. Two weeks later, the boy began to speak with authority on aesthetic matters and to write poetry. He wrote beautiful poetry.

– It's like he swallowed Wallace Stevens, his father said.

– More like Eliot, scholars said, but not so neurotic.

– Still, an expert on child psychology remarked, there is no necessary connection between the worm and the poetry. The child is a prodigy with or without the gravedigger's worm.

To prove him wrong, Mr. Thomas swallowed one of the worms himself. With the same results: after two weeks, he began to write accomplished poetry.

– The father writes like Baudelaire, scholars said, but not so neurotic.

– Worms have nothing to do with it, a psychologist remarked. The father was obviously a poet before this business with the graveyard.

In any case, within months both the father and the son began to acquire renown for their work. (That is, they were published and sometimes admired, but they were generally treated with the contempt professionals reserve for those for whom things come too easily. And then, so few people cared for poetry, and even fewer could distinguish good verse from bad. They were called "The Worms, père et fils.") These were their happy days, and they lasted two full months. The Thomases wrote like demons.

Unfortunately, their bodies were hosts to the annelids. After three months they were infested. There were worms dangling and crying from their noses and ears and eyes and mouths. Whenever they moved worms dropped from them. And, when the pain of being eaten alive became unbearable and they were confined to their beds, the worms infested their bedsheets. The noise the worms made was itself agonizing, like the cries of schoolchildren heard from a distance.

After six months they were both dead. Their corpses were white as marble, but their hands and feet were ash grey. The hair on their bodies was brittle as desiccated pine needles. The nails had fallen from their fingers and toes, and their skin was light as paper. When the pathologist cut into them, millions of worms, exposed to the light, began to cry out.

The bodies of the Thomases were taken and burned.

The worms themselves also died out. They died when exhumed. And, when the reconstruction of the cemetery was completed they were annihilated, or seemed to be, and it was not possible to conduct any further experiments.

5.

On the 11th of January this year, all of the windows in the old firehouse on Sunnyside cracked. It was a cold and unusually dry night; so dry that it was thought the dryness itself had cracked the windows. There were delicate threads of glass, some as long and thin as transparent hairs, scattered over the floor inside the hall. The shards were swept up with hard-bristle brooms, and a dance scheduled for the following night went on as planned.

Martine Beauchamp and her friends attended the dance together, six fourteen-year-old girls accompanied by Madame Florence Gru, Martine's grandmother. The heat inside the firehall had been turned up to compensate for the cracked windows, so the air in the dance hall was as dry as straw in a drought. The girls took up positions against one of the walls. At the opposite end of the room, the young men stood together.

An older man, perhaps twenty years old, with light-blue eyes and extremely white skin, asked Martine to dance. He asked politely, and Martine's grandmother gave her permission.

– Mais oui, said Mme Gru. On voit qu'il est cultivé.
And the two of them danced all night, finding that they had much to talk about.

The man's only indiscretion came when they were about to part for the evening. He put two of his fingers into Martine's mouth and pressed on her tongue. But Mme Gru was willing to believe that this had been accidental, or else a new custom with the well-bred. (Martine was even more surprised than her grandmother, but not unpleasantly. His fingers had been dry as paper, and her tongue had stuck to them lightly.)

The following week there was another dance at the fire-hall. Martine and her friends went eagerly, dragging Mme Gru with them. And this night was identical to the first. When Mr. Highsmith put up his two fingers to touch her, Martine smiled and opened her mouth slightly. He said goodnight after they had danced and laughed for hours.

It was on the way home from the dance, as she and her friends talked of everything but Mr. Highsmith, about whom she was too excited to speak, that Martine realized she had forgotten her gloves. The girls, and Mme Gru, had already reached the bank of the river. The river was not completely frozen. Near its centre a smooth, black strand of water flowed in the ice and snow. The moon was white in the cloudless sky, and it was as she looked down at her hands that Martine saw that she had forgotten her gloves. Asking her friends to take her grandmother home, she walked back to the firehall alone.

As she neared the firehall, Martine saw Mr. Highsmith leave. He walked away from her, toward Bank Street, and at the corner he turned toward the canal. Martine followed him, anxious to say goodnight to him again, but instead of walking along Echo Drive Mr. Highsmith cut across the snow-covered driveway and walked to the back of the monastery.

Behind the monastery there was a large, stone replica of a church, the size of a small cottage. It had been built to keep the bodies of the priests who died. Their remains lay on a bier for two days before burial so that the confrères of the dead could pay their final respects. Mr. Highsmith entered the building directly, and by the time Martine looked in the window to see what he was doing, Mr. Highsmith had already stripped Father Alfred Bertrand's corpse of its shroud and he had begun to eat the priest's body.

Martine put her hand to the window to support herself, and when she did, the window creaked dryly and ice fell around her. Mr. Highsmith looked up, but by then she was already running. The snow on the monastery ground seemed deeper and colder and almost impassable.

In the days that followed, Martine avoided company. She told no one what she had seen. To her mother and her grandmother she seemed to be pining for her young man. They encouraged her to go out, and when, a month later, there was a community dance at the firehall, they insisted she attend.

– Vas y, ma chère, said her mother smiling, et sans chaperon.

– Oui, said Mme Gru, ce monsieur Highsmith est la politesse même.

Her friends teased her and tried to encourage her, but she hid in their midst until they came to the hall.

Mr. Highsmith approached her immediately, and he was so friendly Martine believed he had not seen her or heard her at the monastery. As they walked to the dance floor, he took her missing gloves from his suit pocket.

– You must have been looking for these, he said.

– Yes, thank you, Martine answered.

– The last time we saw each other was some time ago, said Mr. Highsmith.

– Yes, said Martine.

– You followed me to the chapel, Mr. Highsmith said.

– No, Martine answered.

– What was I doing there? said Mr. Highsmith.

– I don't know, Martine answered.

Mr. Highsmith put up his two fingers and forced them into her mouth.

– Very well, he said. When you return home tonight you will find your grandmother dead.

And then they danced. Mr. Highsmith held her so close she could not move, and to the people around them they seemed happy. At the end of the night, when she returned home, Martine found her grandmother dead.

In Martine's bedroom there is a window which looks out on a garden, and beyond the garden there is a curtain of pine trees. As she looked out the window several weeks later, when her grandmother had been buried for some time, she saw Mr. Highsmith come through the trees. He called out to her.

– How is your memory, my dear? Did you see me in the chapel that night?

– No, Martine answered.

– Did you see what I was doing? he asked.

– No, Martine answered.

– Tut, tut, he said. Your mother is dead before sunrise.

She moved away from the window and she began to cry, but in the morning her mother was dead.

Some time after her mother's death, Mr. Highsmith knocked at her front door. Martine, alone, opened the door to him and before she could close it he put a foot on the threshold.

– And how is your mother? he said smiling. I was wondering, my little cunt, did you see me in the chapel that night?

– No.

– Did you see what I was doing?

– No.

– Well, said Mr. Highsmith, time is finite. If you do not tell someone, anyone, what it was you saw that night you will die within a week. But whoever you tell will die.

And he disappeared. And from that moment, Martine began to die slowly, feeling the life pulled out of her as if it were a strand of hair pulled through her fingers. She did not know what to do, but when the pain of dying overcame her, she threw open her bedroom window and shouted out what she had seen. She told everything to the garden.

This is how I heard the story.

A curse on anyone who reads this.

TERRY GRIGGS

Man with the Axe

One spring Hooligan came home with a wooden leg in his mouth. Erie had been listening all that week to thaw, a trickle of melt tickling her inner ear, the sound of water dripping off the eaves *drip* into that handful of bare stones by the corner of the barn, *drop* off the branches of the forsythia out front. Like tears, she thought, cold tears. Then reconsidered, what with the lake opening up and boats arriving from the mainland carrying news and visitors. Tears of joy, or relief. No, that wasn't right either, and she did like to get things right, finding the exact place that words met events. She had literary ambitions, though not openly nurtured. The evidence was buried in her bureau drawer, well hidden below several layers of underwear. The everyday woollies on top, summer cottons below, next a thin layer of silk surprising to the delving hand as a cold current snaking through shallow water. The silks had belonged to Erie's Aunt Elaine, who had lived for a time in France.

In family lore Elaine was the restless one, the one with *ants in her pants*. She twitched and itched, unsettled as a wild bird on a bobbing branch. In pictures she was the disruptive blur, the streak of light cutting through their

46

tight embrace. No one could hold her. *I'm not marrying this rock pile*, she said at eighteen, and left. She wrote home occasionally – short, energetic messages, the words themselves seeming to sprint and tumble like acrobats off the page. Slow suspicious readers, the family had trouble catching even these. They thought her aimlessly adrift, or saw her wantonly snagged in the silken sly arms of foreigners, when what she clearly needed was the honest anchoring touch of an island man. *She'll die young*, predicted Aunt Velma, who had always been jealous of Elaine. But Elaine was too elusive and early death fell like a sudden obliterating snow on Velma instead. Planted like a target by the kitchen sink, a slab of cake in hand and a lump of lard clogging her arteries, damming her heart, what could death do but knock her flat like a disgruntled and abusive husband. So it was Velma who failed to see forty while Elaine's life flowed on, finally pooling in a small package that Erie one day pulled out of the mailbox.

She unwrapped it reverently, thinking it might contain ashes, or Elaine's delicate bird bones. She certainly hadn't expected to find underwear, *lingerie* rather, slippery and spirited as Elaine herself. It practically leapt out of the box splashing up against Erling who had just come in from the barn. He caught at the flying rat's nest of silk, a shock like fine cold skin pouring into his hands, and dropped it, horrified. Only once before had he touched anything like it, Manny Nearing's bare bum in 1909, and that too had been an accident. He shot Erie a look, a sharp fan of annoyance that flared open and trembled ominously for a moment before snapping shut.

Don't goggle your frog eyes at me, she said in a low growl, stooping to retrieve the pearly soft tangle – almost weightless, like gathering vapour into her arms – and he was gone. The screen door slapped shut and he marched across the yard, ducking back into the barn, where Tidy's and Maureen's hefty brown rumps were scarcely distinguishable in the warm gloom.

Erie had to get rid of their aunt's bequest (or remains, how was one to view it) before Erling returned for lunch. Unmentionables, indeed. Apparently some things weren't fit for words. She tried to picture him, bread and beef stew wadded in one cheek, making a joke of it, this sensual assault. Hardly. He'd forcibly forget the incident; in his mind tamp it down like a freshly buried thing. Over the years they had established a common ground for conversation and you wouldn't dare ruck that up with inventive or silly talk. *Would you*, Erie remembers asking herself as she lay Elaine's gift in her bureau, giving it a place among the hidden inventory of the house. A proper cover somehow for her writing, the broken bits of stories, the letters addressed to no one in particular, the shy stuttering beginnings of a novel. Her soul stretched out in longhand and scattered on loose sheets of paper. She wrote secretly at night while Erling slept. *Moonlighting*, she liked to think. Furtive, shadow-sifting work done by lantern or candlelight, even soft slanting moonlight itself. Ghostly sources of illumination that could lead her anywhere while her brother lay snoring and dreamless in the dark back bedroom.

Of course Erie didn't try to fool herself. She understood that Erling was the real writer in the family. Every Sunday after church he composed his weekly column for their local paper, *The Gossip*. Euchre parties, dances, weddings and births, bake sales, visits paid and repaid – he presided over social commerce in the community like a finicky omniscient author. Unlike the correspondent from Silverwater who padded her column with prayers, poems, and gardening tips, Erling crafted a solid substantial block of Blue Lake news, a densely crowded mirror in which anyone could look and see themselves swinging a bat, singing at the Glee Club, or chatting with their cousin Molly at the Come and Go Tea. He didn't have to scrounge for it, either. News came to him steadily like a wind trained to heel. Wasn't the phone always ringing or someone dropping by? People loved to bend his ear, to fill it with those tids and tads that by the end of the week added up to a full-page report. He'd tinker the whole afternoon, working like a kid on the engine of an old car. He wasn't satisfied until it purred like a cat; a contented, well-fed, benign creature. That was how he presented their island life. The same smiling character dressed in slightly different detail from one week to the next. He doctored unpleasant news, delivered it with pastoral care. Erling concentrated on a specific kind of weather that was man-made and unfailingly clement. No wonder he didn't hear the thief in the ice that Erie heard. All that week her ear itched with a telltale trickle of melt like a tap dripping somewhere, and soon a hundred, then water speaking everywhere through rocks and trees and shifting earth. Distracting, listening to winter weep itself away like that. By the time Erling took notice and announced to the world, *Well, folks, spring has sprung,* an unfurling pouncing vernal light had overwhelmed them all. Strangely unexpected, like Hooligan bounding across the yard and skidding to a stop in front of Erie, a wooden leg in his mouth and a sliver of mischief buried deep in his one good eye.

Hooligan was a real presence in any room. Rock-solid and black as pitch. He had a snake of a tail, fat as an arm and powerful. You got your knees and other low-lying objects out of range when he was happy or excited. Of note among his accomplishments: a short ecclesiastical career (he'd once been owned by a priest); progeny stretching from one end of the island to the other; and murder, quarry all harried to death.

His origins were as dark as he was. He might have wandered off one of the reserves, or swum across the channel from the mainland. Who knows. No one could recall Hooligan as a pup. He appeared full grown and half-blind, having left one of his eyes like a surveillance device in some former life.

Some dogs you can ignore. Shut the door in their beseeching faces and they eventually grow restless and move on. Not Hooligan. When he first came sniffing around the farm, he liked the place and decided right then to stay. He sat on their doorstep the better part of three days, affably tenacious as a salesman, until Erie finally relented and let him in. An irreversible invitation, she realized, like letting a child into your house. Though you couldn't really compare Hooligan to any child. He'd ripped up his innocence like a rag long ago. He was full of tricks. He could get his nose up a skirt faster than the practiced hand of a lover. Something about a woman's startled scream gave him the shivers. He enjoyed a good show of emotion, especially in its extreme forms. You could tell he'd been a priest's dog. He would put his paw in your hand, stare encouragingly, coercively – his one eye focused on you like a pistol – and you'd confess anything to him. Erie had. He knew everything she knew about the boy who courted her for two years before marrying the lake.

His name was Jimmy Brooke. Every Saturday night he rode his bike over from Sheg to see her. He was garrulous and generous, spilling like light into the yard. She'd race down the stairs to greet him, a good-looking boy, with a gorgeous head of hair, thick as a tuft of grass. They used to go dancing in town, or on hot nights steal down to the lake for a swim. He stripped easily – he wasn't shy – and she lost time watching him. Male hands and faces were all she'd ever seen before, and even those were often turned against a woman's looking. He was easy in the water. He opened the lake with a high smooth dive. Once in he moved languidly, admiring her on the shore, so transparently eager to be with him she'd be tearing at the buttons of her dress.

For one so talkative, he went without a whisper. By the time she was ready to join him that night he had already disappeared. She stood gripping and wringing her clothing, waiting for the joke to end, for him to break the surface with a laugh. Unbearable, the peacefulness of the lake, a terrible tormenting calm.

To Hooligan, she cursed her slowness. She might have saved him, or followed him. Hooligan was well acquainted with the possibilities, and, with at least mock-sorrow, would place his head in her lap and sigh loudly.

Sure he knew a few things about them, their hoarded secrets fusty and dry as long-dead mice. Small change really, compared to some lives. Erie said as much, what was there to know? After Mother and then Father died, she and Erling had settled down with each other contentedly enough. Working the farm, meals together, small talk, as good as married except for the sex part of it, and she supposed some brothers and sisters worked that one out to their satisfaction as well. Oh, you couldn't write *that* in your local paper, but you could tell a dog like Hooligan who loved to scrabble in the dirt.

Shameless creatures, dogs. Shit-sniffers and disturbers. Behind a show of obedience they follow their own rules, and their own etiquette, which seems to consist of private acts performed in public. Dogs take pleasure in unsettling things, digging up and dragging into sight what would best stay below ground and forgotten. Like Hooligan dropping that leg at Erie's feet, then gazing up at her eagerly, almost ingenuously.

She picked the leg up, and immediately it pricked her imagination. Comfortable in her palm, snug as a rolling pin or a baseball bat, it made her wonder. Relics. Everyone had them, a wristbone in the silverware, a skull hanging on a nail in the shed. People thieved like crows when it came to that sort of thing, skeletons found in caves, it happened on the island. Bones wandered away in hip pockets and purses before the museum folks could get anywhere near them. She appreciated the fascination for something that had survived death, that glowed moon-white, so smooth to touch you felt capable of stroking the unknown right out of it. At least Jim was safe from looting. Or was he? Erie habitually thought of him as he had once been, but a lover of the water now, held and rocked by mothering currents. Though for all she knew, he might have slipped out of his skin and shattered on a reef like a dish hitting a rock. He may have been carried in countless directions, washing up on shore, spangling the island like a broken bone necklace. Even now re-entering her life in some unforseeable way, borne in a bird's beak, a stranger's hand.

A wooden leg wasn't a bone naturally, though it served. Someone must have been attached to it at one time, a husband or a sweetheart. A pirate, God knows. How did a person lose one of these things anyway? Easy enough, Erie supposed. You get involved in a bar-room brawl. Some tough gets his hands on it, then uses it like a pestle to pulverize glass and flesh.

No, rather this: You've been chopping trees, hewing beams all morning for the new house, and you're exhausted. You find some shade and wolf down lunch. The leg chafes a bit so you loosen it. Settling back, you drift into a troubled sleep, then wake with a start. Just in time to see a large black dog vanish into the bush, jaws clamped firmly – teeth like nails – on the hard flesh of a wooden leg, yours.

The moment the phone rang, one long and a short, Erie knew that someone had picked up the scent. It didn't take long in a place as small as Blue Lake for word to get around. Genuine news, not the old stuff Erling dished out, spread infectiously from mind to mind, enjoying a short feverish existence before turning belly-up into history. Erling was simply the one who gave it last rites before burying it in his column.

Nola Wilks' voice buzzed in her ear like a bee in blossom. "You know, Erie, your dog came ripping out of the bush behind our place carrying something, I couldn't tell what exactly, though it looked like oak to me by the grain. I imagine he's been home with it by now, has he?"

"Yes, he's back."

"Well, this might sound kind of funny, but like I said to Bun, that's no hunk of lumber Hooligan's got there . . . looked like a *peg-leg* to me."

"Why, that's exactly what it is, Nola."

"*Go on*, really? Who could it belong to, I wonder. No one from around here, that's for sure. Maybe some sailor off one of the boats. What's it look like, Erie, is there anything on it?"

"You mean, like a sock."

"No, no, marks, scratches, a bear might have, well, you know. Any moss on it, it might've been in the bush a long time."

"Hooligan's had a bit of a chew. Beyond that I'd say this leg's in pretty good shape."

"Hmph, smells fishy to me. Bet there's more to this than meets the eye. It's kind of creepy, if you know what I mean. I'm telling you Erie, a body hardly feels safe anymore."

Erie paused to consider the safety of Nola's body, which was in fact invulnerable, calling up comparisons to heavy machinery, though she took in the suggestion of danger, nonetheless. Two women talking, that's all it took to spark a birth, a genesis, to entice someone out of the shadows. A lurking presence, someone just waiting to try that leg on, take a few tottering steps, then wheel through the door whole as any man.

Trouble was spring made everyone a bit tipsy and unsteady on their feet. Who could walk a straight line with dandelions popping like burning suns out of an earth that was shaking with life? Minds and tongues quickened, hands speeded up and grew expressive, swooping and carving, trying to define and encompass the thing. The thing being, in most cases, the identity of the man with the wooden leg.

Consensus took on a life of its own, metamorphic and unpredictable. One minute he was a cranky and miserly old trapper who lost his life in the bush; the next he was younger, lithe and cunning, a drifter who had been seen about town hanging out with a bad crowd.

He'd been noticed, no doubt about it. In the Ocean House that one leg *tap tapping* on the hardwood floor made William Porter glance up from the guest book. What Bill saw, against a dazzling background of white light flooding through the French doors, was the kind of person he discouraged from staying at his hotel. Not that this man was a tramp or anything, far from it. He was faultlessly groomed, and his clothing an expensive cut, if a bit out of date. No, it was something else about him, that slight scar above his lip, perhaps some immaterial detail, that told Bill he was a gambler. That he would fleece Bill's customers playing acey-deucy and one-eyed jacks, simple games but effective as leeches in sucking rich veins dry. Then one night he'd skip town, leaving nothing behind but a haze of stale smoke.

Sorry, Bill raised his hands helplessly, *no room, we're all booked up*. A lie that drew poison like a poultice. The stranger narrowed his eyes, moved closer, breath cool as fog. Bill froze. Blood rushed from his hands and squeezed his heart. Fear blundered out of him, and the man laughed. Then turned, pivoting on his bad leg, he walked back toward the French doors, but slowly, dissolving in light, *tap tapping* on the hardwood so that the sound of it, the rhythm, stayed with Bill and he remembered. He'd never forget, he said.

Memory served William Porter well, as it served everyone, presenting facts of a shifting and malleable property, fluid enough to pour into any mold. The man with the wooden leg was painstakingly, if playfully, restored.

As far as Erie was concerned, the leg might have been a tossed bone that any flop-eared mutt could gnaw on. It seemed all you had to do was shake the dumb inanimate thing until it sprouted limbs. *She* could conjure a man out of it and do a better job than the good Lord Himself, though that wasn't the point, she realized. The man's true identity didn't really matter; he was selfless and sacrificial. They killed him off repeatedly, speculating on this death or that, then brought him back in a flood of words. Resurrected and sustained him in talk. And how he had multiplied. He was an army, a forest of men by the time Erling got in there and started hacking away, working steadily, methodically, in the end finishing him off with a couple of resounding *whacks*.

He dropped a few well-placed hints here and there, then finally came out with it. He ran a story one week about a man on the west end, a carpenter, who had by some crazy mistake received a whole crate of wooden legs from the States. He'd been using them up as best he could, Erling reported, as railings and table legs, but still had a pile of them in the shed, and *he had noticed a black dog, a brute of a thing*, snooping around his place a while back. . . .

Entirely plausible, Erie thought when she read Erling's

account in the paper. Why had a saner explanation not occurred to anyone? This virgin-pale piece of wood they'd been dreaming on held as much interest as a fence post, a lifeless stump. Erling helped them see this in the sharper, unclotted light his prose provided. Reason had an edge and now they could use it to cut back all that nonsense about a mysterious stranger. How like her brother. Given a chance, he'd kill anything with common sense. As a boy, his plodding devotion to literal truth had made playing games with him almost impossible. Any flight of fancy, *let's pretend we're horses, let's gallop away*, would drive a stiff wedge of disapproval into his face. Erling held himself back like land that never touched water. *That's stupid*, he'd say, or primly, *Don't be childish.*

Well, Hooligan wasn't the one who dropped it in the fire, though he was lying on the hearth rug with his eye cocked open, when Erling did. *A cold night*, Erling muttered, unnerved by what he thought was the dog's amused stare.

Entering the room, Erie was startled to see the leg alive again and vying for their attention once more. Surely it was showing off, shooting blue flames, exhaling plumes of smoke, and belching sparks. She sat down before it, compelled to watch it burn, letting it lure her and draw her in.

When Erling at last went up to bed, Erie found a stray sheet of paper in his desk, and in the splashing wavering firelight, with Hooligan half-asleep at her feet, she began to write. She had no idea what at first. She let her mind drift, phrases rising in waves. Then she saw something, someone, just the tip of a bobbing head, features uncertain. Her words, she knew, would have to be quick and strong as hands to grab that lilting silken hair and lift him out.

MARGARET DYMENT

Sacred Trust

This journey began twenty-five years ago, when I stood in a church in Avebury, Wiltshire, surrounded by concentric circles of stones. Avebury is near Stonehenge, but is a village, a place where real people live. Like Stonehenge, it is surrounded by a prehistoric bank and ditch and, in the fields round about and on what we assume are ancient sight lines leading in, are standing stones, some weighing forty tons. Through a prodigious effort we can only partly imagine, these stones were cut and dressed elsewhere and dragged on frozen ground to this place, where they were erected in a circle a third of a mile across. In Saskatchewan and Alberta the cirlces and sight lines are made with cairns and rows of loose prairie stone: people call them medicine wheels. In Avebury I stood stock-still in a wheel within wheels. In early Christian times a little Saxon church was built, square and rough. Its floor then was covered with rushes. People stood or sat on that floor when they gathered to recognize mystery, and to worship it in whatever way they understood. One imagines their heads full of barbaric monsters and heroes, overlaid with the new hero, Christ. Later generations added a Norman slit window to the church; the Tudors, I think, added pews, the Victorians the carved pulpit and choir. These details and more are tersely outlined on an unpretentious typed sheet kept for visitors to read on a table just inside the door. The British are comfortable with their long past. I am not: daughter of the new world, accustomed as I am to clean air and a clean slate, an expectation of future with virtually no hold on the past: in Avebury abruptly mystery rooted me. I saw the long long lines of men and women pulled from their warm beds on a Sunday morning and brought one step after another to the door of this church and then into its shell, caring for it, changing the rushes, carving the wood, adding whole sections, attempting over and over again to give shape to what cannot be expressed, but which far back before anything was written drew other men and women to move stones, strain, grunt, sometimes burst in pulling them erect, to plant them deep in that circle in the fields.

The museum at Avebury has a pair of scissors, notable for being one of the earliest scissors extant in Great Britain. They were in the pocket of a barber who was crushed by one of the stones, at a time when local farming people, fearing the pagan powers of these giants on their land, used to dig a pit at the foot of one, fill the pit with fire, and then upset the stone, where it would crack in the heat and could be broken and dispersed as small, safe rocks along fence lines and in foundations of local barns. This barber was perhaps inspecting the pit, or even lending a hand to help dig, when the loosened menhir fell. It must have seemed an awful reaching-out of vengeance from dead gods, at the time.

Avebury changed me. I found I desired to seek out the sacred spaces of the earth. Slowly I created for myself the position I now hold, halfway between Anthropology and the Department of Religion, in a small university of long tradition and little repute, in a Maritime province of Canada. Mine has not been a brilliant career; neither has it gone unnoticed. I have done what I intended to do: to visit sacred spots, and report.

I have climbed the pyramids, which are the same age as some of the medicine wheels of the west. I have been lucky enough to enter the Ajanta caves in India and to walk and take measurements in Java, at the nine stupa of Barabudur. Last summer I tramped through Irish countryside to visit Cairn L and Cairn U, and the Mound of the Hostages at Tara. Yet also last summer, later on, I visited Israel, ignoring politics and following the Way of the Cross through Jerusalem's noisy streets. After that I stood in the place where Mohammed ascended into the heavens and received his vision of life after death.

In a word, I have collected these places. I bring back my coloured slides, my careful measurements and, in academic journals, my brief, dry accounts. Every few years, illustrated by the photographs, written for the general public, a book comes out. A coffee-table book, full of speculative theory untrammelled by proof, a Christmas gift for dabblers in the mysterious and the occult. The books hold my position for me at this university, and they prevent me from ever going anywhere else. I am that uncomfortable populist, that suspect theoretician, Harriet Dixon Ross.

Next week, I am on my way to collect one more place, a medicine wheel I haven't yet seen, Moose Mountain, southeastern Saskatchewan.

Suddenly I don't care.

One plus one plus one has not equalled Avebury, and has not equalled Avebury Plus. I expected something else – what was it? To come closer, perhaps, to the mystery's heart. On the academic level, to find patterns – but patterns I have found: my books attest to that. My classes are well-attended. Every day I turn down invitations on the lecture circuit. The patterns I sought, perhaps, were ones that would be so convincing, so compelling, would so speak to the archetypal templates of the human psyche that people would know it was true, and as a consequence live more happily, or at least more certainly, from that time on.

Did I want to be a preacher, then, for heaven's sake: a TV evangelist – was this my secret plan? To say to the world: Behold the moon, behold the three stars, Aldebaran, Rigel, Sirius, behold the carven spirals on the entrance stone at Newgrange, Ireland – and to have my listeners fall at my feet? Not my feet, actually, but the feet of Truth. I think I wanted to help make Truth irresistible.

If so, I was wrong.

Even to myself, truth is entirely too resistible. The more of these places I see, the more alternative explanations I invent. Definitely we have proved and we are proving again that early peoples were much more sophisticated astronomically than used to be believed. And certainly if we in the present times connect wind-swept hilltops and sunlit caves with the presence of the ineffable, no doubt so did they.

I, I, though, am going missing. I have lost my focus, or never had one. I do not know why I am taking this trip to collect one more once-sacred place.

And I hate the idea, I find to my chagrin, that I have set myself up for ridicule. At my age it should make no difference. But age is part of the problem. I am over fifty. Some people I respect begin to pity my life: "Poor old Harriet: she could have done so much more. But she went off half-cocked on the semi-occult. Never even focused on, say, one developmental period. If she'd stuck to the Stone Age, perhaps – but she didn't; what a mishmash she has made of it. Not anthropology. Not history of religion. She must have had something in mind when she started, but it looks as if she never thought it all out. She has a good mind, but unfortunately she has let it go. She can still pull out sensational connections for the untrained minds of undergraduates, but academically let's face it: her work is just plain fuzzy."

I wince: I hear Bernard's voice, saying those words. Bernard is the head of anthropology in this university. If I want a more exciting post somewhere else, he is the person who must recommend me. Instead he is hinting early retirement, the golden handshake. He would like to divert my salary to two or three of the sweet young things crowding the carrels in Graduate Studies.

"And she surrounds herself with bright young men."

The young men come without my invitation. I am glad to have their work but I do not set out to draw them in. One of them, Jonathan Wollner, will come with me on this trip. He is my choice for the usual reasons: I need help, there's money left from my grant for the Holy Land, he's keen. I can see he adores me as well, but not to the loss of his good sense. He has invited his wife to accompany us, at their own expense. I am vaguely aware that part of his reasoning is to share this wonderful treasure, me, with her. This neither warms me nor offends me. It is an error which belongs to the young. With it goes enthusiasm, which I do like, and which does warm me, particularly at this time in my life. Jonathan will get over his idolization of me, and meanwhile, partly because he wants to please me, he is turning in good work.

The one person I made a point of recruiting for this trip was Eileen Simmons, a first-year graduate student who joined us last fall. She was in one of my classes as an undergraduate, and it is obvious that she is still deeply unhappy since the collapse of her marriage last year. She still turns in her work, as prompt and thoughtful as ever, but several times when I have come upon her unexpectedly, her eyes have been filled with tears. She spends no time with the other students, does most of her work at home on her own. I like Eileen. I think this trip might do her good. So I have insisted I need her to take my notes. I would be glad to be there when the sparkle comes back into her eyes and her body begins to move again as it used to, in confidence and an openness to her sexual power. I remember Eileen as a delight when I first knew her, and scarcely recognize what she has become, this dull-eyed, dull-haired mouse.

So.

Those are the outlines of this part of the strange journey my life has become. We fly to Regina next Tuesday: right-handman Jonathan, his wife Kathryn (an unknown entity so far to me), reorder Eileen, and me. We will rent a van to take us all to the town of Kisbey. I have a letter of reassurance and introduction from Bernard in case it is needed in obtaining permission from the native people in the area for us to visit the wheel. But there should be no problem: our intentions are benign. We will take photographs, measure distances, camp nearby, and be on hand for several days at the rising and setting of the moon and the rising and setting of the sun. We will line up cairns and see if it is true that these hunters and gatherers who did not need to plant took the trouble to determine the longest day of the year. There are many circles of stones on the prairies: some are also burial mounds, although why and the exact connections with their astronomical uses need much more work.

We will make notes. It will fall to Eileen to collate.

I guess what I want to ask is: so what? Why do this? Another set of measurements: another set of slides. Another breathless expectancy (nothing, it seems, can

spoil this) while we wait in darkness for the first rays of
moon or of sun. And then we will go home. Jonathan will
have a story to tell. I will change my lectures to include
whatever it is we have found – becoming predictable now,
although such a short time ago it was all wildly new. There
will be some unexpected findings, some puzzle or pattern
that has so far proven elusive and now begins to promise
results. I am still interested.

But for myself, although literally we will be on the move,
increasingly I have the sense of standing still.

*   *   *

Kate – are you awake?

Kathryn stirs against his shoulder.

Definitely – no way I'd be asleep on a plane. I was practising deep breathing.

You were very convincing.

Kathryn's lips twitch in a sardonic smile. She leans past
him, her blonde hair parting at the nape of her neck and
falling smoothly across her cheeks. Jonathan catches his
breath, runs a finger up the back of her neck. Kathryn
turns slowly to give him an arch glance.

Yes? What? There is something to see?

Oh. Yes. There. I wish you had taken the window seat.

Love, the view from the window means much more to
you. It would have been wasted on me. I've been quite
happy here, lost in my P.D. James novel and in controlling
my inner fears.

He covers her hand with his as he points to the grid
pattern below.

Thought you'd like to know about Chief Piapot.

She slides her hand free, swings her hair back from her
face.

Pee-a-pot?

Well, I don't know how it's pronounced.

I thought they pee-aed behind bushes?

They may have done, but Piapot also pitched his teepee in the way of the CPR tracks, trying to stop the train.

Right down there?

Further along, actually. It says here it was Saskatchewan's first sit-in. Hey – 1882 – Kate, that's not very long ago at all. My Grandpop was born in 1896.

My sense of time gets all confused out here, doesn't yours? We go through a time warp when we come out to the prairies from the east coast. Think what they went through, though, your grandparents, coming to no history from England.

No history except the native peoples who had been here all along!

Right. So these native people we're supposed to meet to get permission to explore the medicine wheel: their grandparents, maybe even their parents, were living the original nomadic life, weren't they? Are you sure they aren't going to mind if we look at their wheel? I'd be touchy if it were me. Why should they believe we won't take away arrowheads and stuff?

Maybe we will.

Jonathan – you wouldn't, would you? They'll be letting us in on trust.

We certainly will not take apart the cairns – it's really sad the way even some of the wheels that have been discovered just in the past fifteen years have already disappeared. People don't realize what it is they've got on their land. They just see that it's in the way of the tractor. But as for picking up the odd arrowhead or dart-head: we'll see. That hill is probably rich: there's a point where one more doesn't tell us anything new. We may be able to bring home a souvenir.

Kathryn shrinks into her seat.

It seems to me it's a matter of trust.

Hey, Kate – I'm the guy who went with Martin to the sweat lodge. . . .

I know: you were purified. Then why set out to steal from the Indians – you're going to tell me about their different ideas about property. The earth is the Lord's, I mean Manitou's – we only borrow it.

Yeah – something like that. We don't realize how much our heads have been affected by our training in a material-ist, capitalist society.

And some of your best friends are Indians.

Kate, that's shitty.

She glances about her, meets the eyes of Eileen across the aisle. Eileen smiles politely, drops her gaze.

Kathryn leans back against the seat, practising deep breathing again. A quarrel 35,000 feet up. Just what she needs to take her mind off her fears. She thinks, as she breathes, how to approach this with Jonathan, what it is she really meant to say. Then remembers that the breathing won't work when she's still stewing over whatever has upset her. For a few minutes she tries to empty her mind of all the pros and cons. In. Out. In. Out. At the corner of her eye she sees clouds piled like solid mashed potatoes in the blue air. Jonathan follows her glance and for a few minutes the two of them are like children, entranced by the clouds as the 747 hurtles through the sky.

*   *   *

Eileen's notes: Harriet is asleep, I think. She seems to be looking out the window but her eyes fluttered a while, then closed, and her head is drooping. I'll risk taking a few notes here, writing small and disguising it inside my copy of *In*

Flight, the airplane magazine. Decided at home to make two sets of notes, inner and outer. Harriet talks as if these are the same: "To the Amerindians all was sacred and nothing was sacred." But not to us, that's the thing. We make these distinctions: Harriet calls it "fragmentation." Some people would call it other names: "progress," "civilization."

The official notes I am to take for this trip are not, as far as I have been informed, to include either poems or prayers. And maybe this journal won't either. But I can try to record what is happening to me, and I can guess at what is happening to the others.

The lines on Harriet's face now: the light from the sky outside etches the fan of soft lines starting at the corner of her eye, and the corners of her mouth turn down when she is asleep, in bitterness or sadness that is impossible to see when she is awake and sparkling as she does, full of a kind of electricity, making connections, jumping to conclusions, ready or not, and pulling everyone who comes across her path, even the office personnel, into her excitement. At such times she seems as young as her students, but right now you can see that time has passed.

She looks, of course, much like a child, curled away from me in an airplane seat, which for most of us is cramped but for her leaves lots of room. It is always the first thing you notice about Harriet, her tininess. Later it becomes the last thing: you remember instead her vivacity, that excitement. I remember the day she heard she had the grant to go to India: the whole department got caught up in her plans. You forget that her feet don't touch the floor when she sits in a normal chair. You see instead a sort of giant with flashing eyes who can and will scour the world for what she wants to find: India, Antarctica, Lebanon, Israel, Ireland, Colorado, Montana, the Caspian Sea!

I don't know why I agreed to come. Something about Harriet moves me, maybe her size, as if she needs taking care of, although obviously she does not. More likely I want to get a little closer to whatever it is that drives her on. If she is finding something, then I want it too. This is not a good moment in my life. (Self-pity wells up so easily, even when I write that one line. Steady on, here. What I mean to say is:) This trip right now in this plane is a lot like the rest of my life. That is, I'm moving very fast, pretty high up, and I don't know where the fuck I'm going. (And it may turn out to be someplace very small.) The ground has disappeared from under my feet: I'm winging it. Well, to continue the metaphor (this is cheering me up!), both the airplane and I are made of strong stuff and probably won't crash. We both have a definite destination or two before us, the city of Regina for the plane, back to my thesis for me. It's the larger journey that has become problematical.

"Eileen," said my mother, intending comfort, "look at it this way. At least you got out of a bad marriage before it was complicated by kids."

Wrong, mother. Wrong and wrong. It was not a bad marriage but it was very complicated, and the complicating – and terminating – factor was kids.

Why do I still say, even here, where I am trying to write the truth, that it was not a bad marriage? For me it was bad, bad times. I have been jerked around, I have been treated by my beloved as if I were a piece of slime which he had to pick off his person. When all my sin was that I loved him and wanted to bear our child. I am the normal one, not him, with his visions of saving the world. It is incredible to me that for so long I believed it was all my fault, that somehow I had harmed him, had tempted him from his noble path. Early and late I loved Daniel because he was a guy who gave a damn, about the world, about everything he saw. He fought all the way to keep from becoming one more person who could switch it all off. I remember the excitement with which he came to me with what he felt was the key: helping people to empower themselves. I watched him learn patience as if overnight, my impatient man, to listen and to be still: I thought we would raise our children to learn these things and in some way we would make up for the baby we had given away.

Then I found out that I myself had not been treated with respect. My idea of empowerment is not his. I thought you give the other person your power, and they they don't use it, that is what it is all about: in the light of that free decision we grow together into trust. Anybody, I thought, understands that. But Daniel operates on some other system. I found out he has made it permanent: he has found the work he has to do and he and I will never have another child.

I am still wracked as I remember this, as I let it into my gut.

Why, then, do I still think of him?

Those two across the aisle are having a fight. I saw it just now in her – Kathryn's – eyes. What do they have to fight about – they look so beautiful together. And I like Jonathan. It's easy to see he's one of the satellites around Harriet, but he's not the only one to go through that. He has a similar kind of electricity to Harriet anyway. I know the other female students pay attention when Jonathan walks through – and he's a nice guy, he bothers to get to know us, treats us right – which is more than you can say for some of the others finishing their Ph.D.s: on the make, pompous nerds, expecting to be kowtowed to as if they're full professors when they're still sweating over their footnotes same as us.

So there are tensions in that marriage. What else is new.

At the beginning of this trip, then, I set down these inner notes: something tense between Jonathan and his wife, something sad or bitter about Harriet, something hollow about me.

*   *   *

Harriet: We begin the descent to Regina: I wake with a start. My ears hurt. A baby has begun to wail. I was having an anxiety dream about the rented van: in the dream it became a red bus. The rental people assured me that there are bound to be vans available for a midweek trip and that the best thing to do is to wait until we arrive, but now that seems like madness. We really do need a van: I ought to have made certain we had one. In my bag is a list of what we need to buy before we start out, which will have to be tomorrow by the time we pull everything together. Already it's past noon, even allowing for the hours we have gained.

With guilt I remember Alana Podessky, my colleague in the Anthropology Department in Regina. I probably ought to have told her we were coming. But we parted last time on such bad terms: I just want to quickly pass through! I see Eileen stowing away her notebook: I wonder what she decided to write down so early in the trip. Across the aisle, Jonathan's wife is looking white-lipped as we descend. Jonathan is holding her hand. He catches my eye and grins, welcoming me back awake. Hello, Jonathan. Pay attention to your wife. But he is now, I see, being quite solicitous. I don't know about that young woman yet. Jon shows her off as if she were this precious, fragile creature, and she seems to play up to that, but my sense is there's more to her. She teaches Grade 7 and 8: that's not a quiet, easy job: that's the horrible in-between age when the hormones come in. I must ask her about her class.

The plane is making a turn coming down to the runway now: I catch a glimpse past the wing and my neighbour's head of a grid of residential streets, and then the rush of terminal outbuildings, and, now, here we are on the ground. I would have liked to have caught the pattern of the runways from the air. I am interested in the patterns modern men – they *are* mostly men – find useful: it's fun to compare them with ancient ideas of intersections and highways: sometimes there is a stimulating link. But on this trip I never did get an overview – and I need one, I definitely do!

We're taxiing straight over to the terminal. Good. I guess I could ask Jon to pick up our gear while I go see about this blessed van.

Eileen turns to me, smiling. "Welcome back, Harriet."

"I've been back a while. What were you writing – letters?"

It would have been very easy for her to agree. Instead Eileen hesitates and says – "No, I was taking notes."

"Well, that's what you're here for! Keep it up! But what is there to take down so soon? The make of the plane? The map of our flight?"

And then she tells me, this brown-eyed young woman I am choosing to fuss over a bit; tells me what she has decided to do – the inner journey and the outer one. I know what you will say, says Eileen.

"You do? What will I say?"

"About the sacred and the profane being a modern error: that everything is sacred and one set of notes will suffice."

"I think – it will be an interesting thing for us to talk about while we're waiting for the dawn on that hill."

As we scrabble for bags and jackets and find our way into the aisle, I am caught in a surge of happiness. Because *that* surprised me: *that* I did not expect.

Jonathan's wife looks pink-cheeked again, now she has both feet on terra firma. She walks beside me as we go up the long ramp. She confesses this was her first flight. I am a little astonished, then remember that both she and Jonathan grew up in the same town as our university, and do not need to have travelled very far. I am still feeling lifted on a moment of hope and unpredictability when I see Alana Podessky waving vigorously to us from across the mezzanine. We are being met.

There are times when there is no one else I know who can make the speeches this woman Alana makes, arrange the grant money, beat the bushes for the right grad students, find a place on a program for a bizarre idea whose time has almost come. At other times, and most recently, she has been a pain in the ass. In fairness, I expect it must be hard to maintain that rather wonderful Romanian flair here in the midst of the Canadian prairies but Alana tries. I see now she has also put on a few pounds. At fifty or so, the fiery Alana is taking on the unmistakable élan of a hefty Jewish mama. Her grey hair stands out in little curls all over her head. Before I know it, I am enveloped in a bosomy hug.

"Welcome to Regina, Harriet!"

We step back from each other, both aware, I think, that this was not quite an academic hello. But I've never come to Regina before, and I suppose she is pleased. Or else she is pleased with herself that she caught me out.

"Yesterday I phoned Bernard about something else and he told me you were coming and which flight you were all on. So Lance and I decided to come down and meet you."

I become aware of a young boy, maybe thirteen years, who has been hanging back. Dark-skinned, sloe-eyed. Alana introduces us. Lance Starblanket.

"He and I have a favour to ask. But what are you people going to do first? You're not leaving for Moose Mountain today? Let's find your luggage."

Chattering, laughing, Alana takes us in tow. I decide that, after all, it is much nicer to be met than not to be met. I arrange as I had planned for the others to pluck our gear off the carousel. Kathryn seems to have taken a shine to Lance, and he stays with them as they wait for the luggage. Alana and I go off to the vehicle-rental booths. She could and would pull a few strings for me if necessary and I begin to relax. In fact there is no problem: they will deliver a van to the airport from downtown within half an hour. Just time for us all to get a cup of coffee, if the luggage has arrived, and find out what it is Alana wants. I am a little nervous about that. But I seem to be trusting her: probably it will be all right.

*   *   *

Eileen's notes: The first night. I am alone in a motel room on the edge of Regina. Jonathan and Kathryn are somewhere else in this same place. Harriet accepted the invitation of a colleague to stay in her spare room. This colleague has a protégé, a boy named Lance Starblanket, who is to accompany us and be of some help to us, in return for a visit to see his folks. He is a Plains Cree whose family lives near the Moose Mountain medicine wheel. But those are exterior notes. What I want to say here is the inner journey, as much as I can. I told Harriet today on the plane what I am doing and she seemed pleased where I expected her to be annoyed. Now I feel inhibited, worried she is going to demand to see these scribblings, afraid that will keep me from writing what seems to be truth. I have to decide just to go ahead, edit them or something later on –

As I go back over this day of travel by air and then by van and of busy buying and arranging for tomorrow, four moments rise to the surface: I feel as if they were all moments of meeting in some sense or another.

The first was Harriet's response to my admitting to her about these notes. She looked into my face for a moment and seemed to really see me. How seldom people do that ordinarily – and how little of it there has been lately in my life.

The second was that unexpected meeting with Dr. Podessky. I think Harriet was caught off-guard by that hug. Maybe it wouldn't have happened at all if she weren't so small, so easy for even a short woman like Dr. Podessky to reach!

The third was the very special way both Jonathan and Kathryn took to young Lance. The boy was shy initially but in no time at all he was happily telling them about the band he plays in in Regina: he's interested in music and it seems that's why he's come to the city to finish Grade 8 and why Dr. Podessky has taken him under her wing, although he lives with an uncle. He has been learning native drumming from the uncle – the uncle has been "sharing" it, he says – but also is going through the usual teenage phase of forming a band. They call theirs Better Red Than Dead, and according to Dr. Podessky it takes a lot of nerve to make a point about being a native here in Regina. I liked the way Jonathan talked to him, mainly about music (it turns out that Jonathan knows a lot about modern music: something I didn't know). But it was Kathryn who got him talking about his loneliness away from his family – it seems he's the eldest, at thirteen, of seven or eight kids – she had him admitting that Dr. Podessky seems "old," and that around her he minds his p's and q's. You could see, though, that the fact that she lets him practise his drums in her basement was pretty special.

I don't know what to say about that conversation between Kathryn and young Lance. There was love in it, I want to say. But they had just met.

This is what I see: when you're travelling, you are in a heightened state of mind. You leave behind the familiar and you act out an exploration into the unknown. So this makes for different possibilities – emotionally one feels somewhat skinned without the usual excuses and support systems. That must be why strangers in the seat beside you so often relate the story of their life.

Harriet informed us this evening, as she drove us over here in the van, that young Lance's father is in jail, I don't know for how long or what for. This makes more poignant a moment this afternoon when Jonathan and Lance and I were in a stationery store buying notepads and extra pens and coloured pencils. (The others were a block away, stocking up on groceries.) Lance is a small, serious-looking kid, with glasses. He was supposed to be helping us carry things, but wasn't in fact much help. He kept wandering off, eyeing pencils, erasers, loose-leaf binders and things, and I remembered how much I enjoyed stationery stores when I was a kid – still do. After a while we found out what it was he coveted. He wanted the long boxes some of the coloured pencils came in.

"Do you think you could buy these, and could I have the boxes?"

"It costs more. What do you want the boxes for?"

"I can make neat whistles out of them to give to the kids at home."

I saw Jonathan capitulate instantly. "Sure, son," he said.

"I'm not your son, actually," said Lance: I wasn't certain whether he was explaining or protesting. Up till then he'd been extremely polite.

Jonathan could have said the wrong thing, I expect, right then, but he was very relaxed in his reply.

"Hey, I wasn't taking you over, Lance, don't worry; it's just an expression where I come from. I hope I do have a son some day, though. A person can always use another drummer, not to mention someone to fetch and carry. Here." He grinned and thrust the paper bag of supplies into Lance's arms.

I was smiling. "I could use that kind of son too," I said.

Suddenly Lance dropped his super-polite stance and became a normal inquisitive nuisance kid.

"Don't you have any boys?" he asked me.

No, I said, or girls either.

"You don't have a husband?"

"Not at the moment."

He thought a moment.

"You did have?"

"Yes."

"Where is he now?"

I was becoming embarrassed: we were in a crowded store and people could overhear. I glanced at Jonathan and caught him looking amused: I think he was interested in my answers and didn't want to stop the kid if I could handle it.

I said that my ex-husband lived in the same city that I do but that I don't see him anymore.

"Why don't you?"

I'd had enough and decided to be evasive and then if necessary tell him to lay off. He's busy, I said.

"What does he do?"

I hesitated. He helps out people like you, was the irresponsible answer that came to mind. But before I said anything, Jon spoke:

"He thinks of Eileen."

Lance glanced at me as if to see if this were right, but Jonathan thrust an arm across his shoulders and steered him away. "You guys out here ever heard of a group called the Dead Candies?"

Lance had: clearly Jonathan was "in." Before we left the store, we checked farther into Lance's plans for gifts for next day, and then brought him back over to the crayons and colouring books and coloured notepads. We decided Harriet's grant can extend to a few gifts for the current residents and possible descendants of the land once inhabited by the people who built the wheel. It began to seem more real to us that we were going to meet Lance's mother and his brothers and sisters. It seems there are six younger Starblankets, which is almost impossible. As Lance tells it, his family implements the band's decisions about visitors to the wheel. For a while the band had lost control of it, but recently, with land claims, it is back where it belongs. Alana's idea in adding this boy to our trip is becoming easier to understand.

Now I could write some emotion if I dare touch a bit more of the truth. Son. It scares me to use the word, even inside my head, in case somehow I pull you off-centre, distort your straight growing wherever you are. Or let out my hurt. I allow myself this for you: the cool light of my love like a great white balloon, no strings attached. Son – I must box this back in. I can see Daniel's seventeen-year-old face, white, tense, sitting across the table from me as I filled in the form and we both signed our names. It isn't as if he forced me: we both thought at the time it was the right thing to do.

Not for Harriet, this, but interesting for me: after so many years it is all still so strong. And brought back so fast by the questions of one small boy.

*   *   *

"It sure is flat."

"But look at the sky. It's true it seems so high."

"So clear."

"Wait till you see a prairie sunset!"

"That takes care of all the clichés."

They laughed.

"No – you forgot the one about mountains on the prairies being low hills anywhere else. 'Moose Mountain' is really just a low ridge."

"But we're not going to Moose Mountain, are we?"

"Well, to the edge. What we do is we go to the town of Kisbey and ask directions."

"No, you don't have to," said Lance. "Ask me. I'll get you there."

Harriet glanced into the rearview mirror and caught Lance's excitement as he bounced in his seat a little, gazing at the road ahead.

"How long have you been away?"

"I was home for Christmas."

"Quite a long while: you'll notice some changes."

"I expect so," replied Lance politely, and Harriet smiled to herself. There was a pause, and then he offered suddenly: "You'll know we're getting close when you really do start to see some hills."

"Okay, Lance, but we're not used to the west: you might have to tell us when what we're looking at really is a hill."

Miles rolled by. Eileen had bought a guidebook in Regina, and was regaling them with facts. Kathryn and Lance had their heads together over the roadmap.

"These towns were all named after railway men!" reported Eileen. "Sedley, Osage, Creelman – oh here – Kisbey was named after a mailman. What a relief!"

"Where are the Indian names?" murmured Kathryn.

"Kenosee?" offered Harriet. "I saw a sign for Lake Kenosee. Is that Cree, Lance?"

The boy sounded doubtful: "It sounds a bit like 'waiting' but a bit like 'fish' – not really like anything at all."

Jonathan hooted. "Is there a tourist bureau in Lake Kenosee? Seems like they could do something with 'wait and fish!'"

"It's one or the other," said Lance, again seeming to explain carefully. "So they couldn't use both. Maybe it's neither one."

They were on flat prairie, mile upon mile of wheat. Their eyes had become accustomed to subtle change in shades of brown and green. Now they could all see that the land was becoming more rolling. Lance was enjoying the navigating. As they came closer to his home, he stopped looking at the map and directed Harriet onto grid roads, which Kathryn stopped trying to find on the map. Harriet found she trusted the boy's directions, and she liked the feeling of rocking across the prairies as if they knew where they were going. She was glad she had insisted on driving. Even the cushion she was sitting on, which brought her high enough to see out comfortably, she had thought of in advance and brought along in her bag. All the items on her list had been duly checked off: pup tents, sleeping bags, transits, tripods, tape, cameras, Coleman stove, gas, food, plates, cups, cutlery. . . . At this moment the journey had its own momentum. Harriet was content with roadmaps, place-names, and the constellation of young people gathered in the van.

Lance directed her onto a gravel road, buffalo grass growing in at the sides. Harriet drew to a stop.

"What's this?"

"It's the road to my house."

"No, Lance – I mean the thing on the road."

On either side of the road the land was fenced. The boy explained quickly to these easterners that the bars laid in across the road over a dug ditch let traffic through but kept cattle in.

"We had them when I grew up, too, in P.E.I.," announced Eileen, unexpectedly. "The cows won't go across because they're scared. But it's safe to drive over, or it should be."

"It's safe, Lance?" asked Harriet as she started the car moving again.

"Sure it's safe."

"I could get you a drum, Lance, maybe," they heard Jonathan say suddenly. In the mirror, Harriet saw Kathryn look at her husband with a frown. She looks like she did on the plane, Harriet thought.

"I have a drum, thanks. Dr. Podessky helped me get a set of drums. You saw them, Jon."

"I guess I meant a native drum. Don't you need something special for that stuff?"

"I'd have to ask my uncle. Usually one of our people makes the drum."

"Yeah, I suppose so. It was just an idea." He paused. "I took part last summer in a sweat lodge ceremony – " he began.

Kathryn cut in awkwardly. "Does your mother know you're coming, Lance?"

*   *   *

Kathryn is holding on to the edge of the back seat of the van with her hands. Dust blows in at the windows: everyone else exclaims and rolls them up. Kathryn is in the middle, balancing: there is no seat belt for her space. She has been trying not to meet Harriet's eyes in the rearview mirror, and to cope with feelings of frustration and anger that are running out of control. What is the matter with me, she wonders, unhappily: I just want out. Beside her, Jonathan is growing more and more excited, pointing at things outside and peppering Lance with inane questions: at least, Kathryn thinks, to me they seem inane; nobody else seems worried. She realizes she might be overreacting and does a swift calculation: yes, her period is nearly due; yes, she does have tampons in her luggage. Okay, the world is not so black as it seems but, dammit, premenstrual insights are true, too, and important to hang on to when the flow of Pollyanna-cheerful hormones clicks in three days from now, and masks what she is seeing clearly right now.

What she sees is a group of self-indulgent middle-class whites, herself included, blithely driving themselves (as they have money and transportation and the ability to do this) to a place where this child beside her, with all his emotional and practical ties to the place, has not been able to get to in six months. She resents the academic confidence Harriet displays, as if she knows what they are going to do. She feels increasingly uncomfortable and put out with her young husband, who seems to her in his exuberance and boyish bumptiousness to be putting on a kind of show, for Lance, for Harriet, certainly for herself and maybe even for Eileen, and to be missing, maybe, the whole point. Which is? she asks herself, and feels irritation again. How should I know: just that we are going for a visit, it can't be understood and planned for in advance because this isn't our place: it is the boy's place, and the place of the people who placed those fieldstones in peculiar formations on the hill she does now see rising slowly near her. But she, Kathryn, would rather be in her classroom: she shouldn't have come. It was Jonathan's idea, this trip – he had been so sure she would love these people he works with, she had seen that it meant a lot to him and she did have the possibility of a week off. So she had yielded to his excitement: now she thinks it was a mistake. In her mind's eye she sees the face of her favourite and most difficult student, bent, flushed, over the basic algebra that keeps defeating him, trying to make sense of it under the hostile gaze of the supply teacher. Last time his response to a supply landed him with the vice principal in charge of discipline. And that young girl, new to the class so late in term, still making her way through the inevitable testing kids do to each other, having to face it this week without the tacit support of her teacher. There was marking unfinished, plans for next week only partly done, committee work missed – Jonathan couldn't understand why she wasn't happy just to leave it all behind.

Lance is explaining about the "Texas gate." What Kathryn hears is a metaphor for her own life: you can't see the fences but you feel that they're there: Am I afraid to step outside, she wonders, for fear it might hurt? Look at Eileen: I see the hurt on her face, in the way she hunches her shoulders, the way she walks and talks and holds her notes close to her body. Jonathan, when I am in a better mood, still stirs me. There are times when I love to be with him. What am I missing, then, what is it seems so dead wrong, like a missed turning, about my whole life and this particular trip?

Lance, who has been holding the roadmap in front of him, folds it and puts it between them.

"There's my place," he says. Harriet stops the van.

Kathryn sees a house that reminds her of the pavilion at Long Lake where she used to go as a teenager to dance on a summer night. In summer all the windows were open to the weather and the lake, and she and her boyfriends danced on the board floor to music from a jukebox left over from the fifties. In winter the glass windows were on and the doors locked, the store closed down, and the building looked a lot like this, like Lance's home.

Lance leaps out and runs to the door. In another moment, children emerge from everywhere, some from where they have been playing under the steps, and Lance's mother appears.

At least, she must be Lance's mother. She doesn't look any older than me, thinks Kathryn. The woman is thin, long hair pulled back, but bright-eyed, full of smiles, laughing a lot with surprise and possibly embarrassment.

"Do come in. It's so nice to see Lance. I had a message he might be coming out, but I wasn't sure. You'll have to excuse the mess. Are you all from Regina?"

"No, no Mum: they're from the east! They want to measure the medicine wheel and stay up there overnight! They've brought tents and food and survey stuff: do you think it's going to be okay?"

The woman hesitates. "You couldn't build a camp fire up there," she begins, and laughs a bit. "We found out we had to make that a rule when the people first started coming out here a few years ago. They were moving the stones around to make a fire. But you know about that, don't you? You won't move nothing?"

Harriet takes over, explaining, reassuring, bringing out Bernard's letter and spreading it out. Kathryn notices again how Harriet's small stature helps her to seem more trustable. Behaviour that in a tall woman would seem dominating and controlling, in Harriet looks almost cute. I expect it's a nuisance in other cases, thinks Kathryn, striving to be fair. But finds she still feels upset with the older woman: "I bet she knows how to use cuteness too."

Suddenly Kathryn knows she genuinely does not want to go on with this: she does not want to identify herself with these people going up to measure and quantify what is clearly to the native people a very special place. She looks at Lance's mother, and watches her smiling and trying to stay polite, undone dishes in the sink, a baby in her arms. Kathryn gets up and takes the tray of cups of tea Lance's mother has prepared, and hands it around. Ever stronger in the room is the smell of some toddler in need of a change. From a place she doesn't know she has, Kathryn suddenly finds words.

"Listen, I'm not really part of this expedition. I know I'd really be putting you out, Mrs. Starblanket, but I wonder if I could stay down here in return for some helping out? I've got my own sleeping bag – and lots of experience with kids!" She feels rather than sees Jonathan's start of dismay.

"She's a teacher!" says Lance, and Kathryn is afraid that might make it harder for the woman to agree. So she speaks again, fast, not thinking it out.

"Are you staying here, Lance? You're not going up on the hill?" From the brightness that flares in his face she sees that she is right: he was waiting to be asked.

"You stay for supper, Lance," says his mother firmly. "I'm not letting you go again that soon! It's walking from now on anyway: you folks will have to park your van. He could go up later on if you want him to – but won't he be in the way?" She smiles at Kathryn, "Sure you can stay with me if you want to, and you don't need to help out none neither. I'll be glad for somebody to talk to."

Kathryn doesn't dare turn her head for fear the look on Jonathan's face will make her change her mind. She knows he will be bitterly disappointed.

But inside herself, a little bird begins to sing. This is what I wanted to do, it says. With it comes a spurt of hope: maybe after all Jon understands: he did do that sweat lodge thing and. . . . But as the groups quickly separate, pulling out bedrolls and gear from the van, and she goes to him for a quick kiss goodbye, his face is bleak. He thrusts her sleep-ing bag at her and turns away.

"Good riddance," she says defiantly under her breath, as the two anthropologists and their note-taker trudge off up the long low slope. She picks up Lance's five-year-old sister and whirls her around, twirling among the foxtails and buttercups and brown-eyed Susans outside of the glass-walled house. The girl squeals with delight.

"More!" she cries. "More!"

*   *   *

"We don't realize how high we've come because the slope was so gradual," remarked Eileen. "Look how far we can see!"

They stood catching their breaths after the long climb, between two of the spokes of the great wheel.

"Of course, you don't have to be very high on the prairies to be able to see for miles," answered Harriet dryly.

Still, it was impressive. Jonathan gazed into the distance, smiled at Eileen's moment of excitement. Uncharacteristi-cally he said nothing.

Drat that woman, thought Harriet. It was so obvious how much he has been looking forward to sharing this.

They set to work. For the first few hours they were busy. Then, basic measurements made and their tripods set up, the three of them sat together on the grass, drinking cups of hot soup and looking out over their bit of the world.

"I'm so glad I came!" exclaimed Eileen. "I thought these things would be like archaeological sites, which I think would be boring places unless you know where to look. I didn't expect this" – she waved her hand at the lines of fieldstone laid out in neat spokes from where they sat – "and definitely not this!" She gestured at the central cairn. "It must be twenty feet across! And almost as tall as me!"

"Taller than me," said Harriet, looking wry.

"Why didn't you tell me it was this big?"

Jonathan laughed. "We didn't mean to keep it from you. I guess we thought you knew. They say it weighs sixty-four tons."

"Wow! And was put here –"

"John Eddy from Colorado figured out this wheel worked as an astronomical instrument from 150 B.C. to 300 A.D., isn't that right, Harriet? Some of the stars they used then are other places now, so it's hard to figure out. Maybe they used it earlier too. The Majorville wheel in Alberta seems to be at least a thousand years older than this one, and that's lot of time to account for. It's possible people used them for different things at different times. That cairn over there seems to be lined up with where a star named Capella was at the time of Christ. They think the Majorville wheel is as old as the building of the pyramids. This baby is old, too, but probably not that old."

"It's so fragile," said Eileen. "So easy to destroy. Just stones in the grass. But people have respected them, and left them in place, through all this time." She cupped her palm over one of the stones, and smiled. "It's warm."

For a while they sat in silence, the wind lifting their hair. Then Harriet got up. The student and the note-taker followed her instructions as they finished preparations for a long, wakeful night.

*   *   *

Moonrise came and went. Harriet was right: no amount of cynicism or academic frigidity could spoil that moment when the moon rose and they marked its place halfway between two of the spokes in a line with the central cairn.

They took it in turns to nap as they waited for dawn. By 4 A.M. all were again awake. Eileen spent time with Harriet at her outpost, taking notes using the pen-light Harriet had provided, then walked across the wheel to where Jon crouched at his transit, sighting at stars.

*   *   *

Harriet: I see patterns here, in this moment on top of the world. I see this wheel, the stones glimmering white under the moon, the cairn like a sleeping woman at the centre, a goddess lying close to the earth. I see that house where Kathryn snagged and left us, its windows looking out round about, like a minor turret guarding the sacred place. Lance's mother said that local folk hold this hill in respect. You would think young people would drive up from the village on the other side, and use that access as a lovers' lane. In fact, I rather like the idea. The woman said they don't: she volunteered this information, looking guarded. It was obvious she didn't expect us to understand. People come here just as we did, to sit at the top and find out how far they can see. It seems to me that the taking of measurements, far from being a desecration, is almost a religious rite. It is exactly what the ancients intended for this place. And now in the middle of a June night under an enormous prairie sky I see very far: the stars wheel in the sky; we have measured tonight one cycle of the moon and at dawn we will see the rising of the solstitial sun. The ancients understood this hill to be rooted in the planet, and tonight I feel those roots tugging at me, holding me to this place.

Am I too discovering a cycle I didn't know about before, dark into light, light into dark? Alana wants me to return, return and stay. She has an opening for a full professor, tenure, graduate students, no golden handshake for some time to come. A chance to publish in a different way. What would it be like here in this flat part of the world, so newly inhabited by people like us, prehistoric artifacts still around to be discovered, arrowheads, spear points, atlatl weights, dinosaur bones? What would it be like to live in the tension of the square grid of Regina's new streets and the circling swirl that is the ambience of my friend Alana? The Bernards and Jonathans of our lives will still be there, but we could, I think, now work together here. Alana is sometimes like a force of nature, but I could navigate those storms. Why believe in this now when all these years of living have told me how impossible it is? Yet I did begin to believe the moment I saw her waiting for me. As if I had lived my life so far in order to see Alana Podessky standing there in the Regina terminal with her grey curls tousled, and that hug. But what an odd place this is on the face of the earth, to come home.

*   *   *

Eileen's notes: Harriet says she'll be fine by herself for a while, a nice way of saying she wants to be alone. I have moved away from her, physically and, I feel, psychologically. But I don't want to go back to Jonathan just yet. Something happened over there on my last visit, something I need to think about some more. Probably he does too. I have sat down halfway between them, between the woman who brought me to this place and the man who unexpectedly has moved and confused me on the night of all nights when I would like to be clear and to know my own mind.

Jonathan is responsible for the sighting between the large cairn, one small cairn and the brightest of the pre-dawn stars. He explained to me this afternoon than the stars have moved since this wheel was built, and at least one is now hidden in the light of the sun. However, he has had his transit lined up for hours, and has been using his binoculars to look at other stars. I asked him if he could see anything through the transit in the pitch dark, and he said yes, the glimmer of starlight did make a shape. I bent my head to take a look, and as he reached to adjust the thing I found his hand instead in my hair and I was being kissed for the first time since I left Daniel. What I felt were two things: absolute trust: I hardly know him, but my body warmed (how fast it warmed) without the least problem about what was going on, about who he is or I am or where was Kathryn, his wife. That was the first thing. The second is a lot harder, and it is not new, but it is as solid to me right now as this stone is under my hand, and I do not know what to do. I knew this was the wrong man. I knew the right man is Daniel. I am crying as I write this, because I think it is stupid and wrong for me to go back. What could we build across this bitter abyss? I am still so angry, I still feel so profoundly puzzled and betrayed, so bruised, as it were in my sex. I don't think it is possible to let that much hurt just go.

I stand beside this cairn, built so long ago by the hands of people I have difficulty picturing at all. It stands beside me like a companion. It really is on the highest point of land. Jonathan told me this afternoon about his experience in the Mohawk sweat lodge, and about vision quests: how a high point of land was used as a place to seek one's identity, in oneself and in relation to the tribe. We whites tend to look overhead for our metaphors of meaning, he said, but native people looked more to the ground under their feet. Jonathan said some people believe now as well that there are lines of force under the earth, magnetic or other mysteries that influence the course of our events, and are much closer to us than the stars. I can see the hills a little now: I couldn't before. Surely the sky is beginning to grow bright. We will soon be at dawn. I try to imagine the people of so long ago, coming up here as we have come, carrying stones from the fields; later, carrying confidence and knowledge and power as they found they had succeeded in predicting the moment when summer beings.

Something is moving out there: I seem to see what I have been imagining, dark shapes coming up the hill.

*   *   *

Someone touched her hand. Eileen jumped hard.

"Lance!"

"Hey, Eileen, I didn't mean to scare you!"

It was obvious from the mischief in his voice that he had, and was delighted with himself that she hadn't heard him creep to her side.

She sent him to talk with Harriet. "Don't scare her now! The sun is going to come up any minute and she has to pay attention!" Eileen made her way to where Jonathan stood tensely at his post. In spite of her better judgement, she laid her palms on his shoulders and began to massage his upper back.

"That feels good," he said. "Were you talking to someone? Did Lance come up the way he said he might?"

"Yes, and he nearly scared me out of my wits. I've sent him to watch the sunrise with Harriet. Jon, Kathryn is coming up the hill, with Lance's mother and all the children. They're bringing breakfast: a feast, Lance says. It's supposed to be a surprise. Kathryn learned last night how to make bannock, and they have saskatoon berry jam."

"So Kate isn't going to miss the sunrise after all!" She heard the cheerful lilt in his voice, and for a moment felt alone. She stopped massaging his shoulders and stepped away.

"Eileen, something happened last night."

She found herself smiling. "Something nice. And so is this, this is a nice moment, your wife coming back up that hill and bringing all those little Amerindians with her. She's awfully good with kids, Jon."

"Is she? Maybe you're right. I thought she hated kids. She doesn't want to start our family, keeps putting it off. But now I think of it, she's so damned involved with those students of hers that she doesn't – "

He stopped.

"Doesn't have time for you, is that what you were going to say?"

"Yes. But if she's so good with kids, why doesn't she want to have one of her own?"

Eileen kept her voice steady. There are zillions of possible reasons, she thought, and only one Daniel. Kathryn's reason was probably standing right here in front of her. Neutrally she drawled, "Yeah, think again, Jonathan." You big sap.

The sun arrived, a ball of fire seeming to zoom into the sky, blazing across the cairns into their eyes, right where it was supposed to be. Frenziedly Jonathan and Harriet took sightings, shot film, called out numbers to Eileen. As light blazed in the sky, the children rushed up the last part of the hill, shouting their delight. Behind them came the two women, Kathryn with a bulging knapsack, Lance's mother carrying a basket and a cloth bag. Jonathan stretched his tape one more time, to the edge of a shadow, called a last measurement to Eileen, and went to meet his wife. She was glowing with exertion and excitement. He was reminded of the way she had looked when he had danced with her first in the pavilion at Long Lake. Impulsively, Jonathan dug into his jeans pocket.

"Here, I had an idea I'd give you this when we got home," he grinned, "but I just figured out you were right. You wouldn't appreciate it." He brought out an exquisitely chiselled, small white arrowhead, and laid it in her hand. About them, the children, with whoops of glee, were finding others everywhere and bringing them to show to their mother.

"Now – you kids leave those up here," they heard her saying.

"Thanks, Jon," said Kathryn. "As a matter of fact, since you did give it to me here, I appreciate it very much." She smiled: the sun shone gold in her hair. "The kids say that in spring this whole mountain is purple with crocuses. They call them prairie tulips, they're so tall. It must be beautiful here, the whole hillside moving with purple flowers."

"We'll come back," Jonathan said with conviction. "We'll come back with our kid."

Kathryn looked at him. "That will give you a chance to bring back that other stolen stuff you have in your other pants pocket."

Jonathan looked sheepish, but made no move to take anything else out.

Kathryn glanced about her, then went over to the central cairn and carefully, in an almost ceremonial gesture, laid her gift at its base.

"Hurry up!" Eileen was calling. "Harriet says we can't start without you two. Sit down here, make up the circle. We're into ritual here; Harriet says we're on sacred land."

"Well, as much as anywhere," smiled Harriet, looking about at their faces and the long distances behind and before them, new this day as every day since before these hills were made, and bright under the morning sun.

JENNIFER MITTON

Let Them Say

When her husband stopped speaking to her, Fadimatu worried and could not sleep. She knew the women at school were wondering what was wrong.

"You are giving a tired appearance," said Mrs. Okosun. "I hope you are not anaemic." Mrs. Okosun's sister had recently haemorrhaged after delivery.

"You are not looking fresh," Comfort said. She was a strange-looking girl; her skin was black, but her eyes were clear, pale green.

"It is not a question of fresh," said Mrs. Okosun, who liked to say that Comfort had obtained her green eyes from a curse. "In Calabar you will find those that sold their own to the slavers," Mrs. Okosun said. "They must be cursed with slaver's eyes." Depending on their moods, the women ignored Comfort and said bad things about her to her Christian Religious Knowledge students. "Let those women say," Fadimatu told Comfort. "They are only prac-tising tribalism. I myself think your eyes are as jewels." She pitied Comfort, who was age twenty-six, and unmarried, and had those green, green eyes.

After morning assembly, when the teachers passed around the dustcloth and were exchanging news, Fadimatu leaned back against the cool chalky wall. Monitors shuffled in and out of the staff room to collect their teacher's lesson notes; students knelt to explain their tardiness and receive their lashes, and sometimes, in the middle of all this, Fadimatu fell asleep with the blue curtains blowing gently past her face.

More than a month passed and her husband did not resume speaking to her, and Fadimatu cried often, and brought a toilet roll to school. She talked with the women, of her pregnancy and their pregnancies, but she was afraid to tell them her problem: Ibrahim was a private man. "I tell no one the details of my personal life," he said. "No one." And now he told her nothing at all.

His friends and relations brought her messages. One evening a boy came to her in the kitchen area of Ibrahim's compound.

"Ibrahim, he says, *No dey* you name his new baby 'Mwa-kapwa,' if a girl and 'Ahakapwa,' if a boy," said the messenger. "He says, 'Why are you thanking this Bachama god?'"

Fadimatu ran out to Ibrahim, who was with a friend under the tree taking food.

"Can't I thank the god of my ancestors if I am given a new baby? I will thank Pware and Allah and Jesus Christ." But Ibrahim turned and began to talk to his friend as if Fadimatu were not kneeling at the edge of the mat.

Fadimatu cried and could not stop. She sat in the staff room knitting instead of going to teach her classes, and she did not bother to put the toilet roll back in her drawer, but kept it beside her on the desk. Finally she told the women her problem.

Comfort was the first to offer advice.

"Be silent," Comfort said. 'Your husband is weary."

"My husband is weary? If you are asking who is weary, I am the one," Fadimatu said.

"Not this way," Comfort said. "Listen to God's word: 'Let the woman learn in silence with all subjection.' First Timothy 2, verse 2."

"This means what?" Fadimatu said.

"It means, 'But I permit not a woman to teach, nor to usurp authority over the man, but to be in silence.'"

"I do not wish to be stupid," Fadimatu said. "But are we not teaching at this very school? And is it not rather my husband who is silent up to now?"

Comfort nodded, "And here is the reason," she said. "Listen: 'For Adam was first formed, then Eve. And Adam was not deceived, but the woman, being deceived, was in the transgression.' Transgression means woman is to blame in the matter," Comfort added quickly. "All from Timothy again."

Fadimatu frowned. "Do I refuse to speak? No. Ibrahim is the one. Kai! This Timothy."

"Not Timothy but Paul," Comfort said. "Paul writing to the Corinthians. Anyway, it is only that you are now paying for the sin of Eve. But listen, all will become okay, because of your pregnancy. Listen to the Word of God: 'Notwithstanding, she shall be saved in childbearing, if they continue in faith and love and holiness with sobriety.' Timothy, verse 12, I believe. Are you not with child now?"

"In less than one month, I will deliver, God willing," Fadimatu said.

Comfort smiled. "There is one thing again which will help your condition," she said. "We will become prayer pals."

"Prayer pals? What is pals?"

"Close friends like this," Comfort said. She made a cross with two fingers from each hand. "Every day we must join in prayer on your problem."

"And on weekend?"

"Every day without fail even as our Lord can never fail us."

Fadimatu was unhappy and so she agreed to pray with Comfort. They waited for the other teachers to go to their classes. When they were ready to begin, Fadimatu saw a student walking toward them from the classroom area. He shimmered under the already hot sun.

"Don't worry, he is one of us," Comfort said. "He prayed over Mrs. Degbe's broken sewing machine last Wednesday."

"Did he fix it?" Fadimatu could not help asking.

"Not our time but God's time," Comfort said. She leaned across the desk and took Fadimatu's hands in her own.

"Dear Lord," Comfort began, "we ask just that your will be done in this matter and that Fadimatu cleave to her husband who must be head of her house even as you, that is to say, Christ our Lord, are head of the church."

Comfort's eyes were tightly closed. Fadimatu breathed evenly, but kept her own eyes open to keep from falling asleep.

"Do you want to pray now?" Comfort asked.

"No," Fadimatu said. The boy who had prayed over Mrs. Degbe's sewing machine was kneeling in the staff room doorway.

"Make we close with the Lord's Prayer," Comfort said.

The boy prayed with them, and when Fadimatu left the staff room to go to her class, she heard him talking to Comfort.

"Hallelujah," he said.

"Praise the Lord," Comfort said.

Fadimatu prayed with Comfort every morning, but after two weeks, Ibrahim had not said a word. At night, when he sent for her, she lay beside him, trying to understand him from his breathing, and sometimes she was still awake, stiff and lonely, when she heard the scraping of the neighbour women's buckets on the sandy concrete as they fetched the morning water from the compound well.

She decided to go to the clinic. There were many women sitting outside with their babies in the hot sun, waiting to see the one doctor. When her turn came, and the doctor asked what was worrying her, Fadimatu felt dizzy and could hardly remember her problem.

"I have no appetite," she said. "I am eating only for my unborn child. And I am so tired. And my husband refuses to speak to me." She said it all in a rush.

"You have quarrelled," the doctor said. "You should rather go to a priest, since you do not share your husband's Muslim faith. Which may be the cause of your quarrel. Take this to the dispensary." He wrote out a prescription and gave it to her.

Fadimatu crumpled up the paper. On her way home she stopped to see her friend Baby.

"Do I need injection?" she complained. "Do I need a priest? Am I Catholic?"

"What do you expect?" Baby said. "Your husband hardly goes to mosque and you pray not at all. At Christmas you put on your new wrapper to go to the Lutheran church with Sunday who is not a believer herself, then when you feel like singing you come to Mass with me. You are all mixed up. When you agreed to marry Ibrahim I knew you would have yourself to blame."

"Ah ah!" But Fadimatu caught herself. To talk of love and loyalty was useless with Baby.

"You want western love," Baby went on. "Does Ibrahim give you money to buy food?"

"I am a teacher; I have my salary," Fadimatu said.

"Then you are independent: be happy," Baby said. "Does Ibrahim's senior wife Jummai complain? Do I complain?"

"You have no husband," Fadimatu said.

"Exactly," Baby said.

Fadimatu grew annoyed, but she did not cry. "Listen," she said. "Ibrahim has not spoken to me for an entire season. What is my sin that I deserve this thing?"

Baby was astonished. "But he must speak. He is your husband."

"He will not speak," Fadimatu said, and for the first time, she felt despair, and the walk back to Ibrahim's compound was long.

Some mornings everything was almost right: the cocks crowing and the sweet smell of the dirt, the children's high voices and blue checkered uniforms. Fadimatu felt strong, and she was cheerful in her greetings at the market. One day she was at Obadiah's stall looking for hair cream.

"What of Alhaji?" Obadiah asked. "Will he not make the Haj this year, and bring you another radio? Then you will gift me one radio, customer."

It was true that Ibrahim had been generous: he had brought her jewelled wrappers from Kaduna, a camera from Hong Kong, covered shoes from London. He had loved her. "Obadiah," she said. "You must help me with medicine against silence."

"You say?"

"Against troubles of the heart."

Obadiah looked at her. "What is worrying you?" he asked. When Fadimatu told him, he said, "One season? Since which time precisely?"

"Since before the rains."

"Ah." Obadiah thought a moment, then went to the back and brought her a blue bottle. It smelled like Johnson and Johnson's Baby Powder, but Fadimatu said nothing.

She tried the powder in several ways. First she patted it on her skin, as was her habit after her bath. Then she made a paste with a small amount of water. When the powder did not mix well, she added groundnut oil. This made a smooth paste, and she rubbed it on her face, hands, and then, inspired, on her heart. All the time she knew it was only Johnson and Johnson's Baby Powder. And still Ibrahim refused to talk to her.

Fadimatu's friend Sunday wrote long letters from London, where she was studying to be a doctor. Sunday did not give advice; in fact she did not address Fadimatu's problem directly at all. She said that a girl left her father's house, which was her first prison, to go to school. School, Sunday said, was her second prison. There the girl had to satisfy her principal. Fadimatu looked up from the letter. For once, Sunday was wrong: Fadimatu had refused her former high school principal, and he had expelled her. But Sunday wrote, "I know you will say, 'What of Abubakar?' But even though you refused to friend Abubakar, you entered the third prison: your husband's compound." Sunday had enclosed a book.

"In my previous life I have sinned a thousand times: this is why I was born a woman." This is what one woman in the book had said. Fadimatu read the book at her desk, and when she saw the agriculture sciences teacher, Mebele, walking towards the staff room, she put the book away and picked up her knitting.

"You are suffering from this your *katarrh*," Mebele remarked.

Fadimatu wanted to say, "Mebele, you are still pregnanting the female students." Recently one of these girls had been sent back to her village. But Fadimatu said nothing, because Mebele was a relation of Ibrahim's.

"It's not head or chest cold," Fadimatu said. "Not *katarrh* – only that I'm tired."

"You must pray on your condition," Mebele said. "What of your husband – I hope everything is moving smoothly with him?"

"As we would expect, thank God," Fadimatu said flatly.

"And yet he is still silent with you?"

Fadimatu looked up.

"It is because you are not from the same tribe," Mebele said.

"Also there is clash of religion. Also, try to bother him less about money for gowns. Prepare his favourite dishes. Be tolerant if he takes a second wife."

"I am the second wife," Fadimatu said. But she thought about what Mebele said, and she tried to atone for the differences he had mentioned. By this time, however, Ibrahim refused to eat her food. And she was not able to judge the benefits of her new program, because soon after she had begun, she gave birth to a girl child. Ibrahim did not send fried meat to her room; he did not even ask to see his child. Two days later, the baby died.

"Her name was Mwakapwa," Fadimatu told everyone who came to her room to grieve with her. But Ibrahim did not come, and at the funeral, he stood alone by a tree. Girls from the school danced and sang. They sang:

"Naked I came from my mother's womb,
Naked I shall return,
The Lord has given and He taketh away
Blessed be the name of the Lord."

The girls sang until the sun dropped down, and Fadimatu sang with them, and cried. Ibrahim did not stay, and no one knew where he had gone.

Fadimatu decided to leave him. "And return to your first prison." This was what Sunday would say. Let her say.

Fadimatu went first to Ibrahim's senior wife, Jummai, who lived in a small village outside Kano.

"There is no need to leave him," Jummai told her. "Take it easy: at least he can never put you away. How will he pronounce the words, 'I divorce you, I divorce you,' when he cannot speak?" This made Fadimatu smile.

The next day at school she sat thinking at her desk. Her monitors did not come to remind her about lessons, because they knew she had just lost her child. She decided to tell Ibrahim very frankly all that she was feeling. Perhaps she had not been completely open with him.

The next morning she went to him while he was dressing. "I have been selfish," she said. "I have been thinking only of myself. And of the baby. And of you," she added. She looked into Ibrahim's eyes, but they were dark and unmoving. It was Friday, and Ibrahim would later go to the mosque. He patted cologne on his hair and the front of his gown, and then went out.

Fadimatu did not go to school, but walked instead to the motor-park. The taxi drivers called to her. "Madam!" they cried. "For Jos? Take this taxi. Yola? Madam! Enter here! Madam!"

And Fadimatu thought, if she was no longer Madam, then she had no name. She entered a taxi and at mid-day got out at her father's compound.

No neighbour children ran out to greet her, and the place was quiet: her junior brother Ahmadu was away schooling in Bauchi. Fadimatu cooked soup, and brought it to her father, who was resting under the flame tree. When he woke, he welcomed her, but for the rest of the day he left her alone. In the morning he came to her as she was preparing porridge.

The kitchen was already hot, because he had chopped down the tree that had once shaded the cooking area. Now he pointed to the stump. "Am I to sweep dead leaves?" he asked. "I am an old man." He followed her around, tasting the porridge and the stew as he had done when she was a girl. She had forgotten this, and she thought of Ibrahim, who said, "Women must be equal to men, but it is foolishness for everyone to be cooking at the same time."

Then her father spoke abruptly. "Daughter, what have you done that your husband has put you away?" he asked.

"Not anything," Fadimatu said. "I myself have come to you."

"Then what is your complaint?"

"Only that I am feeling tired."

"*Menene*? What is tired?" her father asked. "Does he beat you unfairly?"

Fadimatu told him no.

"Does he take your salary?"

She told him no.

"Does he shame you by bringing girls to his room?"

Fadimatu said no.

"Does he drink every night and behave badly?" her father asked.

Fadimatu told him no: none of these things.

Her father stared at her. "Then what quarrel do you have with your husband?" he asked. There was a flicker of anger in his voice. For a moment Fadimatu could think only of how it used to be when Ibrahim held her above him in his bed, laughing, telling her that she was his joy. He let her kiss him on the mouth; he let her sleep with her head on his smooth, warm chest.

"For over one season my husband has not spoken to me," she said. Her voice was a whisper. "I cannot sleep. I am tired all the time, more tired than when I was pregnant . . ."

"*Haba*," her father said. "What is this thing that you are telling me?" But his voice was gentle. He followed her as she swept the sand in tidy fan shapes all around the entrance hut. Finally he said, "I have been thinking on your problem."

Fadimatu waited.

"You have discussed the entire matter with Ibrahim?" her father said.

"One half, anyway," Fadimatu said.

"What of Obadiah? You have tried a few western medicines?"

"Yes."

"And what of Ibrahim's relation – the one in your school?"

"Mebele? He says we have difference of tribe."

"Then here is my plan." Malam Aliyu mentioned for her to sit on the stool, and while she shaded her eyes against the sun that would have been blocked by the tree, he told her of his new ambitions concerning his bicycle trade. He wanted her to decorate the side and back panels of the lorry he had just purchased.

"With your education you will have an easy time," he said.

"I did not read Fine Art," Fadimatu said. She did not see how choosing a proverb and arranging for the artwork on her father's mammy wagon would restore speech to her husband, but she knew it would help her forget her trouble, and she told her father she would go to Didango, who had gone to high school with her and was a gifted artist.

"Gifted or not, all the same to me," her father said. "Only the thing must be completed by Friday. Then the driver will take my bicycles to Jos."

Didango was at his mother's compound under a tree sketching a lion. He was a thin, boyish-looking man who had not yet married because he could not afford any bride price.

Fadimatu greeted him and stood observing.

"But this your lion, he has no mane," Fadimatu remarked.

"She is female," Didango said. "Is better for drawing the skull."

"She is very fine," Fadimatu said. "If you paint this lion on my father's lorry, he will pay you one hundred naira."

"Kai! But for the lorry I must give it mane," Didango said.

"No mane," Fadimatu said.

"But what will the people say when they see the lion without mane?" Didango said.

"Let them say!" Fadimatu cried. "'Yes. And for proverb, you will put 'Let Them Say,'" she added.

On her way home she stopped to greet the old woman who sold onions by the side of the road.

"And what news of Alhaji?" the woman asked.

"I have left him," Fadimatu said.

"Ai!" the woman said, putting her hands to her face. "This is a terrible sin."

Fadimatu thought, If I have sinned a thousand times to be born a woman, what is one more? She asked for a basket of onions, and the woman carefully placed each one in a plastic *leder* bag.

The next morning Fadimatu helped Didango mix paints, and she watched him work. On Friday, the paint was dry. When the driver started the engine Fadimatu jumped in the cab beside him. She put her small suitcase between her feet. "You will drop me by Jos at my friend's village," she said. But when they reached Jos, Fadimatu told the boy to continue.

"The place is past Jos small, small," she said. "I think you know Bukuru?"

"I know it," said the boy. "I know all cities and every state in the Federation."

When they reached Bukuru the driver asked for directions, but Fadimatu said, "No, continue straight, straight.

Don't worry about my father's bicycles. I think you know the road to Makurdi." She pointed her way with her chin.

"I know the road," the driver said. By mid-afternoon they reached Makurdi. The driver was in a terrible mood, and did not ask for further directions, but pulled over abruptly by a row of women selling fruit. "I will go chop," he said. Several women were already at the cab windows.

"Buy banana!" they shouted. "Mango! Orange!"

The driver swung down from the cab and pushed past the women to the street. Fadimatu saw him enter the Don't Mind Your Wife restaurant but did not follow; she was not at ease in Makurdi. When the driver came back he looked angry. He walked to Fadimatu's side of the cab, and when the women jumped up again with their fruit, he shooed them away.

"Enter! But why are you standing there?" Fadimatu said.

"*No dey*," the driver said. "This lorry is very bad. Why your father bought this lorry so cheap like that, I know the reason: this lorry killed two men. On this very street. Will I drive this lorry again? *No dey*?"

"*Haba!* Somebody is telling you stories. It is only lies."

"No," the driver said. He was shaking. "Excuse, Madam. I will check my relation who lives in the new town. I think you have your own taxi fare, *ko*?"

"I have money," Fadimatu said. "But we will not go back to my father. We will go to the Lagos."

"Lagos! *Na wa o!*" And the driver walked away, half running, pushing through the people until he turned into a side street and was gone. The women were still shouting up at Fadimatu. Their headtrays of bananas and mangoes were so close she could have reached out her arm and taken several. She bought bananas and ate three, and then she slid across the seat and practised pressing one foot against the hot clutch pedal, the other against the brake, and pulling, with her eyes half closed, the gear stick through the gears, but she did not know how to start it. She jumped down to the group of boys who stood watching.

"Is condemned," she said. One of the boys threw down his chewing stick, pulled himself up into the cab and started the engine with a great show of noise and smoke. The other boys shouted and laughed and slapped each other.

"Not condemned," the boy said as he jumped down. "Only spirited. This lorry killed two men."

Fadimatu shrugged. "Let them say." She thanked the boy, and drove off slowly, with one hand steady on the horn. She saw a beggar hold his hands to his ears, and she laughed.

Outside Onitsha, she thought of petrol. She traded a bicycle for a small amount of money and some coconut to a girl who was hawking slices by a hotel. Fadimatu ate her coconut and watched in the mirror as the girl arranged her headtray on her new bicycle bars. A man came out of the hotel and grabbed the tray; the coconut slices flew off. The girl did not move. Fadimatu looked away. She wanted to drive off; she wanted to imagine that the girl was about to jump at the man and fight him, or that the man was about to apologize, about to offer to find and wash each piece. But she did look back, and she saw the man shrug his gown up over his shoulders for coolness, and she saw the girl bend at the waist and begin to pick her coconut slices up from the sand.

KENNETH RADU

A Change of Heart

When he hit upon the idea of murdering his friend and neighbour, Ronald was staring at the swishing water in a washing machine. A careful launderer, he never closed the lid until all the clothes got thoroughly soaked and agitated. In some laundromats, anything placed in last stayed on top throughout the entire first cycle, dry as dirt, until the spin and rinse cycles began. Perhaps the twisted arms and legs of the shirts and pants suggested agony of some sort. A mild-mannered man who loved "Family Ties" on television, Ronald didn't have a lingering death in mind. Something clean and sudden.

"Excuse me, but could I possibly borrow a cup of your detergent? I've run out and the dispenser here is broken."

"Surely."

It was the kind of gesture Ronald liked. A believer in the community spirit and helping out friends, family, and, yes, even strangers, Ronald could be relied upon to participate in blood drives, winter carnival committees, save the parks campaigns, and to stop by old, arthritic Mrs. Bulletin's apartment every other day to see if she was still alive.

"Thank you."

"Don't mention it."

He handed the young woman his box of Oxydol, then returned to his agitation. Good. Completely submerged. He shut the lid quietly, disapproving of people who clanged it down and made a noisy nuisance of themselves in public places.

Of course Ronald would have been the first to admit that he liked Bela, his neighbour. Everyone liked Bela, who was one of the few men who could make love to another man's wife and remain friends with the husband. Liz didn't much care for him as a man, she said, finding him "too obvious," a comment Ronald could take as a back-handed compliment to himself. Bela could be a lot of fun. Two summers ago they had taken their children, all five of them, on a camping trip to New Brunswick. Bela had led the group in pitching camp, taught Ronald's two and his three kids as much as he knew about Indian petroglyphs, quite a lot actually. He had also strummed an old mandolin, one of the few possessions his family had been able to take out of Hungary during the uprising against the Soviet Union thirty years ago. Proficient in half a dozen Slavic languages, he sang Hungarian, Croation, and Greek folk songs. When the children finally fell asleep after an exhausting day of hiking or canoeing or fishing, he and Bela shared long and deep secrets. Fire sparked off the logs and the chill of a summer's night sank to the ground.

Of all the men Ronald knew, it was Bela whom he trusted with the story of his one and only extramarital love affair, then in progress, with a rather exuberant bank clerk.

"Sometimes I feel awful, Bela. It's not right, not fair to Liz."

"Feel what you feel, Ronnie, but take what the world's got to offer. Did you desert Liz? No. Have you stopped loving your wife? No. There isn't a woman I've loved whom I wouldn't love again if I had the chance."

"What about Anna?"

"What Anna doesn't know won't hurt her."

"You think your wife doesn't know about you, man? Everyone knows you're an alley cat."

"Anna knows I'm crazy about her and would die for her. What more can a woman ask of her husband?"

In the light of the camp fire, Ronald could see that Bela's thick moustache and dark face surrounded by luxuriant, black hair, his Roman nose and his long sinewy legs (Bela jogged daily) were physical attributes that would appeal to many women.

"Is there some way I can pay you back?"

"What?"

"The detergent. How can I give it back?"

"Don't even try. My pleasure."

"But it was a whole cup."

A pretty enough woman, despite the two-tone dye job of her hair, Ronald wondered if she would find Bela attractive. She sounded earnest, a sincerity somewhat undercut by the green and blonde, bizarrely arranged head of hair. She was probably new to the world of suburban laundromats, Ronald suspected and, quite possibly, to the task of washing clothes. If it weren't for the hard water, the general disrepair of the machinery, the number of tenants waiting their turn, Ronald would have used one of the two washing machines in his apartment building.

"That's very kind of you. Next time, though, if I happen to see you here, I'll return the cup."

"Suit yourself."

Bela, of course, would have moved in on her, offered to drive her to a grocery store, taken her out for a drink, and wooed her with one of his soulful Slavic melodies of separated lovers and broken hearts.

In a foolish attempt to carry two plastic hampers filled with clothes and an orange garbage bag stuffed with sheets and pillowcases, Ronald had dropped one of the laundry baskets outside Bela's door in the hallway. He was bending down to pick up Liz's delicate underthings when Bela's hand covered his.

"Here, let me do that."

"I can do it, Bela."

"I'll carry the baskets, fella, you carry the bag."

"I can manage, Bela, thanks."

"So I see."

"Just put that basket on top of this one, then the bag."

"Remember, fella, the doctor said to take it easy."

So he placed a basket under each arm and took three steps at a time down the two flights of stairs to the back door.

"Where's Liz?" he asked, opening Ronnie's car door and throwing in the laundry. It fell over the back seat.

"She took the kids to the rummage sale at the school."

"You want me to go with you?"

It was hard to resist the dark intensity of Bela's brown eyes and the lilt of ancient songs in his voice. He also wore compassion like a suit of comfortable clothes. Ronald's lax muscles and breathlessness responded to Bela's concern, but he didn't like being made to feel weak. A giant of a man at six foot four inches with a 200-pound frame, Bela cast shadows. Ronald felt chilled and he heard his heart shake ever so slightly.

"I can manage, Bela, I'm not entirely helpless."

The doctor had in fact said that. "Take it easy, don't exert yourself." Ronald, who had since grown acutely sensitive to his heart as if he had a stethoscope permanently stuck in his ears, had promised that he would. He now sat on the green park bench provided by the management of the laundromat. The other seat, also a park bench, was gluey with gum stuck on its slats. The waxed floor and the bleeding hearts spilling out of their hanging baskets gave the place a minimal level of decency.

It really wasn't much of an improvement over his basement laundry room except that here a solid wall of capacious dryers, sixteen of them, made his task tolerable. Twenty putrid-pink washers in two rows, six of them sealed shut with Out of Order signs taped over their coin slots, reduced the waiting time. On the whole, Ronald preferred driving once a week three blocks to the laundromat in a corner plaza (a video store, a delicatessen, a gas station at one end, a convenience store open twenty-four hours, and a discount drug mart) than hauling his dirty clothes down three floors to the basement room where, if anything worked, it was usually busy with someone else's laundry.

He and Bela were in the basement, clearing out the goods and debris in their storage lockers when the attack struck, almost a year to the day. Ronald felt as if his lungs had burst and expelled all their air. After momentary breathlessness, he heard veins pounding in his head. He thought he heard his mother, dead for ten years, warning him to be careful and to look both ways before he crossed the street.

"Bela," he remembered saying, before falling over his son's Canadian Tire tricycle, the one that Bela had assembled, onto several rolled sleeping bags. His mind went black. He knew that his eyes were open, but whatever they saw was not recorded. Bela began breathing into his mouth like some Carpathian mountain deity blowing life into a peasant of clay. Ronald felt as if parts of his body were turning to stone. He fainted. Later, Bela said that he had carried him in his arms, right into the hospital emergency room, hollering at the top of his voice for help.

"I didn't pound on your chest. That's your imagination,"
Bela told him in the hospital room several days later when
Ronald, having survived an operation, was well enough to
receive visitors.

"That's funny, I could have sworn you pounded on my
chest."

"No, you don't need to pound, not really, with CPR. It's a
good thing for you, fella, I was around."

Ronald carefully folded the sheets as he took them out of
the machine to prevent them from dragging on the dirty
floor. After the attack and subsequent hospitalization, he
took an extended leave of absence from work at the water
filtration plant and broke up with Janine. He did not want
to die in the middle of a love affair although the doctor said
that he could live a more or less normal life for many, many
years. Who really believed doctors? Besides, still loving his
wife, Ronald could no longer look Janine in the eye, having
come so close to death and the meaning of life. He felt
unfaithfulness and deception in his bones like an incura-
ble disease. A residual, inarticulated belief in God and
judgement urged him towards fidelity once again.

The real problem was method.

"Sometimes I wished I lived in Florida."

"You and me both," the young woman who had bor-
rowed his detergent mumbled through a pillowcase held
between her teeth as she folded a blouse printed with black
orchids. Ronald smiled and took out Liz's granny nightgown. In Florida he understood that one could simply walk
into a store and buy a gun, claiming constitutional rights
or some such thing. He didn't know what the rules were in
Canada, but he couldn't very well buy a hand-gun without a
licence, he imagined. How about a hunting rifle from a

sporting goods store? In any case, shooting struck him as too obvious and messy. He had never shot a gun in his life.

When he thanked Bela from his hospital bed, Ronald cried. After a year he could still blush over that little, emotional scene. Bela had leaned over and wiped the tears away with a yellow tissue.

"For you, anything, you know that, fella."

And so Bela visited him every day, bringing magazines, books, candies, flowers, puzzles, and a portable Japanese television set. Ronald only noticed something was wrong when Liz took to sitting in the corner chair as Bela crowded around his bed, sitting on it, puffing up the pillows, talking non-stop about the guys at the plant, the Russian-Canadian hockey games. Ronald could feel heat radiating from Liz's corner where she seemed to burn over a magazine. In the last week or two of his stay in the hospital, Liz said that she wasn't coming anymore.

"There isn't room for the two of us there. You'll be out in a week or so and, thank God, home. I'm changing the bedroom around so you can see out the window."

Janine phoned him once while he was convalescing. Bela answered instantly, knew who it was, and winked throughout Ronald's short, breathless converstions.

"Don't call here. No, I'm sorry, I can't. Yes, I'm fine, now. A minor attack. Of course I care for you. Yes, no, maybe, we'll see. I can't talk now. I'll call. No! Don't come here! Bye, yes, bye. Thanks."

"You watch that pecker of yours doesn't get you another heart attack." Bela hung up for him and laughed quietly but deeply.

In the laundromat Ronald regretted having told Bela about Janine. Suppose he joked out loud about the affair? He was also sorry to see that the dark blue colour of a new cotton shirt had washed out. He should have washed it separately, as the instruction said, but that would have meant more time and work. Knifing? How could he stab Bela? Even if he could, where? In the back? Ronald's heart skipped a beat. A chest muscle vibrated. He couldn't very well do it while Bela was looking. What kind of knife? A bread knife with its jagged edge? God, disgusting! A stiletto? What did the Japanese warriors and court ladies use when committing ritual suicide? Bela wasn't about to fall upon anyone's knife and Ronnie certainly couldn't bring himself to thrust it into his guts. After all, the man had saved his life!

In the last week of hospitalization Bela timed his visits to last a half hour.

"Can't stay any longer, fella. Need to pick up Anna downtown and Liz can do with some help."

"With what?"

"Well, changing the furniture around in your bedroom for one thing."

"You're helping Liz in my bedroom?"

"Take it easy, fella, before your heart goes zing again. Liz is safe with me, you know that, don't you?"

Well, Ronald supposed that he did. Convalescent in hospital for several weeks, however, feeling his body weaken, despite the physiotherapy and forced marches up and down the corridor, had led to vivid dreams of black, moist tunnels, speeding trains, falling trees, and erupting geysers.

A knife was out of the question. He finished unloading one washer and began taking out the pastel summer cottons from the other. Liz's pale lime dress, the one that made her look like a mint julep, cool and inviting. Ronald pressed it against his face and inhaled deeply. She had assured him that Bela wasn't her type. Poison? More difficult to get than a gun unless he fed Bela tons of mouse bane, the kind that slowly incinerated the insides of a rodent. Too cruel, too lingering. Everybody would know.

Out came his own pink, short-sleeved shirt, followed by his ten-year-old daughter's yellow nightgown and his bone-coloured cotton twill slacks. The spaghetti sauce stain had almost come out. He would have to work on it some more. The result of Bela's dinner for them last week. He had cooked a huge pot of spaghetti, prepared his own garlic-ridden sauce, and poured glasses of Szekszardi wine down his throat. At midnight he danced with Liz, nuzzling her neck, Ronnie noticed, as he and Anna stared at each other over flickering candlelight.

Too obvious, Liz had said. Yesterday he had dropped by Mrs. Bulletin's apartment to see if she was still alive.

"Let me open the windows, it's pretty hot in here." It also smelled like mothballs and urine.

"No, no, no. Please, I can't bear the street noise coming in."

Ronald imagined that she did get up once in a while, but whenever he visited her, Mrs. Bulletin was ensconced in a Queen Anne chair as if she and the stuffing had merged. Had he ever seen her wear anything besides the tartan skirt and two grey sweaters? An old woman with pearl black eyes, she spent most of her days following the soaps on television or, she often said, talking to the church ladies on the telephone.

"How nice of that Mr. Hunyadi to help your wife so much while you were sick. A fine man."

"Yes, here's your tea. Can I get anything for you from the store, Mrs. Bulletin?"

"Please, if you would, some mints, you know the kind I like, and a box of instant potatoes on sale at Provigo, maybe you could get me half a dozen eggs, dear me, am I out of milk?"

"I'll check, drink your tea."

For months following his release from hospital, Bela wouldn't let him do anything. He drove Liz to do the shopping, even met her outside the Bell Telephone office to drive her home. You'd think Anna would have had a fit. No one paid her much attention. She spoke very little English and spent hours in the kitchen baking tons of cookies for one charity drive or another or sewing clothes for her three children.

"Jesus, Bela, I'm not helpless. I can do the laundry!"

"Sure you can, right before another attack. What did the doctor say?" Bela also took the kids to their various appointments and activities and had run both households while Liz went to Edmonton for a week to attend a relative's funeral and Anna was sick in bed with the flu. Bela practically carried him to the john.

It didn't seem to matter that Ronald had recovered some of his strength. Bela still treated him like a sickly or fragile, half-lunatic member of the family.

"I can do it, Bela, I can do it!"

"Take it easy, fella, I'm here for you."

Then his children began talking about Bela said this, and Bela said that. They would rush into his bedroom, their faces hot with excitement.

"Daddy! Bela's taking us to the zoo! You should see what Bela can do with a piece of string! Daddy, Bela's showing us how to carve whistles! Do you want to hear the joke Bela told us, Dad?" And when they left he sometimes felt for his heart to be certain it hadn't been replaced by chill winds and the sounds of desertion.

If he drove Bela somewhere, could he rig the car so it would explode while he got out for a leak in the bushes and Bela remained inside? All the clothes out of the second washer, Ronnie gently closed the lid. He was feeling hungry. Across the street there was a small restaurant where the men from a construction site down the road ate dozens of greasy doughnuts and drank thick coffee. Many of them looked sinister to Ronnie, but almost anyone who wasn't pale and narrow as he looked odd to him. Could he hire one? How much to knock off a friend? He had five thousand dollars in bonds in his name, another five thousand frozen in RRSP's in Liz's name, and seven hundred dollars in his savings account. If a man were desperate enough, he would surely agree to anything at reduced rates. He heard his heart whine a bit, then suddenly rush, forcing him to catch his breath. Good, just a meaningless flurry.

He certainly didn't want to be accused of ingratitude. If he weren't grateful, any number of people reminded him religiously that gratitude was in order. Ronald had thanked Bela profusely, had searched his conscience for any sign of ingratitude hiding in a remote corner like contraband. For Christmas he had given Bela an expensive Timex watch. Carrying the second hamper, heavy with wet laundry and which caused his chest to hurt, Ronald didn't want to think murderous thoughts about his "best friend." Well, not really friend, more like a good neighbour who lent a hand.

"Honey, Bela's taking me to a movie tonight. I really need to get out." Three months home, growing soft and vegetable in his blue terry cloth robe, his mind counting the beats of his recently renovated heart, Ronald had to admit that Liz did have a right. He wasn't much fun and it possibly did get boring for Liz. Except she looked rather eager to go, and too appealing in black slacks and a shocking pink and purple cotton sweater that made Ronald think of lovers in a summer sunset.

"Oh, Bela's much too obvious for me," Ronald mimicked as he slammed the back door of his car. So he stayed home with the kids who watched the videos Bela had brought them that afternoon. As the kernels exploded into white puffs under the plastic dome of the automatic corn pop-per, Ronald listened to his heart beat cautiously with quiet, persistent, immeasurable rage.

Before pulling out of the parking spot, Ronald checked the number on the piece of paper the man in the café had given him. At first Ronald sat and stared at the construc-tion workers who probably thought he was hustling them. On what basis had he chosen a short, pit-bull-faced man with hair growing out of his nostrils? Was it the red neck? The bitten-down fingernails? Very respectfully he asked permission to sit down at the man's table. A reasonable request. The restaurant was crowded. Comments about the weather, about the construction down the road, led to gen-eralized suggestions about work of a highly complicated, discreet nature. Did the man know someone?

What kind of work? In construction? He couldn't say here, Ronald said. Hey, you're not some kind of nut? A pervert? The man blew smoke sideways then stubbed out his cigarette in a coffee cup. No, no, nothing like that. Honest. It just has to be very quiet. The man was interested. He did in fact know someone who knew someone. You can call this number. He wrote it down on the back of an envelope with a stubby pencil. This guy will tell you who to call. He knows someone who'll do anything if the price is right. Even kink. Ronald blushed. No, he said, it's nothing out of the ordinary.

Ronald's safari shirt stuck to his back from the sweat his nerves generated. He was glad that he had decided to hang the clothes from the lines in the back of his apartment building, provided by the management. The day was blue and dry. He put the paper in his wallet, then drove away. So far he had done nothing criminal. Just a number. Desperation. The lure of a few thousand dollars. Could the man be trusted? We'll just have to play it by ear. Nothing needs to be decided right away. We'll just have to see. He could feel his heart picking up speed.

Checking the traffic behind him, Ronald thought his eyes in the rear view mirror too watery-blue to inspire confidence. Did black, luxuriant hair indicate potency the way his own limp, dust-brown hair did not? Sure enough, there was Bela in the back lot behind their apartment building, arms outstretched, ready to help the aged and the infirm out of their cars.

"I can manage, Bela, I'm not helpless!" Ronald heard the temper in his voice.

"I'm just trying to help, Ronnie, why rush it? Give the heart a chance." Ronald got out of the car, tried to smile as he grabbed hold of Bela's hand, and wished that he could look Bela in the eye. He stared into the man's Adam's apple. He was about to push the hand away, ever so gently, when his heart opened its red mouth and roared. Ronald's entire body jolted into Bela's arms.

"Oh my God, no!" And suddenly there was silence in his veins.

"Bela," he gasped as he shook against the man's chest and blacked out.

"Ronnie, don't worry, fella. Bela's got you!"

CYNTHIA FLOOD

My Father Took a Cake to France

My father stands before the bakery window. He is going to buy a cake for my mother.

This is a young man, twenty-six in 1928, and he is tall, bony, of angular visage. His hair is pale, his glasses extremely clean. Thirty or fifty years hence he will look, as they say, distinguished; at present the clothes affordable by the son of a Canadian Methodist minister simply cover his limbs.

In his left coat pocket is Eliot's *The Waste Land*, of which he has been mentally reciting the opening passage as he walks the noisy London streets in search of a bakery. Irony, pastry, flowers, death – my father relishes the contrasts and stirs Eliot's metaphors in his mind, sure that no other graduate of Toronto's Victoria College (motto: The truth shall make you free) thinks such thoughts.

My father is happy, desperately happy, to be in England. His brain has brought him here. The happiness soars from his faith that England is better than Canada: older, deeper, stronger, more highly patterned, more richly and complexly flavoured, more romantic – oh, infinitely more romantic. And here he is, *he* is, in London, en route to Paris from Oxford, to the City of Light from the city with her dreaming spires. Hogtown is far away.

In Paris is my mother. She is there because a married Oxford student is so far outside the norm as to be inconceivable to the university authorities. Somehow, from that fact, my parents have moved to a decision that while my father studies in England my mother will live in France. Soon my father will see her. He is desperately happy, though from his looks no one would guess either the desperation or the happiness or their entanglement within him. Dour, stiff, critical – that is his aspect. (Say the word "Toronto" and I see him walking toward me down the cold white street, his hat firm on his head, his briefcase swinging, the long thick tweed coat swinging above the snow as he advances sternly. Because I am a girl, he will take his hat off to me.)

He now faces the confections displayed within the bakery window.

My father has a tendency to stick his lower lip forward, and thus his chin; the latter is sharp and long, just like mine. His blue eyes glitter. As he ages, his eyes will not change, will always be blue like shadows in snow or ice in sunlight; although his infrequent smile smooths the chin's point and softens the steep drop from temple to jaw, the eyes do not change. They look now through the glasses through the bakery window through the glass display shelves to a woman back there in the shop. She glances away. My father's heart contracts.

He opens the shop door, and with delight he hears the little English bell tinkling, pinging – not a harsh North American buzz or ring, not a machine: a bell, attached to its string, silver trembling in the sun, the sounding centre of the fragrance that fills the shop, a warm yeasty floury doughy sugary fragrance with undertones of almond essence and ginger. My father inhales, inhales, and begins to smile. Then he looks at the woman behind the counter and is silenced by a rush of shyness. His mouth goes tight, straight, thin. For she is a fair English flower. Oh, she has it all – her eyes are grey, her hair curled light, her complexion apple blossom grafted to cherry, and she is freshness and cleanliness incarnate in a pink short-sleeved dress with a white bibbed apron. On her forearms and the backs of her hands is flour, which also powders her right temple just below a dip of curls.

My father takes off his hat.

"Good morning, sir," she says, and my father's heart dissolves.

In the spired city my father is the Canadian student. He is intelligent, yes, highly intelligent, a remarkably good writer, really a most distinguished mind – but still he can never be what he feels, he *knows*, he should have been. There will always have been Humberside Collegiate instead of Marlborough or Stowe, always Long Branch summers and the house on Hewitt Avenue in a modest Toronto neighbourhood (of which my grandmother said, departing thence after twenty-five years, "I never liked the West End"). There will never have been the small English manor house, sparely furnished with good, old pieces, never the youthful rambles in the tender English countryside and the boyish familiarity with spinney and copse, or possibly tor and moor. . . . Instead, my father has canoed on Lake Muskoka. The generations of quiet educated sensibility, of sureness that *This is how we have always done things* – no. The Ontario farm is too near. And on this side of the Atlantic, in Paris, Mme. Papillon, my parents' landlady, points frequently to alleged scratches on *her* furniture and says to her Canadian tenants, in tones at once depressed and threatening, *"Voyez comme il s'abime!"* So, even as my father feasts on the Oxford libraries, exhilarates in recognition, relishes the exercise of his intellectual musculature, some part of him feels he is beaten before he starts. As he would say, will say frequently throughout his life, "All, all is ashes."

But not here. Here in the warm quiet bakery the sun is yellow in the window, he has money in his pocket, and a pretty woman stands before him to do his bidding, sir. Soon he will take the boat-train for Dover. On board the ferry, he will stand alone and ecstatic at the bow and recite "Fair stood the wind for France" and "Nobly, nobly to the northwest Cape St. Vincent died away" (both, like "Dover Beach," learned by heart at Humberside).

France: hungrily, my father will watch that legendary country rise from horizon into actual earth where he can set his flat Canadian foot. Soon he will hear French all about him. Not the crude ugly patois they speak in Quebec (all his life he will rejoice in the belief that every Québécois who travels to France meets incomprehension and contempt), no, *real* French, France French. My father regrets very much that he cannot pronounce a rolled French R. His tongue simply will not make that sound. . . . But France will come later, Paris, the little apartment in Mme. Papillon's building, my mother. Right now he must buy his cake.

He looks again at the beautiful young woman behind the counter. His shyness begins to go away, subsumed by another emotion: pleasure, at the thought that this beauty will soon fade. In my father's other coat pocket is Arnold Bennett's *The Old Wives' Tale*, a wonderful novel, a master-piece, no one writes like that anymore. . . . On the train from Oxford that morning he has read and reread Bennett's introductory description of the book's genesis, is well on the way to memorizing it. Decades later, my father will recite these paragraphs repeatedly, interminably, as he will also the scene in which Sophia, sitting by Gerald Scales's frightful corpse, is brought to the door of her own death by the understanding that "Youth and vigour had come to that. Youth and vigour always came to that. Everything came to that." By preference, my father will select as audiences for these recitations people who are near either the beginning or the end of life. He will also take inordinate and lifelong pleasure, laughing helplessly, in Constance's embarrassed description of her sister's exotic pet: "It's a French dog, one of those French dogs."

Now my father looks at the youth and freshness behind the counter with an aesthetic pleasure that is distanced because for him these are obstacles that stand in the way of the status and respect he knows are his due. Further, although he readily imagines the speed with which these attributes will become their hideous opposites in the person now facing him, he does not refer that process to himself. Too many scholarly achievements, honours, points of recognition lie ahead.

Looking at the young woman in the bakery, what my father feels is nostalgia for the moment, right now while it still is the moment. He may even feel desire *for* nostalgia, that wrenching union of mournfulness and delight.

"Would you be kind enough, miss," he says, speaking formally, though aware in helpless annoyance that his accent instantly marks him as non-English, possibly in her ignorant ear even as American, which annoys him still more, "would you be kind enough to tell me the names of these cakes?"

"Of course, sir."

Her small plump hands, dusted with flour and springing with gold hair, move pointing along the upper shelf of the display case.

Ratafias, gingerbread nuts, macaroons. Snow cake, sponge cake, Savoy cake.

"I'm sure I don't know why Savoy, sir. There's orange-flower water in it."

My mother, marrying my father, carries mock orange. Characteristically impulsive, she breaks the sprigs off a shrub they pass while walking towards their ceremony in the little London church (it will be bombed flat in the Battle of Britain). Because she loves the smell of the mock orange she overrides my father's objections, his wish to buy her a *real* bouquet. She will plant mock orange in the garden of every house they rent and in that of the one they finally own, when he retires.

The plump hands and the soft voice go on. Lemon cake, pound cake, seed cake. A Pavini cake.

"Eyetalian, sir. They use a rice flour."

My father is delighted at the incorrect pronunciation in the gentle voice, for he is developing a nice ability to rank British speakers of English. Her respectful attitude, also, the way she looks repeatedly up at him under lashes to confirm that she is to continue naming the cakes – most satisfactory. Holiday cake, plum cake, almond ca –

My father holds up his hand and the young woman stops in mid-word. That gesture of his, so powerful, so characteristic, has even stopped Mme. Papillon, that stalwart bearer of the arms of the French *petite bourgeoisie*. How? When my father, having heard the *Voyez comme il s'abime* accusation once too often, says in his solid Ontario French and with his right hand raised, *"Eh bien, nous allons. Nous partons, ma femme et moi,"* the landlady stands speechless before him.

"Is there a queen cake?" Now where has he picked up this name? I cannot imagine.

"Queen cakes here, sir? Oh no, sir. You must make your little queens at home, sir, and eat them fresh from the oven."

And she smiles, to soften the response. She is so sweet, so blooming, so feminine, that though there remain several unidentified cakes my father goes right off into a kind of trance. His hand is still upheld and he exudes such an atmosphere of *Do not speak to me* that the young woman remains silent, transfixed – just like Mme. Papillon, who finds her apologies and assurances blown to powder before the cold wind of my father's displeasure, and who only finds out that my parents do not intend to leave her apartment through the fact that they stay.

Which cake? Perhaps the one with the small white roses. Or that one, with what seem to be daisies, eyes of the day – some small white flower. A cake for my mother, in Paris. My father thinks of my mother. He extends his fingers before him towards the glass case and moves them back and forth in the air as if composing, or running scales on the piano.

No, resentfully, he does not play the piano, although God knows he has the hands for it, long, broad, agile, because his sister got the childhood lessons purely for being that: a sister. And what did she do with her training? What? Nothing. Nothing. Fifty years later, after my father's funeral, I learn from my aunt how she bowed, and willingly, to those terrible grinding loving pressures of family, and sacrificed – there is no other word – her own hopes (not even plans, so young were they) for travel and the study of music abroad. Abroad, abroad, that radiant word and world abroad: she diverted carefully saved funds into the channel marked "postgraduate education of gifted elder brother." A girl.

My father moves his fingers along the air and the young woman looks at him, bewildered. What is this odd plain bespectacled commanding young man about?

My father is no longer aware of her. He feels only the intense need to find the right cake, the cake that will say what must be said, the cake that will be for my mother.

Now my mother is and always has been a handsome woman, energetic, with snapping hazel eyes and a lively play of expression and a nose as strong as her will; yet all his life my father yearns, or part of him yearns, for her to be fragile, delicate. He yearns for himself to be the lover who gives gifts to this being who is other, oh very other, mysterious, unknown, in fact unknowable, as strange and distant as the inner reality of France or England to a Canadian (this though my mother like my father is Canadian born and raised). A perfect metaphor for this prism of my father's relationship with my mother is his present status as an Oxford student. As such, he has attained an ideal separation between the life of the intellect and that of the heart and flesh, between a world of many men and a world of one woman, for he has literally to journey from one to the other across land and water, to cross national boundaries, to go through customs. And the one world knows the other not at all, not at all (although Mme. Papillon probably disapproves of my parents' living arrangements as sharply as an Oxford don). Also, my mother speaks French much more fluently than my father does.

My mother, this other being, if correctly presented according to my father's fantasy, would be adorned, no, would be veiled in lace, silks, embroidery, furs. She would wear jewels. She would recline, beautifully; my father thinks of pictures in the *Illustrated London News*, sees the languid hand trailing over the edge of the cushion-heaped chaise longue, the curled tendrils of hair clustering delicately about the slender throat. . . . As the marriage moves on through the decades to its golden jubilee, my father will develop an entire verbal routine (one of many, on various topics) about my mother, more specifically about his own failure to make her a marchioness. He will elaborate on his failure to provide her with a suitable establishment, a suitably lovely house – in England, of course, not in ratty raw Canada where he has been compelled to eke out his miserable sordid existence and where she too has therefore been immured – no, a suitably lovely Queen Anne house, with flanking pavilions in perfect symmetry and formal gardens sloping to the lake. . . . In my teens I find this routine amusing, in my twenties embarrassing. In my thirties I despise it. Now in my forties I feel a sour pity that slowly sweetens.

The woman in the English bakery keeps thinking that my father is pointing, finally, to his choice, and moves up and down accordingly behind the display case. But my father is still not aware of her. He has dropped her into that enormous wastebasket where he keeps people whom he does not currently need. So he moves, and she moves. Which shall it be: the one with the long sliding curls of chocolate? with the stippling of jam? with the corrugations born of a special pan, and these all glazed and shining? Which? My father's hands, duplicates of mine to the last crease and wrinkle, go up and down along the glass.

My father stops. He points to the lower shelf. The young woman bends down. The fabric of her clothing bends too, with a gentle cracking sound, and seems to exude yet stronger, sweeter wafts of that marvellous baking fragrance with which the shop is suffused. With her two pretty hands she removes the cake that my father is pointing to, and she lays it silently before him on the counter. The clean grained wood, white from scrubbing, might be an altar.

He inspects his choice. This cake, of the sandwich type, is softly round; its sides are innocent of icing; in the crack between its layers lies a streak of golden glossy stickiness;

and on its white-iced bosom it bears three beautifully modelled fleurs-de-lis.

Then my father smiles. The dour face splits and everything except the blue ice changes so forcefully that the young woman, astonished, taken all unawares, smiles back, dimpling at her customer in the most enchanting way. She answers his quesion before he even asks it.

"This, sir? It's a French cake, one of those French cakes. Gat*to*," she finishes.

My father in turn is charmed, taken, completely, and only by continuing to smile can he signal his intention to purchase. He and the young woman, smiling, together contemplate the cake.

Then, as he gazes on the ancient armorial bearings of the kings of France, my father feels three tears rise.

The first is for the pain of exclusion. He does not want to be a king, no – in fact a long way down inside my father is a belief that no one, no one in the world is quite so good as a scholar – but he would dearly love to be a citizen of a nation ruled by kings. He wants real, resident monarchs, not people thousands of miles away across grey cold ocean who turn up in Canada every few years and wave from the rears of trains. He wants to be bound in his own person to all the glittering bloody sonorous history of Europe, where century lies on century like the multiple towers of Troy. And he wants *not* to live in a nation that is at best a blueprint only, laid thinly on hostile earth that scarcely knows the plough.

The next tear is for irony, beloved irony, for here collapsed into a cake is that same heroic, embattled, glorious tale of Europe. And is this not always the fate of human enterprise? Aspiration, promise, struggle, heartbreak – all come down to dust, an evanescent sugariness, an ache in the teeth. An aching sweetness. With that is the third tear, for here is my mother.

"What is in the middle?" my father asks, pointing to the filling.

"Jam, sir. Mirabelle."

My father sees my mother, right now, in the Paris apartment. She is wearing her favourite dress, cream with broad vertical stripes of indigo. The dropped waistline suits her. He sees her short dark shining hair and her broad-lipped smile that comes quickly. Her eyebrows, strong and black, lift up and down as she talks and laughs. Her arms move vigorously – perhaps she is polishing the furniture so that it will not s'abime, although this is unlikely, for all her life my mother lacks interest in housekeeping. She values literature and talk and good food and rose gardens much more highly. Probably she is telling a story, which she does better than anyone. The gestures enliven the fabric of her dress so that the loose panels of linen move about over her large beautiful breasts. My father makes a terrible face, standing there in the English bakery. This contorted flesh startles the young woman. What is happening to her customer? What happens between my mother and father is not as his senses tell him it could be. If, if, a thousand impossible ifs – impossible as the manor house, the public school, the panelled library, the heat of summer silence on the Devon Lincoln Hampshire Sussex Cheshire hills. Mirabelle: beauty to be wondered at.

Half a century later, my father will be torn with rage at the construction of the new airport in Quebec: Mirabel. Storming, bullying, rasping, erect at the end of his long shining dinner table (polished by his own cleaning woman to the point where he can see his own face reflected in his own table), he will harangue friends and family into impotent seething submission as he spits out his hatred of the French Canadians, the damned frogs with their hands in the till, spits it out all over the well-done roast beef he is simultaneously and perfectly carving. Then he will fall silent. He will sit down. He will cover his own meat with horseradish and eat it in large pieces, and ignore the timid resumption of conversation at his table. He will not recognize anyone else's presence, not even my mother's, so deep will he be in the caverns of his rage, his freezing resentment that the world refuses to order itself as it ought. Laying his large knife and fork parallel across his plate, he will grimace terribly. For dessert there will be my mother's trifle: his favourite.

"Have you changed your mind, sir? I'll put it back, shall I?" The pretty hands take hold of the cake plate.

"No," says my father, his voice angry and low. "No. I'll take it." He has taken my mother. He has married her. He will buy the cake, and he will ride the Dover ferry to Calais, repeatedly, for he will love her, love her above all others, all his life long. He will do his best to give her the French kings.

Meanwhile here is this shopgirl who has witnessed him in the act of emotion. He feels the cold rich anger rising.

"How much?" he asks roughly. The young woman is disconcerted. Her answering smile is not full. She names the price.

Now this is calamity. Calamity, indignity, catastrophe, insult, humiliation.

Buying the cake will mean that he cannot have lunch before he boards the ferry. Obviously a missed lunch is no great matter, but that *is* not the matter. A man of his gifts should not have to make a miserable paltry puny choice like this. Both a gift for his wife and a pleasant lunch for himself should be easily possible. He should not have to give a second thought to their cost. My father stands silent in the bakery, chill with rage, while the mordant juices of resentment eat into his consciousness.

Why is he poor and why are so many unworthy people rich? Stupid vulgar Canadians who could not write a shapely sentence if their lives depended on it, who know nothing of Greek mythology or the French impressionists or Dickens or Macaulay, who say *anyways* and *lay down*, who holiday in Florida (in later life he will reserve a special loathing for these), who are Jews or have funny names from Eastern Europe or both, who do not have university degrees, who wear brown suits. . . .

My father glares down at the young woman in the English bakery. He stands tall, rigid, barely containing explosive movement. His face lengthens. The prominent cheek and jaw bones elongate.

In the young woman's body, the smallest possible movement occurs: a shrinking.

My father senses it, tells the direction of her feelings, presses in immediately, concentrates his gaze so that it is chilled metal, cold and killing, and sends its force out to nip her warm flesh. He will not let her go. Concentration, intensity, strength. He makes the glare persist. Do that long enough, and the other person will collapse, he knows. I know that. My father grips the counter.

She moves, she takes two little steps back. The fatal shining appears in her eyes.

My father is glad.

Deliberately counting out the money for the cake, my father piles it on the white wood surface between himself and the young woman. As always following anger, he breathes quickly, harshly, but the rage-induced blotches on his face begin to subside.

Trails of warm water move down the young woman's cheeks as she rings the payment into the till. Then, taking a sheet of scored white cardboard, she begins to form it into a box for the cake. She works quickly, neatly, and the tears stop coming, but a damp glossy track runs down each cheek.

My father is charmed. How pretty she looks, how endearing, with those little silver designs on her face! Already the cake is in the box. The string whirls off a ball suspended from the ceiling. She manipulates it deftly so the fibre goes over and under and round and about. Quickly, there is the finished box. She has even provided a pair of carrying loops through which my father can put his fingers; hers leave the loops and so push the cake box across the counter towards him.

"That is very pretty," my father says admiringly. Surprised that the young woman does not respond, he rephrases his compliment. "You do that very well."

To this she does respond, in a manner archetypal among people interacting with my father. She smiles – a little, not fully – and utters a null, monotonous answer, not meeting his eyes. "It is a butterfly knot, sir."

Then she walks through a doorway behind the counter and closes the door.

My father stands alone in the warm quiet fragrant room.

A few months before my father's death, he sits with my mother in their sunny garden, near the roses blooming by his study door, and reads aloud a letter from an old friend on holiday in France. This friend refers, amid descriptions of landscape and weather and food, to the servants at the country house where he is staying.

My father cries. Beating his thin hand on his thin knee, he asks shrilly why he has been stuck in this hole in Canada, why he has not been the one chosen for the sojourn in the well-staffed French chateau. Why has he been exiled to the Siberia of the scholar's life in this country where no one appreciates him or his abilities? Why did there not exist, when he was young, the plethora of scholarships and fellowships for study abroad available now to every Tom Dick and Harry who manage for God's sake to scrape through a general arts B.A.?

Around him flowers the radiant garden that my mother has created, loving every hour of the labour involved. The flower beds give way to plain lawn, where crab apples stand, and this lawn in turn slopes down to a duck-spotted brook overhung with willows. Inside, in the study, the walls and drawers and shelves are thick with honours garnered from every possible Canadian source.

Soon he will have lunch. The delicious Italian chicken soup, with tortellini, is based on a stock that takes my mother a full day to prepare; in these last few months of his cancer, this is one of the few dishes he enjoys. His digestion is much disordered because, after several surgeries, his long body lacks some of its original innards, these having been substituted by a revolting and unsatisfactory American contraption made of plastic and intended to prolong his life. *Il s'abîme.*

Several times my parents' cleaning woman, a constant in their lives for fifteen years, finds my father's beautiful slippers – blue suede, a Christmas gift from my mother – stained with excrement. Surreptitiously, she sponges them clean and sets them in the sun. She tells me sharply not to let the professor know that she knows about his little accidents; my father tells me sharply not to let her know that he has seen her taking his stained slippers away. I watch him standing alone on the sunlit deck, looking down at the slippers drying there, and I can tell that there are tears in his eyes.

At twenty-six, my father stands on the sidewalk – no, the pavement – out in the cool April sun, with the bell's music fading on his ear, breeding lilacs in the dead land and tears in his eyes. . . . He has been humiliated. The day is ruined. The journey is spoiled.

But. In his left pocket is Eliot and Bennett is in his right. He is a student at the greatest university in the English-speaking world, which means the greatest. He is about to take ship to Europe where he will see my mother again, again. And he has the cake. He has it at a sacrifice, true; it has not come as he wanted it; all the context was wrong, awkward, difficult, unseemly. But the plain fact remains that he has got it. Who ever has been such, done such?

In his last illness, when he is if anything even more bad-tempered than he has been habitually since youth, he mentions this cake to me, apparently en route to another retelling of the *s'abime* episode. He tells me that he bought a cake in London and took it all the way to Paris, to my mother, as a treat for their weekend together. He tells me. "I took a cake to France," he says to me insistently. "Wasn't that a romantic thing to do? Think of me, that young man, all his life to come." And then, contemptuously, "You've never done anything like that." He abandons the story. His face resettles into its customary bitter folds. He turns away.

And so my father took the cake to France, to Paris, to that small apartment of Mme. Papillon's where the furniture did or did not *s'abime*. There he presented it to his wife, my mother. She. . . .

LAWRENCE O'TOOLE

Goin' to Town with Katie Ann

Phonse Malloy's car, which operated as a taxi to take all and sundry in Heart's Longing to town, left, as a rule, at five o'clock in the morning while it was still dark, thereby arriving in St. John's at the beginning of business hours. Except for the time his Da took him out to the cod-jiggin' grounds, Toddy had never gotten up so early. There was not a sound. No birds. Not even a rooster. Toddy had to make a long face to keep awake.

Outside, a thick mist blanketed the ground. Toddy watched by the window and waited.

"Come 'ere," said his Da. His Da pressed a whole dollar bill into Toddy's hand. "Have a good time fer yerself an' get yerself somethin' nice."

When Toddy returned to the window he saw a speck of light far up the road. Could that be it at-tall? The speck of light grew bigger until it grew and split into a car's headlights, which in turn grew brighter in the fog. They came closer and closer until they stopped in front of the yard, flooding the foggy darkness like two big flashlights. Hearing the honk, he ran to his Da and kissed him and out the door.

His steps shied as he approached the car. The faces staring at him from behind the dew-drenched windows seemed half rubbed-out, as if they belonged to people not real. The back door swung open and he got in next to Katie Ann. She was wearing a dress he had not seen before, nor the old black purse in her lap. She smelled strongly of rosewater, so very different from how she'd been at the first of the summer. He could tell that everyone else in the taxi felt queer with Katie Ann being in the car, on account of Katie Ann probably not being right in the head. Nobody uttered a word. Katie Ann patted his hand with hers. As the car left the last of Heart's Longing behind from a hill, and the mist was all but gone, daylight lifted sluggishly from the woods as the car rattled above the gravel. Toddy snuggled back in his seat to review his summer with Katie Ann.

*   *   *

A purplish light had begun to invade the evening. The ball, to Toddy, seemed to be a travelling pocket of darkness. *Thwack!* He heard the satisfying smack of it in the mitt's pocket. The field, which the bigger boys used as a diamond, and the two figures of Kevin and Adrian, his best friends, were blurred. Across the road to the back of it a series of small cliffs sloped to the beach, beyond which the waters of the harbour drank in the last light of day. The three of them had been savouring these final, precious moments before they would have to officially and regretfully declare the day over.

It was just then their attention was drawn to a figure moving up the road alongside them. From its stoop, Toddy knew it to be Josey Nail, who was not right in the head and who lived with his sister, Katie Ann. They lived in the grey-boarded two-storey house listing to the side at the other end of the field. Josey, who was harmless, greeted them in his muffled gibberish, as muted as the evening itself, and then laughed to himself, as he always did whenever he said something. They watched and waited until he passed on, a slow and stooped shadow on the road, then resumed their play.

Though he was only ten, Toddy wondered whether the bigger boys would let him join their league, the Heart's Longing Larks, once school began again. Everyone said he was a wicked hitter. Wrapped up in his future, Toddy didn't see Adrian wind up, take a quick run, and pelt the ball which, misjudged, went way too high and landed in Katie Ann's yard. He and Adrian ran over to the fence.

"Now," whispered Toddy gravely to Adrian. "Look what ya did. Now we're in fer it."

Kevin came up behind them, out of breath. "Did it go in?"

"Ssshhh . . ." they both hissed at him. "Git down, b'y, git down!" They huddled in silence behind the fence considering what they might do. Short of landing in the middle of Hell, the ball had plopped into the worst place possible. Not even the bigger boys dared retrieve a lost baseball from Katie Ann's yard.

"She burns 'em, ya know," Adrian said. "She goes out an' collects 'em an' burns 'em. Ever see that dirty ol' smoke what comes up from her chimbly? Balls. It's all the balls she burns."

"It's the only ball we got," said Toddy, "but I'm not goin' in after it."

"Sooky baby," said Adrian.

"Yeah, sooky baby," Kevin added.

"I'm no sooky baby," he told them. He rose and peered into the yard. The grass there just grew and grew until it died and rotted, creating an ugly tangle of weed, straw, and stink. And inside Katie Ann's house was said to be wall-papered with old newspaper. She never went out anywhere, but she was always there, peering out from behind her yellowed lace curtains the moment she heard the traipse of feet on the road. She was reputed to have not washed in years. Her real name was not Nail – it was O'Neill – but everyone called them Nail and left them to themselves. Every once in a while Toddy's Da sent her over a fresh fish.

"How many dresses d'ya think she wears at-tall?"

"Least ten."

"I heard twenty."

"Rats nest in her hair."

"I heard tell of that."

Gathering his courage once more, Toddy poked his head over the fence and saw the glow of Katie Ann's oil lamp from the kitchen window. "Yee better yell if she comes out with her broom," he charged Adrian and Kevin.

"Yes, b'y, us will."

"Us will."

The row of old rotted palings that excused itself as a fence was difficult to scale; Toddy landed shakily on the other side. He began to make his way stealthily through the yard, the dried weeds and straw snapping under his feet. Soon, he saw it: the white globe of the ball about four or five feet from the doorstep. Arched like a cat, he crept over, but stopped in his tracks as he heard the creak of the door and saw the spill of light on the doorstep.

She fixed her gaze upon him. Toddy's heart wanted to crawl up into his throat. She wore an enormous bun of hair, kept from falling all over the place by four or five hair nets. There was definitely room enough for rats to nest in it. At least she didn't have the broom with her. That was a charity. They both stared at the ball. Finally, she bent to pick it up, the enormous bun shifting to one side of her head. Erect again, she held out the ball to him. "Yer Paschal Boland's little fella, aren't ya?" Her voice was deep, like a hand reaching down into a barrel."

"Ye-ess . . ."

"Here," she said with a curious smile, stretching her hand out further.

He half expected her to start cackling all of a sudden and was tensed to run. In the queer half-light from the oil lamp in the kitchen he saw that her eyes were slanted. They were like a Chinese. She had Chinese eyes. Taking the ball, he ran like the Mick's hate of Hell to the fence. "You might of been kilt," Adrian congratulated him once he was on the other side.

That night as his Da played skin-the-rabbit with him, hauling off each article of clothing with a single yank, Toddy, having already related his evening's adventure breathlessly, asked his Da if he thought Katie Ann was in league with the fairies. "She's just an ol' woman," his Da replied. "She was good to me once when I come back from the war."

"Kin I bring her over a fish tomorra?"

"Yer not afraid of her?" his Da laughed.

"I'm no sooky baby," he told his Da.

The next afternoon after he had picked up the codfish – a good one, with a charcoal shadow fanning out from its spine – Toddy heard the cries of the gulls as they circled, dipped, and dived around the wharf. The cries seemed to mock what he was about to do. Some people said Katie Ann kept rats for pets as well. But Toddy determined he was no sooky baby. Before he knew it, or was ready for it, he was standing outside on the road. His heart juddered as he lifted the latch on the gate and saw the curtain move at the corner of her kitchen window. At the door, shaking, the fish still alive and flapping, he rapped gently. Presently the

hinges creaked and the door opened a crack. Then her
face, her Chinese eyes. In the daylight her eyes were dark
and bright, like buttons. She squinted at him and blinked
twice. Toddy shoved the fish at her. "Me Da sent it."

She blinked again and took the fish. "Thank Paschal fer
me." Pausing, she seemed on the verge of some decision or
other. "Wait here," she commanded and went into the
house. Returning, she had her fist rolled up into a ball, held
at her breast. She held out her hand, fist still closed, but
withdrew it and said, "Come in."

The hallway was so dark Toddy had to feel his way blindly
along the walls. He recognized the texture of the papering:
old newspaper that shirred at the touch of his fingertips. At
the end of the murky hallway dusty shafts of sunlight
spilled into a single spot. There was an airless, almost sick-
making smell about the place.

"Come in, come in," she urged him at the kitchen door.
He went over and sat on the daybed, trying to accommodate the newness of everything around him. But the newness was oldness. The yellowed newspapers wallpapering
the room. A dirty coal stove with a grey hill of ashes fallen
to the botton of the grate. A small and old wooden table
covered in a balding oil-cloth. Her toppling mound of hair
as she took a seat on one of the chairs. Her Chinese eyes.
"What's yer name?" she demanded.

"Toddy."

"Queer name," she commented.

He made so bold to explain it was really Theodore.

"Still a queer name," she insisted. "You afraid of me?"
Her grin showed snaggled teeth.

Toddy shook his head and lied, and this seemed to
please her.

She got up and came over to him and unrolled her
clenched fist, displaying a shiny dime in the palm of her

hand. "They're all skeered of me, but it's the height of foolishness. Here," she said, "take it. Fer bringin' the fish." He thanked her and she returned to her seat. She just sat there, looking at him and through him. "Why d'ya wear all that hair?" he finally asked her.

"It's mine," she said, placing her fingertips protectively to the mound, as though someone might want to take it away from her.

"What d'ya do with the balls?" he inquired, surprised at his own gumption.

"I burns 'em. What d'ya expect me to do with 'em? Wear 'em as brooches? Want some syrup?"

He nodded and smiled. At the cupboard she took down an old bottle of Purity syrup, a rose-red colour, and in a jiffy had mixed the extract with water into two tumblers. He tasted it: raspberry. Then she started to talk. She told him how she liked syrup but preferred tea, in fact drank so much of it that one day she felt liable to turn into a tea bag. She told him he had a fine Da. "I remembers him well as a little fella himself," she said. Her eyes went glassy with remembrance. She seemed to be sailing away somewhere else inside her own mind, the way grown-up people often did. Toddy noticed her coarse, plump hands with the dirt caked into the fingernails. She must have been wearing at least five dresses. "D'ya like school?" she asked, out of the blue.

"Sister Mary Eulalie says I'm smart but as lazy as a cut dog."

"The nuns know nothin'," she said.

"I like jography best."

"Oh," she brightened. "Jography's wonderful. All those faraway places an' different people an' everything." Her voice got dreamy and she began to sing, *"Far-away play-ces oh-ver the sea, far-away play-ces fer me."* She stopped short. "I used to sing in the choir when I was a girl. They all said I had the sweetest voice. Voice of an angel." Her features clouded and she began to drift off somewhere again. "Finish yer syrup," she said. "You haves to go now. But you kin come back if an' when you wants to."

*   *   *

Toddy had fallen asleep, missing most of the ride. As he awoke and rubbed his eyes, he experienced a strange sensation: a smoothness and humming of sound beneath Phonse Malloy's taxi. "We're almost there," Katie Ann whispered to him. There were no bumps or rattles or bounces. And then Toddy realized what it was – pavement! They were travelling on pavement! This was what it was like! The rest of the passengers had the same dreamy expressions on their faces, the way people might look if they were on their way to Heaven. The road there must be paved. A new world whirled by outside the car window – houses of differing shapes and sizes, all painted different colours, and above them many wires criss-crossing each other like trawl lines. Then he remembered: the people in St. John's had electricity.

The taxi disgorged them at the railway station on Water Street. The building, a salt-and-pepper brick was enormous, taller even than the Our Lady of Sorrows in Heart's Longing. Behind it steam hissed and brakes screeched as a train pulled out backwards. People were everywhere, some carrying grips, others rushing madly about. It was like a dance. He felt Katie Ann tug at his sleeve and say, "Let's git goin'."

As they walked down Water Street cars and people passed them by unheeding. Nobody said hello to anybody else. As they turned a curve the buildings gave way to a view of St. John's harbour, every inch of it filled with ships, their spars nearly touching the sun, funnels belching out black smoke. All the ships of the world must be here right now, he thought, soon to be headed for faraway places.

*　　*　　*

When his Mom found out Toddy had been inside Katie Ann's, she scrubbed him sore, fearing he had picked up The Itch from her. And The Itch was the worst thing you could get. Toddy returned to visit Katie Ann Saturday evening after benediction while his Mom and Da had their baths in the big washtub in the middle of the floor, but he didn't tell his Mom; he figured if he told the truth he'd have no skin left.

"I was just givin' Josey his cup of tea," whispered Katie Ann when she answered the door. "An' I'm havin' one meself. Come in." Josey was at the table drinking his tea. He looked up at Toddy with idiot amazement. Drool, mixed with toast crumbs, had dribbled and lodged at his chin. He laughed and made one of his idiot sounds, showing off his one big orange-coloured tooth.

"Don't mind him," she said. "He's just like a Christian. He knows what's goin' on." Her voice changed, becoming lighter and higher as she spoke to him in baby-talk. "Ya knows everythin' that's goin' on, don't ya Josey? Yes ya do. That's me good fella. Finish yer tea an' go to bed." She returned to normal speech. "He knows what's goin' on. He just can't tell a soul about it."

"I just spent nearly all yer dime," Toddy told her.

"On what?"

"Coke an' a raisin square." She seemed unimpressed, or else had no opinion. It was hard to tell with her. Josey laughed and made another of his idiot sounds, like the noises seals made out on the ice. He got up and came toward Toddy, then poked his finger in Toddy's shoulder. Toddy flinched a little. "That means he likes ya," said Katie Ann. Josey smiled and went out the kitchen door. Presently, the tread of his hob-nail boots was heard overhead.

She had made him tea. "Was Josey always the way he is?" asked Toddy as he sipped the hot tea.

The question disturbed her. "No, he wasn't," she finally answered. "He got sick when he was yer own age an' then he was like he is after that. He talks, y'know. Not a whole lot, but sometimes he looks at me real hard an' tries to talk. Takes him ferever to do it, but when he gits it out, gibberish an' all, it makes some kind of sense. He's not mental," she said, shaking her head. "An' he's company." She sighed to herself and sipped her tea. "I likes a bit of company now an' again."

She asked him if he wanted to play cards. They played a few hands and never said much, but Toddy watched her all the time. She was so different from anyone he'd ever heard tell of. When she beat his jack with a king and won the third game, she threw back her head and laughed. It was a wild, rich sound. The shadow on the wall wriggled madly behind her. "Ya reminds me of Josey when he was yer age," she said. "Josey was a lovely little child. I know it's hard to credit, but you reminds me of him, you do."

*　　*　　*

Inside Imelda's Beauty Shoppe Toddy felt like pinching himself to remind himself that he was really here in St. John's. Through the bevelled glass of the shop window he kept marvelling at the odd shapes the people out in the street made as they walked by. At first the woman fiddled with Katie Ann's hair, looking at it as if it were a puzzle before she began snipping it away. When she got up from the chair he had to look twice to make sure it was her. "If I saw meself I'd hardly know me," she laughed when they left the place.

Next they went into a woman's clothing store, Frances Fashions, and he watched her as she tried on dresses and hats and things. She finally decided on a yellow dress with big blue flowers, which she decided to wear, as well as her new shoes and a new purse. And there was a little hat with clusters of forget-me-nots in the netting. He noticed, too, that her breasts were different: lifted up and pointy.

"Ya must of been mildered waitin' fer me," she said. "Well, that's over an' done with." Out in the busy street, she kept fondling the dress, touching it like it was alive on her. "It's a charity I did this fer myself," she said. "It's a real charity."

She took him to a soda fountain where Toddy had two milkshakes and a banana split. Katie Ann said she was too excited to eat a thing. On the tail end of the banana split Toddy felt queasy and told her so.

"With what you just took in I'm not hardly surprised. We better walk it off. We kin walk up to the Basilica."

They headed up the hilly, narrow warren of streets until, panting, they came upon the church. Its coupled towers stood majestically above every other building, watching the city beneath it. Katie Ann, obviously in one of her moods again, said she wasn't going in and sat herself on a stone bench looking out to the many-sparred harbour. She had never stepped foot inside a church in ages, he knew. She was bound straight for Hell, of that there was little doubt. *Outside the church there is no salvation.* His catechism and the priest and nuns were pretty strict about that one. Still, Toddy felt it unfair. Katie Ann was not a bad person. He went in without her.

Everything inside seemed to be gold. A gigantic monstrance shone like the sun itself on the altar, catching the light from the side windows. Statues of saints stood hovering everywhere he looked, but on the stained-glass windows, way up high, the saints seemed small and sad and holy. Candles flickered inside tiny beaded cups in the naves. He went over and lit one, offering it up for the soul of Katie Ann Nail.

*   *   *

"Josey took off in the woods yesterday," said Katie Ann when Toddy came in. "He'll be gone a good long spell, too, if ya asks me."

"What does he eat when he stays up there all that time?"

"Rabbits, birds, God knows what all else." She was drinking tea, as usual, though it was scorching outside. "I needs this tea like I needs another head," she said. "I think I'll go out."

Out? It was a well-known fact that Katie Ann had not stirred outside her yard in years. "Out?" he asked.

"Yes. Out."

"Where?"

"Up to the graveyard. You comin' with me?"

"All right."

"I think I'll take off a dress first."

"I'll go on up ahead an' meet ya there," he told her. He couldn't be seen walking up the road with Katie Ann Nail. Disappointment was written all over her face, but she nodded and went upstairs.

Inside the cemetery he walked around the grave sites to see if he knew anybody, meanwhile keeping an eye on the road for a sign of her arrival. From behind the cemetery he could hear youngsters shouting and splashing in the swimming hole, which was only big enough for the babies to use. When he caught sight of Katie Ann walking up the back road he knew how everyone must be poking their noses out of their windows to gawk, wondering where on earth Katie Ann Nail could be headed.

Entering the graveyard, she looked as though she were in some kind of trance and, as she approached him, her legs faltered slightly in the soft earth. "Let me see," she said to herself as she began to walk up the path. "Let me see if I remembers . . ."

Toddy followed her until they came upon another winding path at the slope near the back where the old graves were. "It's got no marker," she said, "but I used to have it in me head where it was." She stopped and surveyed several unmarked graves. "They're not it." They moved through a cluster of bluebells and wild azaleas. "This is the one," she said, finally, pointing to some blood-red partridge berries clinging to a bush. "That's how I know which one it is." Her features became stony as she stared down at the grave. Lowering herself to the ground, she began to pluck out tiny weeds from the unmarked plot and ran her hand along the ground, smoothing its roughness.

"Who is it?" Toddy asked in a very soft voice, soft because the dead might be listening and didn't want to be disturbed. The cries of the youngsters in the swimming hole had died down. Everything had gotten terribly quiet under the scorching sun.

She seemed not to have heard him until, in a soft voice as well, she said, "Someone I loved."

"Somebody of yer family." Toddy still made sure to keep his voice low because the dead didn't want to be talked about.

"No," she said, "I loved him different than that."

It struck Toddy that, there on her knees, in her own way, Katie Ann was praying.

"Well," she said, "I've had me look," and raised herself from the ground.

As they walked down the path, he said, "Sometimes ya looks the way me Da do."

"How's that?"

"Sometimes the two of yee stares. Like yeer lost or somethin'. It looks sad."

She considered this. "It's because we have memories, I s'pose. We thinks about the memories we haves."

"I don't have much memories."

"No," she said and smiled. "Yer too small yet fer memories. You kin be glad of that fer a while."

When they reached the gate he told her he was going swimming out back. She didn't know it was just for babies and he didn't want to hurt her feelings by refusing to walk home with her. For this, he felt terrible.

A similar anxiety overtook him when he played baseball with the bigger boys. During the summer the bigger boys' games were held in the evenings since all the bigger boys either fished with their fathers or worked in the fish-packing plant over in Heart's Content. When they played in the field next to Katie Ann's, those evenings were saturated with the smell of the sea. No matter how diligently they scrubbed, the aroma of fish clung to their persons. For Toddy it was the smell of his Da, the scent of affection. As he lay on the ground, arms pillowed under his head, he saw the ball arcing through the air and the sky, with its full-rigged clouds, spinning slowly above him, the faint odour of fish in it all. He could not have been happier.

Yet there was always this anxiety he felt on the field. He dreaded hitting the ball too hard lest it should land in Katie Ann's yard. He was in a fix: he wanted to play well, yet feared to do so. Katie Ann probably felt that he was *with* them and *against* her. It was not true. It was just not true.

Then one evening the worst happened. Phil Reddy hit a homer into her yard. Since he was the outfielder, he had to run and get it. When he picked up the ball he was sure she had seen him.

The next evening while creeping through the shadows into her house, he felt little men running up ladders inside his heart. He found her playing a hand of patience. "Ya certainly do need the patience of Job fer this," she said after he had come in and sat down for a while. Her voice was steely and edgy. Turning over the jack of diamonds from the pack, she flipped the card back and forth between her thumb and her index finger. It wouldn't place. "Little Chris-ter!" she spat at the jack of diamonds as if the card could hear her. The violence in her voice frightened him. Then, with a wide and reckless sweep of her hand, she sent the cards flying from the table. Toddy jumped. "Want tea?" she asked. She sounded mean. He nodded. While she was mak-ing the tea, he told her, "I decided not to play ball anymore." It was his having said that that brought about the change in her, he figured. It had even brought them to town.

*   *   *

The sunlight almost blinded him when he came out of the Basilica. Katie Ann was still sitting on the stone bench, looking out over the harbour, brilliant and busy through the heat waves. A large ship, as red as the sunset and send-ing a plume of smoke into the bright blue sky, silently sailed out the harbour's narrows into the Atlantic, headed for faraway places, he thought.

"Ya shoulda seen inside," he told her, startling her. "Ya shoulda seen it."

"Is that right?" She seemed disinterested in any further report. She had not tunnelled out of her mood. Presently she said, "I wonder what I'll git Josey," and sighed. "It's hard to know what to git an idiot." He had never heard her call Josey that before and it struck him as cruel. "God bless the mark," she added and said, "Let's go look fer somethin' down on Water Street."

At Bowering's Toddy bought a gun-and-holster set out of his dollar and Katie Ann bought Josey a snow shaker, inside of which was a tiny house with a tree beside it. Showing it to him, she shook the globe and it flurried artificial snow inside. "It's real nice," she said. "He'll be taken with this. He kin play with it when he's lonesome. Hungry?" she asked.

Across the street they saw a restaurant sign that read CHOP SU Y. "I s'pose they won't poison us if we goes in," she said.

CHOP SU Y was hung with faded and torn paper lanterns above each table. Toddy had seen nothing like it. Two other customers, a man and a woman, the woman looked like she'd been crying, were seated at the back. "These people are Chinamen!" Katie Ann exclaimed in a whisper to him. The owner came rushing over to them and bowed, saying words they didn't understand, motioning them to a table. Flustered and excited, they took their seats at a table as the owner, who was extraordinarily short for a grown man, thrust menus at them and left, bowing and smiling, showing his yellowed teeth.

"This," announced Katie Ann, "is a menu. I remembers it from the last time I come to St. John's, God but that was years an' years ago. We points out what we wants and they brings it to us."

Toddy opened the large menu and began reading, though little made sense to him: egg drop soup, chow mein, fried rice, chop suey, and a continuing list of queer-sounding names. But he didn't care. He was glad he had given up baseball for this and to be with her.

"They could be askin' us to eat worms fer all I knows," said Katie Ann. "I'll tell ya what: we'll pick out things – anything at-tall – an' eat 'em regardless." The waiter came over with two small steaming bowls. "Tea," he told them. "Chinese tea." Katie Ann pointed out their selections and he left. Gingerly sipping some of the tea, she grimaced and said, "If this is tea, then I'm the Queen of Newfoundland. Think they'd give ya handles fer the cups while they're at it, too."

"There's no Queen of Newfoundland."

"An' why not?"

"Because the Queen of Ingland is the Queen of New-foundland."

She mulled this over for a minute before saying, "Well, you'd think they'd give us one of our own, wouldn't ya?"

When the food came, it looked too strange to eat. But Toddy was so glad to be where he was that the rumbling in his stomach seemed such a small and petty thing.

*   *   *

The first change in her after he told her he was not playing ball anymore came a few weeks after he had, indeed, stopped playing ball. One day it was clear she had washed her face. Two days later she was wearing a scent. "It's rosewa-ter," she told his sniffing nose. "I got it a long time ago. It's nearly as old as me." Some time later came the most aston-ishing change of all, which confronted him as he entered the kitchen: she was sitting at the table, obviously waiting for him to come, with nearly all her hair cut off. She looked both expectant and frightened, like a little girl who thinks she might have done something either wonderful or wrong. "Well?" she asked. Toddy didn't say anything. "Is it that bad?"

"No," he stammered, "it's real nice."

"Thank you," she said rather grandly and pampered what was left of her hair with her hands. She looked as pleased as a bird with a worm. "I'm goin' to get a perm," she announced. "I'm goin' to town to git meself a perm."

"Town!" She might as well have just told him that the Blessed Virgin had appeared to her the night before.

"Might as well git a couple dresses fer meself while I'm at it."

Toddy was incredulous.

"Will ya do somethin' fer me?" she asked. He nodded. "Help me clean up the yard."

Some minutes later they were seated among years of debris and weeds, clearing everything away under the blistering sun. The task seemed almost impossible. Katie Ann went to the shed and brought back a creaking wheelbarrow, as well as some rusty gardening tools.

All told, it took them four days to clear the yard. Katie Ann rubbed her hands down the thighs of her stained dress and said, "I s'pose I'll have to condemn this ol' thing. I'll just have to dow away with it, that's all." She looked happy and, it struck him, she was beginning to look like other people did. When they were through with their work she went into the house and made them some of the rose-red raspberry syrup. Returning, she sat and rested on her haunches, drinking the syrup. Sighing with pleasure, she looked up at the sky. The sky was clear and a pale, lovely blue like a baby's blanket. And it seemed to Toddy that she was watching angels. When he looked up at the sky himself, he could almost see them too.

And then she told him she was taking him to town with her.

*   *   *

They had almost reached the train station, hurrying through the throng of people, when Toddy's attention was drawn to a store window displaying a collection of sporting goods, among it a bunch of brand new baseballs. He stopped abruptly and stood looking at them, transfixed.

"D'ya want a ball?" she asked from behind him.

He shook his head slowly. "I don't play baseball no more."

"Well, ya never knows," she said and, passing him, vanished into the store. When she came out she handed him a baseball. He took it, feeling its wonderful weight and smoothness in his hand. He wanted to throw his arms around her, but she had moved on ahead too quickly. "Thanks!" he shouted and saw her head nod slightly in front of him.

In the taxi on the way out of St. John's he found himself locked into one of those faraway stares into which he had so often seen Katie Ann disappear. Now he had his own memory. He was holding it in his hand. Pretending to fall asleep, he cautiously edged his head over to her shoulder, but he kept his eyes open a crack sufficiently to see the glint of a smile as she looked down upon him. She soon shifted her position as well so that his head could rest more comfortably there at her shoulder once they left the evenness of the pavement behind.

MARUSIA BOCIURKIW

Mama, Donya

She makes coffee in the morning, makes it while I'm still asleep, so it's not like I actually see her doing it, or can tell it's for me. But it's always there, in the percolator, strong the way I like it, stronger than she'd drink it herself. Sometimes she joins me as I sit on the couch, the old floral one in the family room, incongruously covered with embroidered pillows from the Ukraine. We gaze out the window to the backyard and sip our coffee, not talking. The silence of the house is temporary, as is this wordless moment of truce between us. My Buddhist friend Janet would call it "being in a state of grace," and in it we are briefly fixed in time and know our names: mama, donya; mother, daughter.

Sometimes when I'm visiting, but not always, my father will wake me for his special breakfast: buckwheat kasha. The smell is powerful: it represents childhood, and being cared for. My father gives me a generous serving, with milk and salt, the way we always ate it, and I don't tell him I never eat kasha anymore. He watches me fondly as I force it down, and then the sweet milk of his attention runs dry, and he's gone, to his books and his study, leaving me with my mother again.

We go shopping. It's her only form of recreation in a life clipped and narrowed by respectability and the demands of my father's career, so I comply. I grab some Tylenol 3, and a copy of *Radical America*, in case I get stranded in some remote corner of the Cedar Grove Mall. All of these malls are named after geographical features that no longer exist: huge, bloated structures that capture women with what my friend Anita calls their "lobster-trap architecture."

The voices of my friends are particularly eloquent today, evidence of sagging resolve at the halfway point of my ten-day visit. I have made a pact with my superego: no remarks about American imperialism while watching TV; no feminist rhetoric as I read the morning paper. I have with me a small library of socialist-feminist literature, some lesbian trash-fiction (for balance), and, for desperate moments, an early, syrupy Cris Williamson tape for secret sessions on my Sony Walkman. And I will call Claire. But only once. With Baba gone and buried just one month ago, I can give them ten days of my life. It's nothing to me; it's everything to them. This is the mantra I repeat to myself as we stroll in a leisurely fashion through the imitation-cedar innards of the Cedar Grove Mall.

She wants to buy me a dress. It's not bad, simple green jersey, 100 per cent cotton, padded shoulders. She's always had good taste. But I tell her I'd have nowhere to wear such a dress, and her smile fades. We go for a coffee to the Forest Glen Café. She starts to tell me about Nadia, the daughter of a friend of hers. She thinks I will be able to relate: Nadia is the newly elected president of the Conservative Party Women's Caucus in town. I choke on my cinnamon-blueberry Danish. Nadia and I used to sleep over at each other's houses and read together from *Cosmopolitan* such articles as "How to Orgasm" and "Masturbation: What Every Woman Needs." Not long after that, we discovered Betty Friedan, and consecrated ourselves and each other to the Women's Liberation Movement. We were all of sixteen; nonetheless, I feel betrayed. "Has she joined REAL Women yet?" I mutter. Mama looks away.

Strike two. One more, and the hard-won truce is over. So I tell her I've changed my mind about the dress, and she buys it for me, $79.99, a month's grocery money for me. And also: black lace stockings, and enormous silver earrings. It makes her happy, I reason. Maybe I'll give the dress to Janet for her birthday.

After that we start walking to the car. Two women are in front of us. They are carrying groceries and walking close together, hips touching. I've never seen such a thing at the Cedar Grove Mall. They must be from out of town. I can't take my eyes off them. My mother is talking about the new extension to the mall they're building over on Orchard Boulevard. The women get into the car next to ours. One of them leans over and kisses the other on the lips, and they embrace. I'm four years old, watching something *bad*: enthralled, horrified, delighted. My mother notices them. "Queers. They're all over the place these days," she says matter-of-factly, and starts the car.

When we get home, she turns on the TV, then goes into the kitchen to start dinner. I ask her if she needs any help, but as usual she says no, so I sit in front of the television, near the kitchen indicating my solidarity. I am simultaneously watching a special called "Women of the World" ("a look at beautiful women and the fashions they wear"), and reading a book called *Labour Pains: Women's Work in Crisis*. I hear my mother humming softly under her breath. For the moment, she and I are content. My father comes downstairs and puts on a record: The Dnipro Men's Chorus, singing Ukrainian folk songs. My mother is chopping cabbage. The three-track sound becomes too much, and I dissolve into my imagination, a survival tactic learned from childhood.

My head is on Claire's shoulder. My hand strokes the inside of her thigh. We are watching "Dynasty," in which Krystle is

*afraid that Blake may have fallen in love with Alexis. This is
our electronic fireplace: we don't really watch it, it just flickers
warmly in the corner of the bedroom, as Claire licks my ears,
kisses my neck and collarbone and space between my breasts. I
caress her legs as she moves down to suck my nipples. Krystle
and Blake kiss and make up as Claire's nimble fingers slide in
and below the waistband of my sweatpants. I am very wet, and
come almost immediately, during a crescendo-filled McDonald's
commercial, my legs wrapped around her, her tongue deep in my
mouth.*

The television stays on all evening. A group of experts
discusses the contra-funding scandal. They cannot decide
whether the money should have gone into a Swiss bank
account or not. At dinner (borscht, pot roast, cabbage rolls)
federal politics are discussed. The Conservatives are too arro-
gant. The NDP's falling apart. Turner's pretty good on multi-
culturalism. Mostly, my father talks, my mother listens. I skip
dessert and flee to the basement for a cigarette. A picture of
the Pope smiles at me from the wall, next to the Ukrainian-
maiden figurines. Tomorrow, I will call Claire.

She has found an occasion for the green dress. The Watsons have invited us to Thanksgiving dinner. I attempt a
pleased smile when she announces this, and make a mental
note to bring along the joint Anita thoughtfully provided for
me. The Watsons are on the wrong side of a great many key
social issues. Mr. Watson is a retired air force general. Mrs.
Watson is a homemaker, and a volunteer for the local Pro-Life
group who regularly picket the only hospital in town that has
an abortion committee. Their son Frank studied communi-
cations on an army scholarship. He got married last month.
Kitty Watson, divorced three years ago, will remarry in the
spring, to Bud, who happens to be a born-again Christian.
Everyone will be there.

My mother fills me in on the breakages and repairs to the Watson family tree while I am dressing. The dress is becoming, though the lacy stockings are a touch sleazy. I pluck some hairs out of my mole, paint on some eyeliner, and sip a beer. At this moment, Claire is at her Canadian Action for Nicaragua meeting. She's one of two lesbians in the organization, but in her endearingly sweet, idealistic way, hopes to organize a gay and lesbian cotton-brigade to Nicaragua. I must call her later tonight. My mother offers me some jewellery. She thinks the eyeliner is too heavily applied. I sigh, and rummage through her makeup bag for lipstick. No sense just going halfway.

Last year we argued bitterly about the contras. The year before, it was the Mid-East war. We're at dessert by the time General Watson and I start to loosen up. By some oversight, we've been seated next to each other, and I know that my excessively seductive appearance has thrown him off. His eyes slip nervously and frequently to my black-lace legs.

Mrs. Watson dishes trifle onto our cut-glass dessert plates. We are discussing The Media. Frank Watson is a radio announcer. "I'm realizing how much power we as The Media have, and it's scary," he says. "Take AIDS, for example. The Media has virtually created an epidemic. People, normal people, with children and families, are afraid to, ah, afraid . . . ah, to be . . . sexual now. . . ." He blushes, suddenly. His new wife Deb coughs into her napkin. Mrs. Watson offers coffee or tea. Mr. Watson cuts in.

"AIDS is a homosexual disease, son, and let's not forget it. It's been foisted upon us by the perverted activities of a mob of . . . child molesters. They should be lined up and shot."

It's not like I planned it, it's just that my arm muscles and the innermost stirrings of my soul were suddenly profoundly in sync with one another. I leaned over to get the cream and nudged a bottle of wine. A half-litre of red Kressman's landed in Mr. Watson's lap.

"Terribly sorry," I muttered, "I'm feeling rather dizzy. I really must go." I gathered my things and left, smoking the joint on the way home.

"Why did you do it, Halia?" she asks me the next morning.

"Do what?" I reply.

She doesn't answer. It's rare that I can really put one past my mama. So I discard the speech I had prepared on premenstrual syndrome and how it can lead to violence and sometimes murder. Besides, my reserve of sweet submissiveness has just about run out.

"Watson is a racist, sexist jerk. I'm sick of hearing him talk like that year after year. It's people like him who kill off peasants in Central America. He makes me sick, he makes me feel stupid, and, besides, he baits me –"

"What do you mean he *baits* you? He was talking about *homosexuals!* Why do you have to jump up and defend every cause on this earth? Why can't you just take care of your own?"

She is crying. I go over to her and put my arms around her, the way I would if it was Anita or Janet or Claire, trying to comfort, saying I'm sorry, expecting to be understood. But her back stiffens and she leaves the room.

Sometimes I'm afraid I'm turning into a commissar, a socialist-feminist dragon-lady. Times in which I long to regain some of the imagined (fabricated) gentleness of my ancestral past. I phone Claire that afternoon, and tell her how I miss her touch, her woman-smell, her body-warmth in my bed, and hear my voice grow soft and calm again. She in turn makes comforting sounds on the phone, shrieks with delight when I tell her about the Watson episode, and tells me I must make peace with my mother. She arranges to meet my train the next day.

It's a cold and drizzly morning, perfect for a train ride. My father is getting ready to drive me to the station. My mother has made kolbassa sandwiches wrapped in waxed paper, and has placed a package of her poppyseed rolls next to my bag. I sit next to her on the couch before I go. We are silent for several minutes, watching the rain trail down the window, and then I take her hand. Her fingers resist, curl in, but she doesn't pull away. "Mama," I say, "I know you're sad, now that Baba's gone. I'll be thinking about you. I'm going to call, every week."

She looks down at the floor. She whispers, "Halia, you and your father, that's the only family I have left in this country. . . ."

"I know, Mama, I know." I wipe a tear off her cheek and tell her that I love her. She looks at me and smiles, almost imperceptibly, and it is as though an old and brittle string wrapped around my heart has unravelled. I have never spoken like this to my mother before.

Halfway to the train station, my father clears his throat. Expecting his usual "Do you have enough money?" I turn to look at him with a smile on my face.

"Halia . . . who's this Claire?"

My heart sinks. My head spins. "Claire who?"

"This girl you phone, I heard you yesterday."

"She's my . . . my Claire, ah . . . she's my friend."

"You, thirty years old, not married, no good job . . . it's not natural, how you live. Your mama, so upset by you. Coming to visit us, how can you hurt her like this, how can you be such a – "

Lesbian. The word has been waiting for me patiently, under my breath for days. It sits in the air, unspoken, still secret, there but not there, a solid wedge between us.

"Agh . . ." he is saying, "What's the use. You stupid, stupid girl."

There is nothing I can say. All the provisional, first-draft coming-out speeches were for later, much later, for a time when we would be wiser and closer. I had envisioned slow recognition, a photograph developing more depth, and slowly, slowly, a familiar image again, the same picture, the three of us, same as before. Here there is nothing but shame, over-exposure; artificial light in a private room.

We are at the train station. I don't have my ticket, and the train leaves in four minutes. I grab my bags. When I lean over to kiss him, he turns away, won't say a word.

Somehow I get through the ticket lineup, garble something to the man behind the counter, and then miraculously find myself on a moving train, bald November fields spinning by. A long, grey corridor for my thoughts to batter about like crippled birds, at the end of which is Claire, and the liberated territory of her strong, long woman's arms.

Claire comforts, with glasses of wine, lengthy embraces, self-help manuals from the Women's Bookstore. They address various topics; she's not sure if I am mourning my dead grandmother, my estranged father, or my oppressed mother. She herself came out to her parents long ago, over drinks on some patio, and brings lovers home for Christmas. "It's only a matter of time," she murmurs. "Wait till your mother meets me. She won't be able to resist my cooking, let alone my charm." Though she never says so, it's clear she is bewildered by my grief.

Claire is a fifth-generation Canadian. Her parents play golf and eat things I've never touched, like Yorkshire pudding and tripe.

I describe to her my Baba, Kateryna, still illiterate in English when she died at age eighty-eight, who came here with my mother on a crowded boat to join my grandfather, who had fled the Polish Occupation. Who, whenever she said "home," meant a small village in Western Ukraine she hadn't seen in over sixty years. My Baba, a seamstress since she was sixteen, who wanted nothing more than to be able to sew for me my wedding dress, for which she had chosen the pattern years ago. And my mama, for whom grandchildren speaking to her in Ukrainian represent continuity and future: the only security she will ever accept as genuine in a culture that daily makes her feel insecure.

I explain to her that in Ukrainian I am "*samitna*," the word for "single," which, coincidentally, sounds almost exactly like the word for "lonely." And yet, in English, I am a lover, I am part of a community, I am a lesbian. I cannot find that word in my Ukrainian dictionary. My mother tongue, no longer mother to me. And me, speaking, loving, working, in a tongue my own yet not entirely mine, estranged from origin.

Claire listens, is confused: by the whiteness of both our skins, by the common culture of our lesbian-ness. Worries I am overemphasizing difference. Then worries that difference, if it exists, separates; somehow manages to learn a phrase or two of Ukrainian, surprises me with "*Ya tebe lyublyu*" ("I love you") on the streetcar. Buys me perogies, and an Easter egg.

One night as we lie in bed I try to describe for her the image I have of a stream, me in it, blocking its flow. The stream is my ancestry, the flow of tradition from one generation to the next. There seems to be no way of opening up this stream, and so I am somehow always trapped in the present, my past there, but closed off. A past only I can see, and impossible for anyone, even Claire, to share.

This time, she says nothing. She takes me in her arms, kisses me deeply, and holds me until I fall asleep.

VIRGIL BURNETT

Billfrith the Dreamer

In his dream Billfrith saw a woodland at twilight and a woman walking naked beneath shadow-burdened trees. Stalking her was a savage beast, shaggy and brindled, going at times upright, then loping on all fours. Sensing danger, the woman hesitated, looked uncertainly about, and in this moment of hesitation, the beast leapt on her, dragged her struggling to the forest floor. There, among the russet ferns, he held her fast and used her viciously, assaulting the flesh of her loins with the gross member sprung from his own. When he had sated his lust, the beast ripped open his victim's dimpled belly and settled down to make a meal of her, lapping blood, cracking bones, feeding as a wolf would feed on a freshly killed ewe.

The finale of the nightmare came with an accompaniment of thunder and lightning. Only then, by the storm's heightened illumination, did Billfrith see that the beast crouching on the woman's corpse was himself.

If the dream had visited him only once, he might have been able to ignore it, but it came often, too often, so very often that it was there, or seemed about to be, whenever he tried to sleep. It came with such persistence that he was terrified of lying down, of putting his head on a pillow, of closing his eyes. His bedroom became a dark forest for him and the dream its stalking beast.

After weeks of struggling with his nightmare, weeks which aged him brutally and brought him to the edge of madness, Billfrith collected his scanty belongings in a sack and set off for home. He had nothing of his own to go there for, no house or land or people. His parents were long since dead. His brothers, wanderers like himself, were scattered to the four winds. Sisters he had never had.

What took him back was the memory of a man he had never known except by reputation. This man was a monk called Mull. He was a member of a community of pious and learned brothers who lived in the monastery that was built on the height above Billfrith's natal village. Throughout his boyhood Billfrith had heard tales of Mull and of his successes as a healer of spiritual disorders – falling sicknesses, hexes, demonic possessions, and the like. If the monk could cure all of these, Billfrith reasoned, it seemed likely that he could help a man who was tormented by bad dreams. Whether he could or not, it was with this possibility, this hope, in mind that he went to see Mull.

Humbly, and as a suppliant, Billfrith presented his case to the famous healer, who by this time was aged, frail-seeming, and more than a little vague. Even so he listened attentively to the tale of Billfrith's troubles. When it was told, he looked Billfrith sternly in the eye and announced that the sufferer must confess his sins and be shriven before any treatment could be undertaken.

Billfrith had expected this and had tried to prepare himself for it. The task was not a simple one. Many years had passed since his last confession. During this time his sins had accumulated to an appalling degree, or so it seemed to him. He had eaten and drunk most gluttonously. He had been in brawls – stupid, angry fights over he knew not what. He had lain in bed when he should have been at work. He had been vainglorious, stubborn, envious. Only his complete lack of wealth had kept him from being miserly. More than all the rest he had been lustful. Confessing to all of this could not come easily.

Even so, he did it. While Mull listened, or seemed to listen, for his eyes had closed and his head had drooped until his chin rested on his meagre breast, Billfrith recounted the catalogue of his wickedness, bringing forth everything honestly and in scrupulous detail, as the old monk had said he must. Disagreeable as it was for him, he even revealed his prodigious lechery, the more salacious moments of which, he noticed, prompted a subtle sort of movement in Mull's face, curious puckerings of the lips and at the corners of the mouth.

The confession was long. Billfrith began in the morning and finished late in the afternoon. When finally he got to the end of it and had nothing left to tell, Mull, who had been paying attention after all, rose stiffly to his feet.

"Bad," he said, shaking his head gloomily, "very bad. Memoria justicum laudibus, at imperium nomen putrescet."

Then he ordered Billfrith to follow him and turned abruptly away.

Together the two men left the church, left even the monastery. Unspeaking they trudged through gardens and fields, exuberantly green at this season, and beyond them onto fuscous moors. The farther they went, the sorrier the soil became, until finally it failed altogether, giving way to bleak grey granite and weather-blasted schist. Even the most modest grasses and herbs could find no purchase in this barren terrain. Several times Billfrith paused to catch his breath and ask where they were going, but the old monk never slowed, never spoke, never even looked at the sinner he had so solemnly taken in tow. Their march ended on a high promontory where the land plunged headlong into the sea far below. On this cliff Mull at last addressed his companion.

"Nam qui erranti comiter monstrat viam . . . ," he began, and went on to tell Billfrith what he must do if he expected to receive absolution and be liberated from the thrall of his dream. The penance was simple enough. Billfrith was to stand on the cliff-edge. He was to look out unflinchingly at the immense sea and to reflect on the immensity of his wickedness. He was to do this until Mull told him to do otherwise. The monk was very explicit about the necessity of standing, of not giving in to fatigue, of not sleeping. So that Billfrith might ward off drowsiness, Mull supplied him with a knout – the cord which had girded his own cassock, expertly knotted – and told him to apply it vigorously whenever he felt the approach of sleep.

It was Mull's plan to return the next day. He had no doubt that a night in the open with only his conscience for company would render Billfrith sufficiently contrite to merit absolution. As it happened, however, he was not able to realize this plan, for just as he got home, a slate slipped off the monastery roof and struck him on the head. The slate was a very old one, worn thin by wind and rain, honed in fact until its edges were very sharp. Like an axe the slate came down on Mull's old skull, cleaving it neatly from pate to palate.

He died instantly, of course, and in a moment of mortal sin.

Ordinarily Mull was a most reverent and moral man, but like all men, he was subject to lapses. They were very occasional in his case, but they did occur, and it was during one of these that his life came to an end. This ultimate lapse could perhaps be blamed on exhaustion, for he had worked long and walked far that day in the service of his calling. Whatever the reason, if there was one, it transpired that as he was approaching the abbey, he suddenly recalled one of the episodes from Billfrith's confession. It concerned a beautiful Levantine girl, the daughter of a physician in a Mercian town, whose vagina was so richly fleshed that she was obliged to draw aside the elaborate curtaining of its lips with her henna-tinted fingertips so that her lover might penetrate its interior. Something about this detail in Billfrith's lengthy account of his amours put Mull perversely in mind of the way the draperies were drawn aside on great feast days to reveal the abbey's reliquaries and the potent bits of saint which they contained. In the very instant that his brain was making this blasphemous correspondence, the fatal slate descended.

The accident of the old monk's death altered Billfrith's penance, changed it from a moderate spiritual exercise to a life-long sentence. Left alone on his rock, abandoned by the unfortunate Mull and forgotten by the world, he carried on as best he could, prosecuting his obligation simply and obediently, struggling to keep his mind free of everything but the immensity of the sea and the immensity of his sin. Often he longed for Mull's return and for deliverance, but he did not break faith with his confessor. He had been commanded to stay awake meditating and this is what he did. He did it principally because he was sincerely sorry for the way he had lived, but he also did it because he was afraid to sleep, afraid to dream. Whenever he was beset by doubts and fears, especially by the fear that his strength might fail, that he might doze off, he flogged himself mercilessly with the knout Mull had left behind.

All through the summer Billfrith stood there, then all through the autumn and the winter that followed. He suffered terribly from hunger and from thirst. He suffered too from exposure, from the cruel pummelling of winds, rain and sleet, from the fierce scorching of the sun's rays. But more than all of this he suffered from loneliness.

With time these sufferings passed, or rather they became something other than suffering, something more intrinsic and more tolerable. They developed a quality that made them inseparable from Billfrith's endurance of them.

With still more time, more summers and more winters, Billfrith went even farther beyond suffering, so far at last that he lost the very idea of it. He lost much else as well: his childhood, his years of wandering, his lust and his fear-some dreams, his confession and Mull. He lost them all, forgot them. He forgot everything else as well, everything but the immensity of the sea.

Not until a whole century later did anyone happen upon the promontory where Billfrith so long had kept his vigil. The man who finally came along was a shepherd searching for a sheep which he imagined to have strayed in that direction. When first he saw Billfrith, who wore a hooded shirt and still held the knout in his hand, the shepherd took him for a monk from the local abbey. When he got closer, however, he saw that the cowled figure was neither monk nor any other sort of man, for it was made of stone, granite as hard as the rock on which it stood.

The shepherd was less taciturn than many of those who follow his trade. On the contrary he was something of a blabbermouth, and when he returned to town, he boasted to everyone he met of the statue he had discovered.

It did not take long for this piece of news to reach the monastery. The abbot, ever on guard against resurgences of paganism in the district, dispatched a contingent of monks to investigate the shepherd's find. The report they made to him on their return was comforting.

"It's one of ours," explained the leader of the explora-tory party, a man of archaeological erudition. "Indige-nous work, fashioned from native stone – difficult to say when."

More trips were made to the cliff beside the sea and more theories were put forth about the origin of the mysterious stone perched so dramatically there. The most popular, and certainly the most ingenious of these hypotheses, was suggested by the abbot himself, who had not for nothing risen to his present position. In his view the statue must be a commemorative monument erected in honour of a distinguished member of his own abbey, a monk from any earlier century, most probably the monk Mull whose learning and powers as a healer were still remembered in the region. By and by this attractive solution to the mystery, helped along by some sermons and a discreet campaign of rumours, was generally accepted and the statue became known as the "Mull Stone."

Almost immediately a local cultus developed around the "Mull Stone." Miraculous cures were reported, not among the mentally ill as might have been expected considering the reputation Mull enjoyed while he was alive, but among barren women, several of whom suddenly found themselves to be with child after visiting the statue. Because of these events the spur of rock where Billfrith suffered so long in solitude became almost populous. Pilgrims came from all over the island, and even from beyond the sea. Hardly a day went by that some woman did not appear to prostrate herself before the granite image, imploring it to make her womb quick and productive. Many of these women were fair. A few were of high rank, noble and even royal.

Inevitably there was talk of canonization. The monks, naturally enough, were eager to see one of their brothers elevated to the ranks of sainthood. They worked accordingly, enhancing Mull's reputation at every opportunity. There was also strong support among the island's women, who had their own rather obscure reasons for embracing the notion of Mull's sanctity.

These efforts might have met with some success, at least in monastic circles, had it not been for the violence which occurred a few seasons after the discovery of the "Mull Stone." A band of Northmen, driven from their own country by famine and internal strife, swept along the coast, pillaging and raping, ferociously crushing all resistance raised against them. The village where Billfrith grew up was quickly overrun and torched. Because of its high position and solid construction, the monastery held out a bit longer than the town had done, but in the end it too was sacked.

When the raiders moved on, there was nothing but blackened rubble left of either the town or the monastery. The fields nearby were stripped, devastated. With the exception of a few women who were carried away as slaves or concubines, everyone was put to the sword. For a while crows provided the landscape with a certain grisly animation, then they too departed, leaving behind them a scene of utter desolation.

Not even the standing stone that Billfrith had become was left unmolested. The Northmen, taking it for a Christian monument, which perhaps it was, tipped it over and tumbled it down the cliff into the sea.

It came to rest in several feet of cold salt water, battered by the fall, badly chipped and broken. At once the ocean went to work on the statue's remains. The mighty surf rolled over them, pounding them, dashing them against each other, grinding them among the sea-floor's boulders, breaking them down, reducing them to ever smaller fragments, to little stones, to pebbles, to sand, reducing them until they were reducible no more, until they were one with the immensity of the sea.

THOMAS KING

The Dog I Wish I Had, I Would Call It Helen

for Helen

Jonathan lay in the tub with just his head and butt out of the water and practised his swimming. "I am swimming because I am four now, and, when you are four, you have to know how to swim."

"That's right," said Helen.

"In case a ghost throws you in a lake."

"It's always good to be safe around water."

"Only the ghost wouldn't do it on purpose. Only if she slipped."

"Let's wash your hair now."

"Am I four now?"

"Yes, honey. Yesterday was your birthday."

"But I didn't get my dog."

"Should I use the bunny soap or the squirrel soap?"

"If I had a dog, it would scare the ghosts away."

"The bunny soap smells like strawberries. Here, smell."

"No, no, no. It wouldn't hurt the ghosts. It would just fool them."

"The squirrel soap smells nice, too. Why, I think it smells like lemons. You like lemons."

"The ghosts would think it was only a pretend dog, and, when they got close, it would jump up and scare them."

"Let's use the squirrel soap this time."

"But I don't have a dog." And Jonathan sat up with a splash and began to cry.

Jonathan stood at the edge of the table and watched the side of his cereal bowl. He stood on one foot, and then he stood on the other.

"Look, Mummy!"

Helen smiled at the book she was reading.

"Look Mummy!"

"That's nice, honey," said Helen, and she shifted in the chair without taking her eyes off the book.

Jonathan went into the kitchen and dragged his stool back to the table. He climbed on the stool, leaned across the book Helen was reading, took her face in his hands, and turned her head towards him so he could see her eyes.

"You have to look, Mummy."

"You haven't eaten any cereal."

"You have to feed me."

"There are some nice peaches in your cereal."

"You put in the wrong cereal."

"I'll bet you could find those peaches if you looked."

"I don't want peaches. I want you to look."

"I am looking. And you know what I see?"

"A dog?"

"I see some yummy raisins."

"A dog would eat that cereal," said Jonathan. "If I had a dog, it would eat all that cereal."

"Maybe there's a four year old who would eat that cereal."

"No, there isn't," said Jonathan, and he dragged the stool into the bedroom closet and shut the door behind him.

That evening, Helen got a cup of water from the bathroom

tap. Jonathan was standing on his bed. He had taken off his sleepers, again. His diaper was balanced on his head. Helen held out the cup.

"I don't want that," said Jonathan.

"You said you were thirsty."

"No, I said . . . I said . . . I said I was werstry."

"Oh."

"That's how dogs talk."

"Which story would you like tonight?"

"If I had a dog, I could talk to it."

"Shall we read the one about the donkey?"

"If I had a dog, I wouldn't need you."

"Maybe we should read one of the new books we got from the library."

"My dog could wash my hair and make my cereal."

Helen smiled and gathered Jonathan up in her arms. And before she could catch herself, she said, "Maybe we should read the one about the Pokey Puppy."

She felt Jonathan stiffen in her lap, and, almost as soon as the crying began, she could feel his warm tears pass through her skirt and trickle down her belly.

Helen had read an article on mothers that suggested that you didn't have to be a perfect mother. In fact, it said that mothers who did everything might actually be injuring their children by removing all the frustrations and obstacles from their lives, things that tended to educate and strengthen. What one should strive for, the article said, was to be a "good-enough mother," someone who loved her children but who didn't try to protect them from all of life's difficulties.

Jonathan's father was in San Francisco, and when Helen called him one night to see how he was doing, she told him about the good-enough mother. "Honey," he said, "you're one hell of a lot better than just good enough." Which was not what Helen had wanted him to say.

"What I mean," she said, "is that you can't do everything for children. They need to grow and learn sometimes that's hard." And then she confessed that she hadn't bought Jonathan a dog.

"I thought you were going to get him a dog."

"I was, but I think it would just be too much work."

"It would give him something to look after."

"It would give me something else to look after."

"I'm sorry, honey."

"It's not your fault."

"You know what I mean."

Helen stood up and moved quickly to the bathroom. Long-distance phone calls brought on bowel movements. Helen didn't know why, and she had never heard of anyone who had a similar problem, though, in truth, she hadn't asked around. The phone would ring; she would answer it and hear that long-distance hollowness, and, before the person on the other end said anything, Helen would feel the sensation of things on the move. If the conversation was short, she found she could tighten her muscles and endure, but until she bought the portable phone, longer conversations were always broken with intermissions.

"Are you coming up at Christmas?"

"Is that okay with you?"

It was not a problem so much as a puzzle. At one point, she decided it wasn't the phone call itself but the person calling. Her mother calling from Prince Edward Island. Sam calling from San Francisco. Local calls didn't affect her at all. But then, one day, Canadian Airlines called to correct an error in a ticket she had booked, and she couldn't get to the bathroom fast enough. She had heard of people experiencing this problem in bookstores and large libraries. It had something to do with the chemicals that were used to make paper.

"Jonathan would like to see you."

"How about you?"

Helen could see the edge of the shower curtain. It was picking up mildew and grey stains along the bottom. The toilet-paper dispenser was almost empty.

"It would be nice to see you."

"I'm sorry."

"It really would be nice to see you."

After they hung up, Helen was sorry she had said it in exactly that way. She should have set up a few more barriers, so that there was some effort involved. Sam would have the wrong idea now. He would think she was lonely, desperately lonely, perhaps, when she wasn't. He would think that she missed him, and, while she did, in a modest way, she only missed him sometimes late at night and occasionally on the weekends, when her law office was closed and she had time to think about anything.

She should have said, "Let me know what you want to do." No, that wasn't it, either. She wished she had xeroxed a copy of the article.

When she picked up Jonathan from the Day Care on Monday, he gave her a heart he had cut out himself. All around the edges were patches of glue and glitter. There was a piece of yarn strung through the top of the heart and tied in a loop. In the centre was a series of colourful scribbles that took on a vague form. At the bottom of the heart, one of the day-care workers had written, "I love you, Mummy."

"This is lovely, honey. Is it for me?"

"Yes," said Jonathan.

"Do I hang it around my neck?"

"Yes, that is what the string is for. You hang it around your neck because it is your heart."

"Is this a picture of me?" And Helen pointed to the lines and swirls at the centre of the piece of red cardboard.

"No," said Jonathan. "That is the dog I wish I had."

That evening, after supper, Jonathan brought out the quilted pad from his crib and a table knife from the kitchen.

"We have to play the game," he said.

About a year ago, Jonathan had crawled into bed with Helen, curled up against her stomach, and told her to push so he could be born. She pushed, and Jonathan was born morning after morning. At first, she was delighted with his interest in birth and his understanding of the process, which included, not without its emotional difficulties, Caesarian section. Some days Jonathan would be born vaginally, and some days Jonathan would have to cut her open so he could escape. On the days when a section was called for, he would run his fingers over her scar and ask her if it still hurt. Later, the game became more elaborate with Helen having to walk the floor in an attempt to turn the baby so it could be born naturally.

The morning game was a nice game because Helen was still half-asleep and didn't have to do much, but as the game progressed and gathered more elaborate rituals and equipment, it also became a burden. She had invited George and Mary and Sid and Elizabeth over for drinks one night, and Jonathan had come into the living room dragging a blanket and a table knife. Helen had laughed and explained the game, hoping honesty would quell the embarrassment. They all said what a clever boy Jonathan was and what an imagination! Then they fell into a conversation about what babies really knew and how they were probably much more aware of what was happening than parents gave them credit for. The whole time they talked, Jonathan tried getting his head under Helen's skirt and later settled for lying across her lap and twiddling with her nipples.

The pad from the crib was the newest piece of equipment. There were elastic straps on each corner of the pad and Jonathan would have Helen put both her arms through the top straps and her legs through the bottom straps so the pad functioned as a cotton womb into which Jonathan could crawl and be pushed out. The elastic straps were not very comfortable, and, in spite of her interest in Jonathan's imagination, Helen, of late, had begun to find the game tedious.

"Mummy's a little tired tonight, honey. Maybe we could play that game another time."

"No. I have to be born."

"Maybe we could put the pad on the floor and you could crawl under it and you could be born that way."

"No. That is not the way babies are born. I am a baby."

"Well, little baby, maybe you could crawl under one of the cushions and be born that way."

Jonathan curled his lip and lowered his forehead. "Babies are not born that way. They have to come out the 'gina, and the doctor cuts them out with a knife. Did they cut me out with a knife?"

"Yes, honey."

"Did it hurt me?"

"No, I don't think so."

"Did it hurt you?"

"Just a little."

Actually, Helen recalled, it had hurt a lot. When she came out of the anaesthetic, the first sensation she felt was nausea. The second sensation was pain, as if she had been cut in half. She lifted the covers and could just see the tops of the thick staples holding her groin together. They reminded her of the staples she had seen her father use to nail barbed wire to fence posts. When she tried to move, the pain roared up through her body, and she was only just able to turn her head to one side before she threw up.

"Did the doctor use a laser?"

"No, honey."

"He used a knife, right?"

"That's right."

"I think we will have to use a knife this time, too."

Jonathan brought home three cardboard birds and a bag of twigs and spent the evening piling the twigs on top of each other. "This is an ostrich nest," he said. "And this is a baby ostrich and the mother ostrich."

That left one bird. It lay on the side of the floor. Jonathan bounced the other two birds about on the pile of twigs. "They are kissing, Mummy, because they love each other."

"That's nice, honey."

"I love you, Mummy."

"And I love you, my baby ostrich."

"No, no," said Jonathan. "I am a baby lion."

"Are you a hungry baby lion? Should we eat some supper?"

"Yes, I am very hungry."

"What should we eat, baby lion?"

Jonathan picked the third bird off the floor. "Ostriches," he said.

The dog had been Sam's idea. He said it would be good for Jonathan to have a pet. Then he said she should get one for companionship. Six months later, Sam was pushing a German shepherd for protection. Finally, he confessed that it was guilt, that he wanted her to be happy and safe.

"I'm fine, Sam. I don't need a dog."

"I know."

"I don't have time to look after a dog."

"I know."

"Jonathan's fine, too."

"Does he miss me?"

"You're his father."

"I've got no excuses."

"We're both fine."

"I'm sorry."

Helen quite enjoyed the graveyard. On her early morning runs, she would wind her way past the markers, trying to read them as she went. She was especially moved by the turn-of-the-century granite angels and women in flowing robes who leaned over the graves casting long shadows on the grass and by the stone crosses that had little oval pictures of the deceased. Sometimes there were Grecian vases and turned pillars or a pair of clasped hands rising out of the rock. The newer gravestones were generally plainer, rectangles and squares, with short, pithy inscriptions, "Beloved Husband," "Together at Last," "Our Mother." There was an entire row of granite slabs set in the ground on the same level as the grass that all said "R.I.P." and then gave the name and the dates.

Helen was most taken with the older graves of children and babies where stone angels and granite lambs were the rule, and where the inscriptions were great romances: "I Will Lend You for a Short While a Child of Mine, He Said," "Sleep Sweet Babe and Take Thy Rest. God Called Thee Home; He Thought It Best." There was a large stone with a harp carved on its face that said "Gone to Be an Angel." Right next to it was an oval stone that simply said, "Ashes and Dust, Angelina, Dead at Birth."

Helen's favourite was a small stone with a figure in a robe holding a lamb. It was the grave of a young girl who had died of cholera at the age of three. "Budded on Earth to Bloom in Heaven" was carved at the base. It was the halfway point on her run, and she always paused a moment to read the inscription. Some days she would shake her head and laugh; other days she would cry. And then she would turn around and run home.

One Saturday, Helen took Jonathan to the graveyard. There was a large, yellow backhoe at the far end of the cemetery and a small group of people standing around a pile of dirt.

"Look, Mummy, a tractor!"

"It's a backhoe, honey. They're burying someone who died."

"They are putting the dead person in a hole, right?"

"That's right."

"Because they died?"

"Yes."

"Is Daddy dead?"

"No, Daddy is in San Francisco."

"When he dies, will they bring him back and put him in a hole?"

"They have graveyards in San Francisco, too."

Helen took Jonathan by the grave with the woman and the lamb. "This little girl's name was Amy. She was only three when she died."

"She was never four?"

"No, she died before she was four."

"Are you going to die, Mummy?"

The stone lamb had had one of its legs knocked off and there was a chip out of the woman's shoulder.

"Yes, I'm afraid so. Some day."

"Yeah," said Jonathan, "me, too."

Jonathan talked about the graveyard for a week and concluded that Amy got sick and died because her father had gone to San Francisco and was gone too long, and her mother didn't hear her crying because her mother was running home but didn't get there in time because she kept falling in holes.

Helen took inordinate pride in Jonathan's imagination. Nevertheless, she stopped running in the mornings and began playing squash during her lunch break.

Sam called in early December to say he couldn't make it up. He wanted to know if she had thought any more about a dog, and Helen told him she had decided not to get one.

"How does Jonathan feel about that?"

"It would be better if you didn't mention it to him."

"I'd really like to get him one."

"I know."

"What should I get him for Christmas, then?"

On Christmas Eve, Jonathan lay in the tub and declared that he no longer wanted a dog.

"What would you like for Christmas?"

"Daddy."

"Daddy can't come."

"Then I don't want anything."

Helen rubbed Jonathan's back and pushed the warm water up on his neck. "Maybe you'd like a tricycle."

"No, I don't want a tricycle."

"Maybe you'd like some books."

"No, I want you to hold me."

"Do you want me to hold you, now?"

"Yes. I want you to hold me for eighty-two minutes."

"That's a long time."

"Did the girl's mother hold her for eighty-two minutes?"

After Jonathan went to sleep, Helen made herself some tea and cinnamon toast and sat in the straight-back chair and watched the night turn blue-black and moonless in the kitchen window.

GLEN ALLEN

The Hua Guofeng Memorial Warehouse

If there had been one thing in Chicken Man Wang's life that never seemed to end, that came back and back again like a meal of spoiled tofu on a hot day, it was loss itself.

He had lost his sturdy mother and angelic father to one of Chiang Kai-Shek's hangmen three years before Liberation. He had lost his only brother, drowned swimming to Hong Kong. He had lost his wife, when, on the day of their wedding sixteen years before, a jealous cadre had assigned her to "northern duty" 3,200 kilometres away (she left within the hour, waving madly from the back of an army truck, so he had not, at least, lost his innocence).

He had lost a year of his life during the Great Leap Forward when he was locked in a windowless barn with thirty-five other comrades, all, like him, English teachers at the Fukien Institute of Foreign Languages. He had lost another seven years during the Cultural Revolution (it was then that he lost his hair), digging yams in the countryside with other banished intellectuals.

He had lost his chance to go to an American University when a colleague, reading a page of a diary he had lost, noticed a politically dubious quotation from John Donne and reported him to the Leadership.

In the heady days following the downfall of the Gang of Four he had lost his bicycle and most of his teeth in the first fight he had ever had in his life (he lost) with a deeply aggrieved Maoist cousin.

Yet it seemed to his comrades that Wang wanted nothing, that he loved his aloneness, the bareness of his room perched out above the nursery where he could hear the happy cries and songs of the commune's children. Everyone saw that he managed to live contentedly without a radio or TV set (he had lost all his consumer points when one afternoon, deep in Byron, he had failed to present himself at the airport for the arrival of the institute's first foreign expert, a fat man from Canada accompanied by his fat family). Indeed he had no appliance beyond a splendid pencil sharpener sent to him by an uncle in Kuala Lumpur (it had stopped working years before).

And Wang had not lost the respect and affection of his neighbours. Everyone, workers and intellectuals alike, loved him for his generosity and resourcefulness. He always had cooking oil left over from his monthly ration and gave it to the most deserving. He was called "Chicken Man" because every Spring Festival he slaughtered the dozen chickens he raised every year, leaving their bald and headless bodies on the doorsteps of the lame, the halt, the blind, the mentally ill, the politically discouraged, and the two hapless teachers of Russian on the campus. He was only sorry there were never enough to go around.

Wang was "correct," they all said, a scholar in his field and a sympathetic teacher who, even when volunteer labour was not compulsory, soon began to spend his Friday afternoons collecting the night soil from behind the Canadian family's apartment, a job no one else would do, for the Canadians, as everyone had remarked, smelled grotesquely of milk and butter.

They also called him "Chicken Man" because, with his uncanny skinniness, the loose wattles that gathered at his scrawny fifty-year-old throat and the way his long chicken limbs flailed at the soggy tropical air when at 4:30 every morning, long before the loudspeakers brayed the morning message, he jogged through the ragged jungles of mimosa and hibiscus all the way to the filthy commune fish pond and back, he looked like nothing so much as some underfed and demented cockerel.

"There goes the Chicken Man," said Old Chen each morning through the baffles of the mosquito net which separated her from her snoring husband. Old Chen, alert all night to the sounds of domestic discord coming from her neighbours on either side, never slept and spent the night hours reliving her memories of the Long March to Yenan, so that when she heard the pad-pad-pad of Wang's light feet passing by she knew that sunrise was near and that the past was again about to become the tedious present.

"There goes a real socialist," she shrilled at her companion, the disgraced son of a Manchurian general who had never worked in his life, who spent his empty days reading bad erotic verse into his giant bootlegged tape recorder and who had disappointed her many times.

But Wang had a dark and terrible secret. His faith in socialism had gone the way of everything else, though fear and endless practice had given him the colours of a true believer. When every morning and evening he scattered crumbs and purloined grain for his fowl, calling out in his chicken man's voice that cut across the searing heat like some antique piccolo – "here Shakespeare, here Hemingway, here Dickens and Dreiser" – to his hungry little flock, he often dreamed of a future full of forbidden comforts: American bathrooms, steam heat, cheeseburgers, long sleek cars, profit and loss. Sometimes in his mind's eye he saw a chicken factory as grand as the East Wind Hotel in nearby Anwei, with tons of glistening chicken flesh, mountains of eggs, riches beyond counting.

"With my money I would buy an office, a position, just as they do in America," he told Grand-Uncle Yu, an unregenerate opium smoker, so ancient that the Revolution had passed him by without leaving a trace on his old capitalist heart. "Something modest but useful," said Wang, recalling a classmate who had become deputy director of the Sixth Ministry of Waxes, Soaps, Foodstuffs, and Footwear in the capital, and a man who every year sent him cards showing himself displayed against the yawning door of a Red Flag limousine.

"Just once," he told Yu, colouring with embarrassment at the great gulf of his greed, "I would like to eat lean pork, see foreign films, wear real leather on my feet."

Yu yawned widely, showing a gobful of black and snaggled teeth. He was not only Wang's only living relative but his only confidant, the keeper of his clandestine ambitions. But Wang's enormous guilt bored him.

"My son," he said, idly stirring a pot of ugly green broth on the charcoal stove in the corner of the little hut from which he dispensed herbal medicines to those who had given up on pills, doctors, and hospitals, "we are all imperfect. We all have dreams. In the old days I had money in seven Shanghai banks, a concubine, a home three floors high, and a leather chair stuffed with the hair of wild Mongolian ponies.

"It will all happen again, just like the turning of the seasons," said Yu, who saw China's recent history, the many years he had lived, as simply a series of circles returning on themselves.

"This," he said, waving out his tiny doorway at the exhausted Chinese earth, the crumbling piss-yellow buildings and a water-buffalo, its impossibly thin body covered with elaborate designs of blue blowflies, that was relieving itself on the front steps of the students' dining room, "this will not last forever. Your moment will come and when it does you will know."

And so it happened that late one night word sped from door to door that China's leader and Party chairman, Hua Guofeng, the man put in office by the great Helmsman himself, had been dismissed. So it had been reported on the public television set that flickered to life from time to time outside the junior teachers' quarters. The camera had shown Hua's bulbous squirrel's face and the announcer had proclaimed that he was "indisposed" and would be replaced in all his functions.

Like priests reading a particularly complicated set of entrails, all members of the community set to analyzing the wording of the announcement, its position and duration on the national news and the conjunctions of the moment. Alone and together they concluded that there was a new order in Beijing, and they were not wrong.

Wang could not get to bed that night and sat for hours in his only chair staring absent-eyed at the comings and goings of a lizard that skated jerkily over the fractured walls of his room.

It was two in the morning when the idea flowered in him. He jammed his feet into his cloth slippers, bounded out of his chair, and hurried off to Yu's hut. Yu that day had got his monthly prescription for opium, a right reserved for all aged and confirmed addicts, and was deep in reverie, his mind illumined with visions of the rich past, his youth, restaurant meals, fine silks on his back, the downy skin of his mistress. He felt himself a tree in early spring, sweet sap rising from trunk to branch to twig to bloom.

"Uncle," cried Wang to his all but unconscious elder. "The time you talked of has come. My mind is full of plans." Wang then told the old man of his scheme, so farfetched and perilous that he spoke in a whisper, so daring and pregnant with promise that he could hardly catch his breath.

Yu, when he heard what Wang had to say, returned to reality, laid his pipe aside, and said, "Yes, it is right. Wait until tomorrow night when I am rested and I will help."

Then the old man groped among the galaxy of vials and bottles beside his sleeping mat for the decanter of Sze-chuanese green bamboo liquor with which he celebrated all great occasions, and the two drank, both sealing and legitimizing their singular enterprise.

The next day at nightfall Wang and his great-uncle rode out on Yu's bicycle, Wang's gaunt legs dragging in the dust, Yu's rachitic body driven by an energy he hadn't felt for years. They headed for the nearest village where, one by one, they entered the school, the Party headquarters and the office of the village tea corporation, all of them unlocked and empty. From each public room they stripped one of the large grinning portraits of Hua that decorated every civic wall in China. Night after night they visited all the communes and hamlets around, returning in the early morning with thick rolls of posters of the fallen leader.

After two weeks they had hundreds, but it was not enough. They ventured into the city, this time in daylight, telling the cadres of the government buildings they called on that they had been sent by the provincial Party office to remove the offending portraits. And they were believed, for as all knew, Hua's face and name both were being expunged from national life. It would soon be as if he had never existed at all: texts would be rewritten, newspapers removed from files, official films would be destroyed.

When Yu's tiny quarters were teeming with rolls of Hua posters, so many of them that he had to cover them with blankets to hide them from his clients, he told Wang that until their work was realized – until Mao's line was restored, until Hua returned to power and the posters could be resold before they could be reprinted (for this was their design) – they would have to be kept elsewhere. They agreed there was only one safe repository for their contraband, a neglected but weatherproof shack, perhaps the only building in the whole county that was not in use, that had variously served as a rough jail, a depot for outdated political tracts, and a millet silo. "This will be our warehouse," said Yu, drunk with his own cleverness. "This will be the Hua Guofeng Memorial Warehouse," he said, cackling wildly at this small deception of the State that had so cruelly and resolutely impoverished their lives.

Wang often wondered in the awful weeks ahead why things went wrong and decided he should have known it all along – in China there was always someone watching, always someone there to see, always a fellow citizen to open the door of a vacant building for no other reason than to be alone. There was no patch of ground, no hill, no valley, no paddy, no vantage point, not even a single tree that could be climbed that ever remained long untenanted.

Why such alarm then that an idle peasant came to the stone shed where the portraits lay in stacks and saw Wang bent over counting them, reckoning the riches they promised? The man, doing no more than his duty, told his brigade chairman, who told the security police, who told the administrators of Wang's institute.

Days later Wang was summoned to a meeting of the Leadership – Director Liu, his thirty-six vice-directors, the chairman of the local Party committee, and six of his colleagues in the English department.

Even before he was asked he confessed all: his infatuation with free enterprise, the theft of the posters, and, worst of all, his conviction that Hua Guofeng (and so the followers of Mao) would lead the country again one day. He was long used to making confessions of all kinds. It came easily to him.

When he had finished speaking there was wide surmise in his inquisitors' eyes. Even Director Liu, who had foregone his nap to chair the meeting, awakened briefly to glare at him. Wang heard a roaring of blood, a train going through his head, and pondered the punishments they could prescribe. Death? Imprisonment? Banishment again to the dead countryside? Most terrible of all, the confiscation of his books? His precious Shakespeare, the illicit compendium of Joyce given him by a visiting tourist, his Byron, Keats, and Shelley, his tattered copy of *Middlemarch*?

"Comrade, we are at a loss for words," said Chang, a fat panda of a man who had never been speechless in his life and who had been named as Wang's accuser. Chang had always hated Wang since a loud and very public discussion in the faculty years before about the uses of the preposition "from," during which he had demonstrated his truly astonishing ignorance of the language he was supposed to teach.

Chang felt moved to bellow at him. "We must think of the students," he said, "of the example you have set them. To them and to us this is no less than treason. News of this will get to Beijing. We will all be disgraced."

Wang stood there in silence, feeling that his dry mouth was full of feathers. He wished they would allow him to sit, and thought of the straight-backed chair in his room, its stern integrity and rigorous angles. He yearned for a chair.

Then his mind raced away from the assembly of his judges and betters to Hsiao Fen, the woman he had married, and settled on the one day in their short and furtive courtship when she had allowed him to lead her into a thicket of bamboo on White Cloud Mountain to hold her doll-like hand, trembling in his like a captured bird.

"You have betrayed us all," shouted Chang, chopping at the long table with his obese paw.

Then there were coughs and much shuffling of feet. A typewriter broke out in a distant room. All heads turned to Director Liu at the end of the long table, who had once again slid open his little red eyes. The verdict would be his. But like so many cadres of his rank he had reached a position of power by never speaking in terms of facts and numbers and issues and things that must be done. Rather he delivered himself of elaborate and ambiguous epigrams in rendering decisions, windy maxims that could almost always be open to any interpretation. When he spoke at a meeting there was always a second or even third caucus of his underlings to decide what it was he had said. Only the week before, examining the case of a newly arrived Peruvian expert who had illegally acquired a dog, Liu said after five hours of wrangling by his juniors that "a black hen can lay white eggs," and left the room. All present nodded their heads at the man's wisdom and at further meetings ruled that Liu had meant that the animal should be commandeered and later serve as the main dish at an institute banquet held to honour the thirty-second anniversary of Liberation.

This day Liu's theme was maritime: as his eyes bore into Wang's he said, "He who rows the boat seldom rocks it." There was little confusion in his message and the words fell on Wang like a rain of stones. He had been condemned.

Two weeks later while Wang was putting out water for his flock, a small grey panel truck carrying two sick-looking men wearing dirty, much-patched beige smocks and plastic sandals drove up to his door.

"We are Doctors Ma and Tang from Public Hospital No. 14," one of them told him, "and you are to come with us."

Though not a word had been said about Wang's fate, he had been expecting them. "They certainly won't put you in jail," said Uncle Yu after the haunting meeting with the Leadership. "Too many people have been to too many jails. They'll send you for a rest somewhere till all is forgotten. You are too valuable to all of us."

Wang knew that Hospital No. 14 was one of two psychiatric hospitals in the provincial capital, and a place children feared in their dreams. But he had to go somewhere. His job had been taken from him, his students and neighbours both would no longer look him in the eye, and only the day before he had found the neatly severed body of a rat resting against his door. He had been put outside the others, he was as much a stranger as he had been when he came to the place years before.

"We must hurry," said the doctors. "We have many more calls to make today." They pored over a long and filthy piece of paper and said, "Our instructions are that you may bring one book with you and, if you insist, one of your chickens."

Wang climbed up above the nursery one last time and entered his room, quickly surveying the pitiful inventory of his life – the enamel tea pot, the coal brazier he used to fight the chill of winter, the crude framed portrait of his murdered mother, an old calendar with its dates clipped off, the lizard frozen on the wall, and the tiny frog hopping about the far and perpetually damp corner by his tumble-down bed.

From his shelf of books he took his copy of the Christian

Bible for no reason other than that he had never had time to read it before. And from his chickens, he selected his favourite, a black bantam rooster named Byron, a gluttonous and bad-tempered bird for which he had the special affection one feels for all rogues and runts. With the holy book in one hand, he scooped Byron into the other and settled into the doctors' vehicle. It occurred to him that he had not been in an automobile for a full decade, and carefully watched the changing of gears, veers in direction and applying of brakes as they passed the commune's pig-killing pen and the minuscule barbershop where those who had hair lined up for the clumsy attentions of Wei the barber, a lunatic ex-farmer who babbled endlessly of the limits of outer space to his customers. Then they drove by the graveyard of perfectly good heavy machinery, rusting away as it awaited replacement parts that never came, then over the black and viscous Lotus River, so full of oil and chemical contaminants that now and then it caught fire.

The hospital was a comely old building that had once been the clubhouse of a polo league for the Europeans who had owned and run all the businesses in the city. It had a rambling open courtyard with two immense banyan trees whose penumbras seemed to fill the sky.

Within a week Wang had blended with his fellow patients, only two or three of whom seemed mentally disturbed. The others, like him, had taken a wrong turn somewhere. There was a prominent mathematician from Hangzhou who had unwisely found himself courting and then proposing to three different women in three different cities using three different names. There was a teacher of Vietnamese so taken with his subject that he had begun an enthusiastic correspondence with the government of the new, unified Vietnam, China's latest enemy. There was a master bricklayer who had made a sumptuous life for himself by casting the I Ching for lonely widows. Another was a professor of Western music, under perpetual suspicion as it was, who had been caught playing the music of Stevie Wonder to his class. A fifth was a plump Christian, born in Macao, who had led a protest against the unseemly racket caused by the firing squads that abutted his house. Yet one more, a choleric Szechuanese doctor, had refused direct orders from his hospital's directors to put unlicenced newborn babies in the delivery room refrigerator. These and the others were joined by the two weary psychiatrists, Ma and Tang, doomed to tending the perfectly well.

The hospital inmates spent their days together sitting on the burls of the huge trees and hovering over their plain meals of lentils and rice – learning from one another until all were English scholars, speakers of Vietnamese, aficionados of Elvis Presley, experts in masonry, mathematicians, and lay psychiatrists themselves.

Wang felt a great ease among his new friends and never once thought of the life he had left behind. Late at night he read his Bible, memorizing the books of Job and Genesis, his busy mind filled with the possibilities of human existence and the good cheer of brotherhood.

When one summer day a year later, the sun beating on the gong of the flat, hard hospital yard, Old Yu wheezed through the gates on his bicycle, Wang felt almost troubled at being reminded, even by so true a friend, of the far-off institute.

Yu, who, as always, had escaped all punishment for his role in Wang's calamitous adventure, bore a letter from Director Liu saying that he was forgiven and needed again.

Wang fingered the letter as if it were something both unwanted and even hateful, gingerly settling it on the scarred table in his room. Then he introduced his old uncle to his friends and offered him a cup of tea from the thermos put outside his door every morning.

Yu was won over by what he saw and said, "I think you'd be insane to leave here. I have never seen you looking so well. America could not be better than this place."

He advised Wang to return Liu's letter with a reply saying he was not well yet. So Wang did, writing "I am still unworthy of your confidence. My terrible error is still much with me," and gave the letter to Yu to take back to the Leadership.

"And it is true, my uncle," he told Yu. "I can never go back. A man alone lives like a wolf. I am no longer alone."

That night came the first of the season's typhoons. Byron, wandering about in the dark and lashing rain, his small chicken brain intent on finding shards of nuts and candy sent to the hospital by well-wishing relatives, was hit by a falling branch and died.

When Wang and the others found him the next morning they dressed his body in fine gauze and buried him deep in the muck by the quickening stream that ran by the hospital's far fence. Before the tiny grave was closed, Wang dropped into it a small scroll bearing a quotation from the bird's namesake.

After the others had left, Wang lingered there, the still angry sky above tinted different shades of grey, his wandering mind brimming with a whole constellation of ideas and memories: the theory of numbers, the raging seas he had never seen, Switzerland and a photograph of the Alps he had once owned, the beauty and economy of English pronouns, the perfect, hurting greenness of young rice, the roundness of buttons and wheels.

Even Byron's death brought him as much relief as pain, for it meant the end of a lifetime of loss. There could only be gains from now on. On and on and on.

JENIFER SUTHERLAND

Table Talk

This story is about sex and it begins in the middle of the kitchen floor. I'm taking a course this semester called History of Ideas, recommended by David who took it last semester. You don't really think about ideas having histories. Professor Dixon, on the other hand, thinks about it constantly and once he gets you going, you're hooked. Sex, for example. Has sex always been an idea? Prof. Dixon asked the very first day of the course. Or was there a time when people didn't talk about it and just did it, like eating?

Well, that got me going. The more I thought about it, the more eating seemed like an idea with a history. So I decided to do my final paper on the idea of food. David's final paper was on the idea of matter. It was more specific than that, something about information and energy and all this computer-physics stuff. He got an A plus. My thesis is that food is everybody's most important idea. I'm sitting on the kitchen floor trying to develop this a bit. The paper isn't due for two weeks so there's no rush, which is a good thing because it's nearly midnight and I'm totally beat, body, mind, and whatever idea might possibly be holding the two together. David is sitting on the floor too, helping me out by telling me about these sticky rice balls his mom used to make. That reminds me of my grandmother's baccala balls which Dad says Mom doesn't make right. Then David goes on about his dad's fish soup and he explains about these little blue crabs which gets me thinking about calamari and how we used to call the tips "little hats." We go on and on like this, making ourselves salivate. There's nothing to eat in the apartment. We've just finished moving in and there isn't even anything to cook with except a roasting pan I found under the sink filled with old Brillo pads and dead cockroaches.

David is wedged between the stove and the cupboard and my legs are doing a V up the side of the refrigerator. It's a small apartment, right. While we talk, David scribbles a list of things to buy. So far he's got:

> cuisinart
> pasta-rolling machine
> espresso machine
> toaster-oven

I give up thinking about food and think about how to describe this scene to my sister Josie. My family's not too thrilled about the fact I've moved in with David. If it'd been Tim Harris, now, that'd be different. But David's last name is Makayama. My last name is Millefontani, which you could say is just as bad, but to Dad, Millefontani is normal whereas Makayama is Japanese. My dad doesn't distinguish between Japanese and Japanese Canadian. Japanese is Japanese and, among other things, he believes the Japanese make lousy drivers. Nevertheless and anyhow, I'm expected to show up for dinner next Sunday, business as usual, or else. Mom will hug me and say, You got dirty laundry? Dad'll grunt and say, Back so soon? Then we'll all sit down for spaghetti. My older sister, Marianne, will be so jealous of me that she'll spend the entire dinner staring at her plate. My youngest sister, Lisa, is on a diet. She weighs, oh, maybe forty kilos, so she's got food under control. Now she's working on words. She can only take so much talking, then suddenly she yells out, Get offa my body! Scary stuff but Dad says it'll pass. Then there's my other sister, Josie. If I'm lucky Josie will be in her So-what-the-fuck's-happening? mode and I'll be able to tell her about David and me and the kitchen floor and the list and the talk about food. After a while she'll say, Hey, cut out the pornography. Just give me the reality.

The reality is that the scene on the kitchen floor happened after what happened in bed. Except that what happened in bed didn't actually happen so it's kind of hard to talk about it. We got all the boxes moved in – basically the apartment's one room with a kitchenette and bathroom – and I started scrubbing floors. If you knew how filthy they were it'd make you sick. David went out to buy a foam mattress from some foam supplier on the Danforth. When he got back, I went out for a bottle of wine and we ordered pizza. So far so good. The delivery guy had a little trouble finding our door. We're on the top of a hardware store but you have to come in around the back lane through this kind of courtyard where everyone sticks their garbage, and by the time we'd shouted directions at him out the window and he'd figured it out, the pizza was cold.

Here I go on about food again. Why don't I just give Josie the reality?

Josie and I are in a booth in MayBee's Donut and Coffee Shop. I have tea and a hamburger and Josie has coffee, fries, and a fresh pack of cigarettes. The booth is my idea. I really don't want anybody to see me at MayBee's. MayBee's is like the major hangout for Donover High which I left almost two years ago and which I'd rather not ever set eyes on again. And plus there's the hideous possibility that Timothy Harris might walk through the door. Tim – alias The Prince – Harris is my old boyfriend. Josie swears up and down he hasn't been sighted in MayBee's since last spring. She's heard he's in Montreal, at McGill. Sure, I say. Josie lights up her first cigarette and makes the sign of the cross.

"All right, so he's in Montreal," I say. Josie looks at me weirdly like I'm not making any sense. She's in her So-what's-your-problem? mode. Not only does she lean away from me into the opposite corner of our booth, she keeps glancing around the end of it towards the door. If she's set up an ambush with Tim, I'll kill her. She was the one who got my entire family calling him The Prince. God knows what they call David. Hiroshima Baby, maybe.

"So anyhow," I say. "Did you ask Dad about the marinated eggplant?" The bell for first-period lunch has just rung and here comes half of Donover High, piling through the door, fighting for a stool at the counter where there's no minimum charge. No sign of Tim. I sit back and kick Josie on the shin. She blows a stream of smoke smack in my face. We share a room, Josie and I, or did, until last night. We put up with a lot from each other. Now I'm wondering if she's thinking what I'm thinking, which is, shit who needs her?

I wave my hand in front of me and the smoke settles between us like a screen. Mind you everyone in MayBee's except for me has lit up a cigarette and the air is striped with blue. I cough and Josie goes back to staring at the door.

"Eggplant," I remind her, without the kick this time. "Give me a break, Jos. I got an essay due in two weeks, not even."

She shrugs, blows out smoke. A guy in a black leather jacket is coming towards us through the haze. Not Tim Harris. This guy looks completely wiped. He comes to a halt in front of our booth and says, "Give us a smoke."

"Fuck off," Josie says. The guy stares at her for a long time with bloodshot eyes. Finally he lurches off.

"Eggplant," I say again. Josie barks out some smoky laughs and jerks her thumb towards the black leather jacket.

"Bagplant," she says. I nod I've got the joke. She means he's a sniffer and a vegetable. I wait a minute before reminding her again about the recipe for marinated eggplant I asked her to get from Dad.

"He says don't bother with the big ones," she says at last. I reach into my shoulder bag and take out a pen and notebook. Josie lights up another cigarette as I write.

"Okay, so they gotta be small?"

"Yeah." Smoke trickles out of her nose and mouth as she thinks. "Get them from the market, from Mario. Or was it Mimo? The guy with the table out front."

"Mimo's the toy man," I say as I write.

"Whatever. Get them small and slice them lengthwise. Like up and down or they fall apart when you soak them."

She drags on her cigarette and glances at the door. "Okay," I say. "Go on."

"You gotta soak them."

I write, You gotta soak them. These are my father's words. As I read them back I can hear his voice. He's sprawled on the couch in front of the television watching Jacques Cousteau and shouting over his shoulder each step as it comes to him.

"Brine, right," Josie adds.

"How much salt to water?"

Josie shrugs and blows out smoke. "Salty water. Fuck."

Salty water. Fuck, I write.

"Then you press them."

"Press them how?"

"Like with a weight. Like with a board with some weight on it."

"How long?"

Josie shrugs. "You soak them then press them, then you stick them in oil, right, that's it."

I write the words down.

"You gotta use glass, like a jar. Or else a crock. A crock is the best. You cut a piece of wood and you put it on top and weigh it down. All the eggplant's gotta be under the oil or it's fucked."

She concentrates on her cigarette. She's finished. "What about garlic? Red pepper? Oregano?"

"Yeah, yeah, all that shit. You stick all that shit in there." Josie butts out her cigarette and rummages through her bag. Josie's bag is made from the bum of an old pair of bluejeans. It's a weird sight when it's sitting on the table. She finds what she's looking for and says, "Dad said to give this to you when I saw you."

She throws me a box of condoms. It's first lunch at May-Bee's Donut and Coffee Shop, the place is wall-to-wall high school students and I'm sitting there holding a box of condoms, gift of my father. I drop the box onto my lap and cover it with my hands. From the booth next to ours some guy's arm is sticking out. He's telling a story about what he'd like to do to the vice principal and he keeps flexing his arm. His shirt's got a design on it like amoebas dividing. I look down at the box of condoms on my lap. My dad has certainly found a very pretty one. Looks like it was designed by whoever does the covers for Harlequin romance. Blue and gold swirls, maybe wind, maybe waves, maybe water, billow out from this woman's head. Picture pure ecstasy.

I squash my shoulder bag onto my lap. "Josie," I hiss. "Being of Japanese origin is not a social disease."

Josie lit up another cigarette and goes back to looking at the door. The air between us is definitely murky. I regret the conversation I had with her after David and I first started going out together. We were up in our room and Josie was in her So-what-the-fuck's-happening? mode. Very casually I mentioned that David's grandmother is originally from Hiroshima. His parents grew up in B.C., right, and during the war they were in an internment camp set up by the government. David was born in Toronto. But none of that is history as far as Josie is concerned. After I'd dropped the word "Hiroshima," she looked at me like I'd been screwing a mushroom cloud and was dripping radioactivity all over the bedroom carpet. Meanwhile the ash fell off the end of her cigarette onto the bedspread.

"What are we talking about here?" I ask now. "Bombs? Or babies?" But the box of condoms slides out from under my bag onto the floor, ker-plip. I try to cover it with my foot. Beads of sweat have broken out on my forehead and the amoebas on the shirtsleeve of the guy in the booth next to ours swim around and divide and then merge again. Josie taps her finger on the edge of her styrofoam cup and starts humming a Josie hum, totally without tune or rhythm. Smoke trickles out of her nose and also, it seems to me, out of her ears. I shove my notebook into my bag and stand up. Then I leave. I walk out of MayBee's first lunch, eyes straight ahead, amoebas swimming in and out of bars of smoke. I walk out with Dad's recipe for marinated eggplant tucked safely inside my bag, leaving Josie sitting in a booth with a box of condoms lying inches away from her black ankle boots.

When I get back to the apartment, the key I've just had made in the hardware store before I went out doesn't fit my lock so I go around to the superintendent and bang on his door for about five minutes. The Super's name is Fred and he's an old guy, a bit deaf, who always wears this red-and-black plaid cap. Now he comes limping up the stairs behind me, scares the daylights out of me, grunts and mutters and checks out my key, then goes into his place and comes back out with a wad of keys. Takes him a while to find the original of my key and a while longer to compare it to mine. Finally we go back down to the hardware store together and the hardware lady cuts another key. I'm dying to get into my apartment and get going on my essay. Something about marinated eggplant has me really excited. The key-cutting machine is making a high-pitched whine. "Hey Fred," I shout. "What's your favourite recipe?"

Fred pushes at his cap and looks at the floor. I seem to have embarrassed him. The hardware lady gives me little looks out of the side of her eye as she cuts my key. "What d'you like to eat, Fred?" I shout again over the noise of the machine. "What are you good at making?"

Fred settles his cap and looks up as far as his hands, which are full of keys. "Pancakes," he says. I nod in my most encouraging way and take out my notebook.

"Pancakes! Great, I love pancakes! So how d'you make them?"

He lifts his cap and scratches at his ear with the clump of keys. "Yep," he says. "I like pancakes. I make 'em real good."

"That's great," I encourage him. The machine has stopped whining and the hardware lady is watching me write. "I'd like to hear how you make 'em."

"Well, I just use pancake flour. Put an egg in it. Milk. Mix it up real good and beat it up and it comes out good. That's about all. It comes out real good. Next time I make pancakes I'm going to put a couple on for you. Make you taste them."

Fred and the hardware lady watch me write. Fred nods and scratches his head again with the keys. "Yep, that's all I do," he concludes. I put my notebook away and go out with my new key.

The new key works. I close the door behind me, lock it, and flop down on the foam mattress. I take out my notebook. Over the past few weeks I've collected quite a few recipes. But now I can't think what it is I wanted to do with them. My clothes and hair stink of Josie's smoke but when I try the taps, there's no hot water. I plunk myself down again on the mattress, squash! right on top of David's box of condoms. I reach into the sleeping bag and pull it out, now partially flattened but otherwise your normal box of condoms, basic blue. I read the small print and try not to think about my father in the drugstore, standing in front of the condom display looking for the box with the prettiest picture. My family is always popping into my head uninvited, not necessarily one at a time, either. Now the scene switches from the drugstore to the dinner table. Mom comes in with a pot of spaghetti and my dad smacks the condoms down in the middle of the table. Mom stares at the box and then at my dad and then forks spaghetti into a bowl. Lisa glances at the box and then goes back to inspecting her fingers for fat deposits. Marianne bursts into tears and Josie hums her little Josie hum. Mom hands Dad a bowl. Dad puts it down and jabs his fork towards the condoms in the middle of the table. Impossible to know what his point is. Everybody except Lisa starts eating. The box of condoms sits in the middle of the table all through dinner, next to the Parmesan cheese.

I'm tired of this scene. I stick David's condoms back inside the sleeping bag and go into the kitchen. David has left a note on the refrigerator door saying that after he gets off work he's going to Steve's to get some smoke. This message is surrounded by exclamation marks and I know exactly what it means. It means David is going to get us some grass to help us out in bed tonight. Help me out of my family in bed. Help get my family out of my head in bed.

I stand in front of the refrigerator considering this message. Then I go back to looking at my notebook. I decide to make a soufflé for dinner. I have this recipe my French Lit professor says is foolproof. Back I go down to the hardware store to buy one of those hand eggbeaters.

David and I are sitting on the foam mattress with the sleeping bag around both our shoulders, giggling. So much for the smoke. I've been trying to explain what happens in my head as soon as we get past kissing but every time I open my mouth we go off into giggles again. Now I'm staring at David from so close that our noses are touching. We stay like this for a long time, quietly. David's eyes are Japanese, but that's just shape. They're black, but that's colour. When you look into them you see they're really a place. Not Japan, not Canada. Somewhere else I've never heard of before. I stare into this place and then it starts happening again. What happens is hard to explain but it's like my whole family is sitting around in my head. I mean, it's like I'm the dinner table. Shit! I shake my head hard, trying to knock them both out, but it never works. "Shit!"

David is moving his hand up my leg. I reach out and pull it away. "Too many people," I hiss.

"There's just us," David whispers in my ear, but I shake my head and pull away. My back is towards him now. When he reaches out to turn me around I feel as sexy as a cheese grater.

"Make them go away," I whimper.

"Shee-it," David says. "Let'em stay. I ain't afeerd of nobody nohow!"

We giggle ourselves to sleep.

I dream the floor is decaying. We'll have to take it apart completely, David tells me, kneeling down and beginning to pull up pieces of rotten wood. Soon there is a big hole and I shout at him to stop. But he keeps working. He doesn't seem to notice that the floorboards are covering a swamp. The mud bubbles up into hideous shapes with sucker mouths and tube-like snouts and squashy underbellies and jelly-blob secretions. David points to the bucket I've left under the window and tells me to put the creatures in there. I force myself to bend over the hole he is making and lift out one slimy creature after another into the bucket. But the bucket is not the bucket I've been using to scrub the floor. Instead it's my dad's largest pickling crock, full of fresh olive oil. The creatures bulge up over the side of the crock and plop backwards into the oil.

I wake up sweating. The sleeping bag is twisted around my legs and David is completely uncovered, sleeping peacefully on his back with one arm raised above his head as though he's greeting a friend. I untangle myself and cover him, then go to the kitchen and switch on the light. David's face blinks from grey to orange. I switch the light off again and stand for a long while at the kitchen counter, staring into the bedroom. Swarms of blue and yellow dots combine and re-combine in front of my eyes. I long to go back to the bed and lie with David but I don't want to disturb these dancing lights.

"Salmon Loaf: you take an entire can of the cheapest salmon on earth. Big."

I'm in the bathtub getting ready to meet David for dinner at his dad's house. This will be the first time I've seen Mr. Makayama and David's grandmother since David and I moved in together. I've boiled water to make the bath really hot and my body is turning salmon pink. My essay is due on Monday.

"Don't bother to drain it. Throw it into the bottom of a not-too-clean loaf pan. Overcooked mashed potatoes, grey. Eggs. The world's cheapest margarine. Mix by hand. Bake in the oven till it's got an inch crust on top. Serve on waxed paper. This was my mother's favourite treat when she didn't feel like doing dishes, which was every Friday night. Oh. And never make enough for the whole family."

This lecture comes from a girl in my Psych 200 class. She spat it at me during a lecture on the limbic brain. "The cheapest salmon in the world. Big." I feel very glamorous in this bathtub. It's got those old-fashioned nobbly legs that remind me of medieval maps of the world where the corners are held up by sea monsters. It's a very romantic bathroom. The hot water pot's in the middle of the floor and David's photographic chemicals are lined up along the walls in different coloured bottles, rust brown, green, clear, even black, with serious labels. Alchemy, I think, not chemistry. In this bathtub I feel I could be anyone, someone new and wonderful emerging out of darkness into soft starlight. It's hard to concentrate on Sheila's mom's salmon loaf. But I know there's an important idea in there somewhere. If only I could think my way through to it, then Prof. Dixon would give me an A plus. But it's hard to think when your body is stretched out naked in front of you. I give up.

David and his dad are still out shopping when I arrive. David's grandmother waves at me and grins. She's standing at the stove stirring beans in a huge enamelled pot. I can smell the sweet bean smell. They're the same red beans my nana used to cook. Gram waves again, beckoning. "Rook, come rook." I am used to her exchange of r's and l's and I take off my jacket and come close to the stove. "I gonna take to od radies," Gram says, chuckling. Gram almost always laughs and smiles when she talks but her eyes tear up quickly, too, especially when she remembers David's mom who died of stomach cancer a few years ago. "Ode radies," she repeats, grinning with what's left of her teeth – a few long yellow spikes. I nod that I understand. Ode radies. Gram teaches Japanese pastry-making at the Japanese community centre. She also visits elderly Japanese Canadians and brings them food. But she herself is very old. She came to Canada in 1920 when she was twenty-four.

She chuckles softly, lost in some thought. I stare into the pot and wait for her to speak. "No vegetables," she says at last. I nod again, tapping my forehead to show that I know she's talking not about food, but about the car accident she was in a year ago. "No mo lide now." She lifts up the thin white hair from her forehead to show me the scar that is there. But there are too many wrinkles. To my eyes her face is a mass of scars.

I nod again. "No more driving for you, eh Gram. We need you here." This kind of old-lady talk doesn't bother me. Before she died my nana lived with us for ten years. I spent lots of time with her. I got out of chores that way. No one else wanted to be with her, specially not my mom. Dad didn't mind her but he fell asleep during her stories.

Gram keeps talking. "God no want me to die yet," she says, returning the spoon to the pot of beans. The beans have a dull pink colour like faded roses. "Prenty work to do. So he save me. Not just body, mind too." She taps her forehead. "God no want me to be the vegetables."

Gram goes on stirring the beans which are turning into a thick paste. Their heavy sweetness fills the kitchen and makes me feel small and warm, like a child. I get up onto the stool beside the stove and watch Gram stir. Nana used to spend hours with a pot of sauce. She kept Hershey Kisses in the pocket of the black sweater she wore winter and summer and gave me handfuls of them whenever I came to talk with her. I peeled off the silver paper and licked out the chocolate. It was always melted from the heat of the stove and the warmth of Nana's body.

Gram pushes the spoon deep into the rose-coloured paste, then pulls it up, shlurp! The shlurping noise makes us both laugh. Gram laughs for a long time, lost some-where. When her eyes come back to me she says, "Swamp!" I don't know if she's making the Japanese sound for shlurp, or if she means the paste is like a swamp. I smile cautiously and point to the pot. "Careful," I say. "Something may jump out." I make chomping movements with my mouth. "Chomp chomp, it may bite you!"

Gram guffaws, showing her spikes. Tears fill her eyes as she laughs and she pats the top of her head. "Horro," she says, when she is calmer. "Horro." For a moment I forget to exchange her r's for l's and a chill creeps up my spine, leaving my head numb. Gram sees that I don't understand. She keeps patting the top of her head. "Horro."

"Hollow? Hollow head?"

She nods, smiles. I've finally understood. "Horro head, yes." She points to the pot of beans. "Kappa."

"Kappa?"

Again she nods and pats the top of her head. "Kappa horro head, yes."

People with hollow heads should wear hats, I think, and smile. But Gram is pointing to the pot. "Kappa come out of swamp. Vely scaly. But vely porite." She puts her hands in front of her, as though in prayer, and bows so low I'm afraid she'll tip over. She comes up leaning on the edge of the stove. "You bow to Kappa. Kappa vely porite, bow back vely row." Gram bows again, this time touching the top of her head with one hand. I can see how the wispy hair grows out of her scalp. "Kappa rive in swamp," she says, straight again. "Got to have water in horro head or go away. But Kappa vely porite. Bow to Kappa and Kappa bow back vely row. Water come out horro head and Kappa gone. No mo scaly. Everyone happy now." She chuckles softly and goes back to her pot of beans. From the living room the clock on the mantlepiece begins to chime. I slide off the stool and go the window. Where is David?

"Because," David says, and stops. I am standing at the foot of our mattress wearing the sleeping bag pulled up to my underarms. David is lying on his back looking at me with an expression that is getting to be familiar. "Because people just like to talk about food. It reminds them of their childhood."

I shake my head. "That's true but it still doesn't answer my question." I want to know why people don't talk about sex the way they do about food.

David reaches out and grabs my ankle through the sleeping bag. I shift my weight to keep from falling. "Who says people don't talk about sex?" David asks.

"I do. You don't. You don't like to talk about it. You joke about it but that's different. We don't sit down and go on about it the way we do about meals we've eaten or want to eat."

"Sex is just something you do. Talking gets in the way."

"Well sure. You can't talk and eat at the same time either. Just ask my dad."

David lets go of my ankle and sits up. "Meals are shared. They're family memory. You go out and shop and come back and prepare and everyone's involved in the whole process."

He's right but I don't give in. I stand there shaking my head. "But sex is about families too."

"Angie!" David is alarmed. "You're not pregnant, are you?"

I let the sleeping bag slide down my body and climb out. When I shake my head and kneel down beside him, the fear leaves his face. But the look of hurt is still there. I dread this look now when we're in bed together. I take his face in my hands. "David!"

He takes my hands away, gently. "You're thinking too much, Angie. Stop worrying. We don't have to make love."

"I'm going to tell you a story," I say quickly. "About Kappa."

"Kappa!" He looks at me startled. "Wait a minute. That's one of Gram's stories. Kappa!"

"Swamp creatures with hollow heads," I remind him. "Horro head. They have to have water on the brain or they disappear."

"Yeah, I remember. To get rid of them you bow and they bow back. The Japanese obsession with manners." He looks hard at me. "What are you telling me, Angie? Have I been rude to you?"

"Lude to me?" I laugh and pinch his nipple and he yelps. "No, no. It's the Kappa. You should've told me about them but you didn't so I have to tell you. Come on. Stand up."

David goes on staring at me. The hurt look has nearly melted into curiosity. Leave it, I think. Forget it. Just make him come inside you, that's all that matters. But instead I pull him up beside me and hold him there, closing my eyes. Nana arrives first. I open my eyes and force her out of my head, onto the edge of the bed under the window. "There," I whisper, pointing. "Kappa number one. Nana. See her black sweater bulging with chocolate kisses?"

David stares at the edge of the bed. "We have to bow to her," I whisper. I squeeze his arm hard, pleading with him. But he pulls away.

"Are you trying to spook me?"

I point to the other side of the bed near the doorway into the kitchen. "Here comes Kappa number two. Mom with a pot of pasta. You'd think she'd get sick of dishing out spaghetti through all these crises. And there's Dad eating it up. Kappa number three: Tom Millefontani. And there's Marianne with her head in her hands. And Josie in her So-what's-your-problem? mode making the sign of the cross with her cigarette. Over there, way down in the corner between those boxes, that's Lisa. Any second now she'll start shouting at me, Get offa my body. No. You get offa mine. Lisa. Look! There's Gram, there, through the doorway. Gram and Nana at the same table! And your dad is over there, fishing for salmon out the window." I laugh and then stop, reach out to touch David. "Where is your mom?" I whisper. "Can you see her?"

David is standing stiffly beside me but his voice is soft. "She's making balls out of sticky rice," he says slowly. Suddenly there are tears in my eyes.

"Where?" I whisper. "Show me where." David turns and points to the pillow he has been lying on. I turn and bow towards it very low, as low as I can without falling. And beside me, palms together, David is bowing too. We name and bow and turn and name and bow until I have seen the hollow on the top of each Kappa head. Gram is right. The Kappa bow back very low. Water is everywhere, spilling and spilling and spilt. David and I are suddenly all alone. I can hear the sound of traffic from the Don Valley and through the floors, a long way off, the bass note from someone's stereo. For a moment we stand listening. Then I bow to David and he bows back. We peer at each other in the darkness, both still there. Beneath us the bed begins to rock gently, like a small boat drifting under starlight out to sea.

WAYNE TEFS

Red Rock and After

Some things fall into patterns. You say goodbye to lovers over checked tablecloths in pizza joints named after Greek Olympians, you see the foreman at the bar laughing with the waitresses and you know the rumours of lay-offs are true. Life turns on an axis of events that repeat themselves.

Whenever my parents moved it was raining.

In May of 1964 the lawyers closed in on my father and forced him to declare bankruptcy for the second time in thirty months. The first was in Red Rock, an iron mining town that went bad in the way of mining towns, taking Father's hardware store with it. He and Mother had worked hard there for twenty years, sinking their savings back into the business. They lost it all when sales of hematite plummeted in the early sixties. I was fifteen at the time. A big orange van backed across the lawn which Father and I had dug and planted and rolled a couple of summers earlier, and two men in blue uniforms shifted our furniture, clothes, and appliances out of the house. Father had built it himself. He'd shovelled in the gravel for the weeping tiles, he'd hung the front door through which our stuff was being carried in a light rain. As they moved back and forth the two uniformed men ducked their heads to keep their faces dry. My mother stood in the kitchen, packing the last of the china. Bravely, she was trying not to cry.

She came from a family of market gardeners who sold vegetables to wholesalers and didn't think of themselves as businessmen, as Father did. They were simple folk who liked cabbage rolls and beer and picnics on sunny summer days. Mother's passion was flowers. We had tomatoes and lettuce and peas in a plot at the bottom of the yard, a regular vegetable garden, but around the house Mother kept her flowers in narrow, loamy beds. Dahlias, peonies, sweet Williams, begonias, tulips, daffodils, many names I no longer remember. She came in from tending them with her face flushed from the sun and perspiration glistening on her brow, saying she felt clean and free. Mother had a youngish-looking face. She understood no better than us kids why Father was up worrying every night over glasses of whisky.

The hardware store in Red Rock was lost on mortgages. Two more years of making payments and Father would have been in the clear. But the market for hematite dried up. Father had gambled on the mine holding out and he lost. According to Father the unions priced Red Rock's iron out of competition with Germany's. He was against Medicare and strikes. But mostly he was against unions. He called the men who went out on wildcat strikes shirkers, and worse things after he lost the hardware store in Red Rock.

The laundry he bought in Fort Frances was another thing. That's where the orange van took us in the rain in the summer of 1962. This was a pulp-and-paper town, a union town, too, with a sister city across the border in the state of Minnesota and a tradition of hard-nosed success. The Fort Frances Canadians had won the Allan Cup twice in the early fifties. But it was more bad luck for my father. The previous owners of the laundry had left some bad debts which Father got tangled up in somehow. Courts and lawyers ate up the little cash he'd managed to salvage from the Red Rock fiasco.

He was a short, wiry man with brown hair and eyes to match. He smoked a pipe. He liked owning small businesses because of the independence they gave him. A coal-yard labourer during the thirties and a private during the war, he'd had a bellyful of taking orders. "No one's my boss," he liked to say – and then add with a laugh, "except your mother." I remember him laughing a lot in Red Rock, and smiling over his pipe as he tamped and fiddled with the tobacco before lighting up. That was his great pleasure, smoking his pipe.

He liked fishing rods and guns, too, which he sold to Red Rock's miners and which he taught me how to use so I would grow up a man. He taught me to squeeze, not pull, the trigger of a rifle, and always just at the point where you started to breathe out. He taught me to walk in the woods without making a sound. When I was very small he hunted moose in the muskeg terrain around Red Rock with a hand-gun. He used a .38 Walther HP he'd brought back from the war as a souvenir. I had the job of blowing into the moose horn while Father positioned himself behind a tree twenty yards downwind. The sight of a thousand-pound bull moose crashing down on us through the scrub is etched on my mind forever. When it was fifty yards away Father stepped out from behind his tree, aimed and fired one bullet into the moose's chest. I never knew him to take more than one shot. Or to think he'd done anything extraordinary. He liked moose steaks. He liked fishing on warm afternoons, too, and always predicted we'd catch our limit. He was an optimist despite everything.

Just as the laundry in Fort Frances was beginning to turn a profit there was a disaster. The phone rang about three one night, waking us. I lay trying to listen to my father's side of the conversation. I couldn't make out what he was saying but I heard the scree and scraw of trains in the yards near our house, the distant hollow thump of cars being coupled together. We lived in a rented place near the tracks with a yard too small for a vegetable garden or flowers. When Father finished talking he put the phone down and went into the bedroom where he spoke to Mother in hushed tones. Minutes later I heard him leave through the back door, his steps echoing down the walk. He was in a hurry.

There had been a fire at the laundry. It took three pumps to put out the flames in the roof. Sirens, police cars. One fireman had collapsed from smoke inhalation when he was trapped between two upright mangles that toppled over. That wasn't the worst of what had happened, the Chief said. He was a big man with soft hands and a pencil moustache. He had driven Father home from the laundry at dawn and stood in the kitchen, drinking a mug of coffee which Mother had made. I lingered in the doorway, knowing something important was happening. Father sat at the table drinking whisky. His shirtsleeves were rolled up, his eyes were wild. He looked up from time to time but he didn't focus on anything. He stared into space and then back at his drink. The Chief whispered to Mother that Father had nearly killed a man. He'd taken one of the fireman's axes and started hacking at the machinery, all the while shouting. When two policemen had tried to restrain him, he'd turned the axe on them.

Father clenched his hands on the whisky glass as the Chief spoke to Mother. I remember his knuckles were white. Blood had smeared on the tabletop and then dried.

"You were good to bring him home," Mother said to the Chief. To Father she said, "Wasn't he, Tom?"

Everyone was speaking softly, like after a death, and I could hear the electric clock in the display panel of the stove whirring and ticking. My father raised his head. He looked at the Chief as if he hadn't realized until that moment that he was in the room. He looked back into his whisky glass.

Mother asked, "What happened?"

The Chief said, "At first there was so much smoke it was hard to see anything. Clothes burning, I guess." He looked at Father for confirmation, but when he got none, he went on. "Then part of the roof caved in and the boys were hosing it down when Tom here grabs an axe and leaps through a flaming window."

"My God. Didn't you even try to stop him?"

"We were caught off guard. We saw him duck under the smoke and make for the front of the building where there wasn't any fire." The Chief squinted over his coffee, work-ing to recall each detail as if he were giving evidence in court. "He hacked down the office wall first," the Chief said, nodding at Father. "Plaster and wood chips flying through all that smoke." He waited to see what Father did, and when he said nothing, the Chief went on. "It might have been funny except that Tom was so crazy."

Mother nodded. "How'd he cut his hand?" Blood was pooling on the table from the cut on Father's wrist.

"We circled to the front of the building, the cops and me. After we shouted for him to come out, the sergeant and one of the other cops went in after him." The Chief drank some coffee. He added in a bolder voice when he saw Father was quiet, "I didn't see how he cut himself, but I saw him turn the axe on the sergeant."

Mother looked terrified.

"There was a scuffle and the cops brought him out with his arms pinned behind," the Chief said gruffly. "That's why I brought him home. They wanted to lay charges, you see."

"Charges?" Mother asked.

"Obstruction of justice," the Chief said, lowering his voice again. "Assaulting an officer."

"Tom," Mother said.

Father looked at her and then at his bloody hand. He seemed to rouse himself from the trance he'd been in. "Why are you talking about me," he asked, "as if I wasn't here?" There was anger in his voice. I'd heard him say things around the table about police and firemen and I'd always thought he admired them. But his voice was filled with rage. I took a step backwards.

The Chief studied his mug of coffee. "I better go," he said. He looked for a place to put the mug and settled for a space on the counter between the coffee canister and the whisky bottle.

"You talk about justice," Father said. He stood suddenly, nearly tipping over the table, and said, "What the hell do the cops know about justice? With their pensions and their fat-cat wages?"

"Tom," Mother said.

He added as an afterthought, "And you firemen with your soft jobs and frigging union."

"Sit down," Mother said. "You're talking nonsense."

"Am I?" My father stood in the centre of the room, looking wildly from my mother to the Chief. "Am I now?"

"You broke the law, Tom." The Chief pulled himself to his full height. He had a potbelly but he stood a head taller than Father. "That's all I'm saying. You attacked your property like an animal, you resisted restraint, you abused an officer of the law." The Chief drew a deep breath. "You attacked a man with a deadly weapon, is what I'm saying. That's wrong, and that's all there's to it." He hiked his pants up by the belt. "You're lucky to get off without charges being laid."

"Lucky?" Father said. He came around from behind the table, pushing at his shirtsleeves. Since his days at the hardware store he's always worn a white shirt, and this one was smudged on one shoulder with soot. "Lucky?" he asked again. His face was white and his brown eyes bugged out of their sockets.

"Tom," Mother said. "For goodness sake, the man brought you home. He's trying to help."

"Get out of here," Father said in a loud voice.

"Don't you lay a hand on me," the Chief said. He was backing up toward the door, his big rubber boots clumping across the floor. I don't think Father had any idea what he was going to do until the Chief put the idea of physical violence into his head.

"I'll do anything I want to. It's my house, isn't it?"

The Chief said, "You lay one hand on me and there'll be charges. So help me God, Tom."

My father leapt at him then, pushing the Chief's chest with both hands. It was a gesture of impotent anger, not violence, the kind you use in the schoolyard with the class bully. You can hit a man in the face or even in the chest with your clenched fist and mean to hurt him bad. But when you shove with both hands you're only trying to get something out of your way. My father had taught me that, too, along with how to break a man's nose with one snap of your elbow. "I'll damn well do what I please," Father said. "This is my house, see. I've still got that."

"Oh my God," Mother said. She looked wildly about the room, realizing suddenly that I was there.

The Chief stumbled backwards into the door. There was a bloodstain in the form of a handprint on his chest. He wrenched the door open. "You'll see," he said to Father, who was standing with his face upturned to the Chief's, maybe a foot between them. "I'll get the law on you."

After that my father went to the window and watched the Chief get into his firehall station wagon and drive away. He stood looking out into the night with one hand up to cut the glare from the glass. He was there a long time after the car was gone. His shoulders looked small to me. Mother and I stood in the room, not looking at each other. Mother had her hands folded over her stomach like she had a pain there. Maybe she was thinking about how her life would change in the future. Maybe she was wondering how on one night Father could have gone after one man with an axe and fought with another in his own house. Maybe she was just numb with what had happened and was waiting for something ordinary to occur. I don't know what she was thinking.

I remember clearly what I was thinking because it was the first time it occurred to me, though I've had occasion to think it many times since. I realized that anyone is capable of anything. A father on the church board could be forcing his teenage daughter every night. The lady you meet in the aisle at Safeway might have killed her child and buried it in the backyard. I realized that if my father could take an axe to a man, anyone was capable of anything. I began to realize, too, that I was.

After a while Father turned away from the window and looked at us. "I don't know why I did that," he said. He sounded like a child puzzled about misbehaving in class. His eyes shifted from one of us to the other. They were normal again, sunk back in the sockets.

"Let me put a bandage on that," Mother said, meaning his cut wrist. She crossed to the cupboard and took down a first-aid kit.

My father said to me, "I was way out of line there." He seemed to be waiting for me to speak. "I don't know what came over me. You'd think when a man lost his head that way he'd at least be able to say why afterward, wouldn't you?"

"Yes," I said. My voice sounded small in the room.

He looked me up and down, though I don't think he was actually thinking about me. "You would?" he asked.

"I would."

"Yes," my father said. He was calm now, not the tense silent he'd been when he'd sat at the table drinking whisky, but ordinary calm. He looked about the room as if he were only now aware where he was. "I wanted us to be happy here," he said. "Just to be happy."

"I did too," I said, thinking of the friends I'd made at school and would have to say goodbye to. I felt very weary of life.

Father must have too. He sat with his chin in one cupped palm and looked blankly at me. There were lines around his mouth, a spot of blood on one cheek and the white welt of a scar he'd got in hand-to-hand combat during the war in Italy. His breathing was laboured and after a while he said, "I feel so hot." He touched his brow and added, "Right from my feet on up. Just hot."

Mother said, "Here." When she was done putting a bandage on Father's wrist we sat around the table and drank coffee. We looked at each other, but no one had much to say. We were thinking private thoughts. Father got up and poured himself more whisky. He splashed some in a glass for Mother, and when she shook her head, he pushed it in front of me. I took a sip. It was my first taste of whisky. I felt the raw burn of alcohol down to my gut.

"I don't blame any of them," Father said. He shook his head. Some of his hair had matted to one temple with dried blood. "I did for a while, but I don't anymore."

I listened to his voice. It was a soft, gentle voice which rasped a little from the pipe smoke he'd inhaled. I thought of all the stories I'd heard him tell around the kitchen table in Red Rock, building to a slow climax while he tamped and fiddled with his pipe. He used wooden matches which he struck on the sole of his shoe and shook once quickly to extinguish after he'd lit up. When I was a child he'd let me blow out those matches, and I remembered sitting on his lap saying "bwow, bwow" whenever he lit up. I felt the urge to tell him that I loved him, but I did not. I sipped my coffee. I watched the dawn creep in at the window.

The Chief didn't lay charges, but the law came down on Father just the same. Lawyers dragged him through the courts over the bad debts while he was planning how to get the laundry operating again. I remember him standing amidst the charred machinery with a push-broom one Saturday when I was helping him tidy things up. His gaze roamed around, appraising the damage, calculating how to put things back together. I don't think his heart was in it. That day he sent me across the street to buy Pepsis and when I came back he had the classified section of the paper open on his lap. "There's a hardware for sale in Stone Creek," he said. "What do you think of that?" He told me about the town. He was impressed by its clean streets. He'd never liked the chemical odours of Fort Frances or the effluence that blew out of the pulp mills' stacks and settled on everything in the town. He thought he could make a go of that hardware store in Stone Creek. Like I say, he was an optimist.

We drank Pepsi and swept broken plasterboard into heaps. From time to time Father lit up his pipe and gazed out the window. There were a lot of places a man in his fix would rather have been, with a family to feed and a second bankruptcy looming. He never said anything about that. He never said anything about the burdens of family life or railed about injustice the way I've heard men do since. He never said anything about what happened on the night of the fire either, though his gaze shifted a lot after that night and he didn't lecture me anymore about seeing things through to the bitter end or taking the bull by the horns.

He must have been preoccupied thinking of money. There was the insurance pay-out but that got held up waiting for the Chief's report, and then the adjustors found out about Father taking the axe to the machinery and things became more complicated. I remember him going off to court, carrying his cardboard briefcase bulging with papers. His wrist had healed but he smoked more than ever and in a desperate way, as if he were trying to get as much smoke as possible into his lungs. He was talking about an out-of-court settlement then, and starting fresh somewhere else. Mother went to work at Eaton's where she was a clerk in the Accounts Office. One day I dropped by to bring her the sandwich she'd forgotten on the kitchen counter. There were pockets under her eyes and she seemed to get paler by the day, but she smiled at me over her files in her brave way. She was worried about Father. "Don't hold it against him," she told me.

"No," I said.

"If you want to blame something, blame this cruddy town." That's the closest I ever heard her come to swearing.

"It doesn't seem fair," I said. "He tries so hard."

"That's just it," she said. "Bad luck." She opened the wax-paper her sandwich was wrapped in and took a bite. "It seems to follow us around. I mean it seems to follow *me* around." She looked out the tiny window of her office. "I remember during the Depression how your grandfather had us kids load up a wagon of watermelons one fall. That's when we had the farm in Pine Ridge. We'd tended those watermelons all summer, hoeing and watering them so they'd be round and juicy for the market, the way he insisted. He drove to the city to sell them. With what he made he'd hoped to buy flour and salt and maybe some shoes for us kids. They offered him five cents apiece. Five cents. You couldn't buy two chickens for that. Do you think he took it?" She looked at me to see if I understood the point of her story. "He did not. He turned the horses around and drove the wagon out of the city without stopping. About a mile from home he threw the watermelons in the ditch." Her voice choked a little as she remembered. "That's what this is, I guess," she said. "That sort of kick in the teeth."

She ate the rest of her sandwich in silence. I went out and brought us two paper cups of coffee. "But don't let it get you down," she said later. "As soon as we get out of this town things will be better."

It was raining when we left Fort Frances. Father and I were up most of the night, loading our stuff onto the three-ton truck with the driver the company had sent along. Toward dawn a light rain began to fall. Father roped down the furniture. He arranged the boxes of china Mother had packed last thing so they wouldn't be damaged. The driver pulled the overhead door down with a clang and sealed the compartment for the customs officials who had to inspect every truck crossing the border. The light drizzle misted on the skin of his face as he walked around the truck, checking its tires. Father and I say goodbye to Mother and my sister who were joining us by bus after they cleaned the house and returned the keys to the landlord.

We followed the truck's tail-lights to the edge of town where Father stopped to get gas and buy some tobacco. Along the streets house lights were coming on as people woke to a new day. We stood beside the car, breathing the morning air.

"Smell that crap from the mill?" Father asked me. "That chemical crap?" His nose twitched.

I looked at the mill. "I won't miss that," I said.

When we got back into the car Father turned on the wipers. A mist hung over the highway. "I never did like this town," he said. The wipers beat steadily against the windshield.

I felt close to him at that moment. "I hated it," I said. "The smells, that black crap in the air. Even the kids at school."

"That's it," he said. "Hate." Father speeded up as we hit the edge of town. Rain spattered the windshield, making it difficult to see the highway. At a curve there was a thump under the car. We looked at each other. Father glanced in the rearview mirror. "I hit something," he said, a note of surprise in his voice. "A cat, I think. Its eyes flashed at the side of the road." He was a man who cared about animals. Once when I shot a woodpecker with my .22 he made me search for it in the bush and make sure it didn't suffer needlessly. He took his foot off the accelerator and hesitated for a moment, the car drifting along in silence. Then he drove on. After a while he relit his pipe and threw the match out the window. "The hell with it," he said. The tires of the car swished in the water gathering on the asphalt. We sat staring out the window as the highway snaked into the distance, misty, grey, and flat.

DOUGLAS GLOVER

Story Carved in Stone

I thought my wife had left me, but she is back. What she has been doing the last two years, I have no idea. She's thinner. She has a Princess Di haircut, and she's wearing three-quarter-length tight white sweatpants and a black blouse. She's sitting across from me at the kitchen table, looking self-possessed and aloof. Her name is Glenna. She won't speak to me.

I made her a cup of instant coffee which she ignores. I do not press her with idle questions because, to tell the truth, she terrifies me. (This though, at six-three, 224 pounds, I outweigh her by 122 pounds.) Brent Wardlow down the street had his wife leave five years ago and, when she came back six months later driving a spanking new El Dorado with fluffy dice dangling from the rearview mirror, he asked her one question and she was gone the next day. Sitting down at the Dunkin' Donut of a weekday morning, Brent allows as that he has learned his lesson and will keep his mouth shut the next time she returns.

I am not saying that my situation is exactly the same as Brent's – everyone in Ragged Point knows he drove his wife out with excessive golf-playing and sexual demands – but a word to the wise, et cetera. Also, I have checked the driveway and it appears that Glenna did not drive home in an El Dorado; in fact she did not drive home at all. Her sole possessions are packed in a brown United Airlines shoulder bag with the zipper popped and a small black pocketbook decorated with spangles.

We sit for a couple of hours like this, not talking. Glenna just staring at the kitchen window where the lace half-curtains she made are turning somewhat dingy for lack of a woman's care. As she watches, the window fills with purple sunset then blackens like a bruise. The only sound comes from the bug zapper in the breezeway, killing insects. At 9 P.M., she heaves a sigh, whether of relief at being home again or of sadness, I cannot tell. Then she gathers her shoulder bag and pocketbook into her arms and walks down the hall to the guest bedroom.

I hear the guest bedroom door lock; I hear water running in the bathroom. Presently, I am disturbed by the sound of sobs, the sound of Glenna weeping with wild abandon. I am torn in myself as to whether or not I should run to comfort her. Glenna crying is about as heart-rending a spectacle as you can imagine because she is, or was, such a normally cheerful person. But I recall Brent Wardlow's experience and decide to leave well enough alone.

Instead of knocking on the guest bedroom door, I head outside into the darkness. Turning past the bug zapper and the lurid pink neon GULF HAVEN, VACANCY signs, past the nine identical one-room holiday housekeeping cottages (painted coral with red trim) with matching concrete parking pads, past the azalea hedgerows and the peach trees just coming into blossom, past the oyster cookery and the little dock where I keep my John boat, to the tenth cottage (not identical – forest green, unpainted trim, cracked panes in

the windows, porch roof buttressed with two-by-fours)
which is where Mama lives.

"Glenna's back," I say, bursting in.

To tell the truth, I am pretty excited. Nothing this big has
happened since Glenna left, and before that, not since my
father died in a boating accident (he was leaning out of the
boat to retrieve his oyster fork, fell overboard and suffered
a heart attack – his last words to me were, "Shit, E.A., the
fork's stuck!").

Mama's cottage is dark as a cave. She's sitting at a deal
table, the glow of her cigarette lighting up her face, a frozen
orange juice can full of butts in one hand, a glass and a pile
of wrung-out lime slices in the other. She takes an extra
long drag on her cigarette, breaks into a coughing spasm,
then, catching her breath, says, "The whore."

Stung by her insensitivity, angry with myself for having
let down my guard, I rush out again. For an hour I stand
watching the bug zapper, its eerie blue glow and the flashes
and sparks it gives off as it does its work. A young couple in
Cabin Six is making noisy and acrobatic love; the Firbanks,
old regulars who've been coming here since my father built
the place just after the war, are listening through their
open window. My wife's sobbing has subsided, though I am
convinced she is not asleep, only staring at the ceiling,
listening to the bugs dying and the distant love sounds.

In the morning, I rise early and drive to Biloxi for supplies:
croissants, real coffee, fresh butter, Glenna's favourite marmalade, a *Times-Picayune*, white napkins. While I am making breakfast, I hear her stirring at the other end of the
house. I hear the shower running, then I hear her soft voice
singing. I can't make out the words, but I know it's a hymn.
Her family were Seventh Day Adventists ("The Cult," as

Mama used to say – she always disapproved of Glenna's singing and religion), and, though she's fallen away from the church, she still remembers the old songs when she's feeling relaxed and alone.

I am stirring my coffee, listening to Glenna, when Mrs. Firbank knocks at the back door. She has come to complain about the young couple in Cabin Six. If there is anything Mr. and Mrs. Firbank (to think that when I was young I used to call them Uncle Ted and Aunt Netty) cannot stand, it is young people having fun on their vacation. During the Firbanks' annual two-week stay, Cabin Eight becomes a veritable black hole of joy, and I am under constant pressure to turn Gulf Haven into a police state.

Needless to say they are great friends of Mama's and there is much toing and froing between their respective lairs where they drink and reflect together upon the bitter emptiness of life. Though my father willed Gulf Haven to me, all three of them regard me as a form of renter, a temporary interloper with no idea how to run a successful business.

Mrs. Firbank believes that something "funny" was going on in Cabin Six last night. She has noted a "peculiar odour" and heard "nigger music" played on the radio. Above all she wishes me to demand to see the young couple's marriage licence.

"Maybe I'd better get Sheriff Buck to run their tag number through the computer," I suggest, having learned from past experience never to argue a moral point with a guest.

When I finally get the door shut on Mrs. Firbank's righteous back, I turn to find Glenna sitting at the table with a knowing smile on her lips. She's wearing the white sweatpants and black blouse, but her pink feet are bare and her hair is swathed in a towel turban.

The most difficult thing about life at Gulf Haven for Glenna was dealing with people like the Firbanks. She much preferred helping Effie, our black chambermaid, serving the public. She could never adapt to my style of secretive politeness; "mealy-mouthed" is what she called it. Though mostly we shared a sense that it was all a silent comedy – even at the worst moments she could flash me a special smile as if to say, "I know what you're up to, you."

To see her smiling now in our kitchen feels like a gift from God, and I turn quickly to hide the mist that comes to my eyes. It is like old times, except that I dare not say a word (remembering what happened to Brent) and Glenna will not speak to me. I am almost paralyzed with fear and hope. I know she is capable of leaving again the minute my back is turned, the first mistake I make.

Out the window I see Mama conversing with the Firbanks next to their vintage Dodge Satellite. They keep looking in our direction and I know Mama is telling them the good news about Glenna. Mama has a glass and a cigarette in one hand and a claw-hammer in the other. The claw-hammer is a constant silent rebuke to me. She is always "repairing" something on the property and holding up her own cottage as evidence that she doesn't have a moment to spare to look after herself.

The truth is that Effie's husband Bubba and I keep the place in pretty good trim with very little effort. We are always trying to fix up Mama's cottage, but she throws a fit every time we go near it. She says Bubba "watches" her. It took us three years to remove a limb that fell on her roof during Hurricane Camille.

When I turn back to Glenna with the tray of croissants and marmalade, her face has gone cold again and she won't look at me. She sips her coffee but refuses to eat the meal I have made for her. This is a riddle, for she always used to be a hearty eater. Yet, if anything, she is more ravishing now than when she left, her body a geometry of angles and curves like one of those magazine models. Her breasts are like pale ghosts beneath the black cloth of her blouse.

I bite my tongue to keep from saying, "A body can't live on coffee alone." I sense that this would be precisely the wrong thing to say, almost a spell for getting her out of the house.

Presently my watch alarm sounds and it is time for me to go outside again to supervise the help. In fact there is little supervision to be done. Only I must be on hand to prevent Effie from barging in on the young couple in Cabin Six. Effie is a large, lusty woman who delights in breaking in on guests, especially when they are in the throes of passion, sometimes scaring them half to death with her booming laughter. She is a great displayer of used condoms and is always on the lookout for signs of perverse practices.

As I stand to leave, I allow myself a quick glance at my wife who is staring at the wall. Her expression is a sermon of loss and it is with great difficulty that I restrain myself from throwing my arms around her. But I am prevented by the fact that I do not know where she's been or what she wants or what she has lost. She's become a complete mystery to me. With Glenna now, anything is possible.

At 11 A.M. I am sitting on a stool at the Dunkin' Donut, Bubba on my right, Brent Wardlow on my left. The place is crowded with fishermen, shopkeepers, resort owners, hardware salesmen, and local clergy all shouting, laughing, and gesticulating. Everyone by now knows that Glenna is back and I am the centre of attention. The booths and counter are alive with noisy speculation on causes, motives, itineraries, and outcomes. Each new topic is quickly exhausted for lack of evidence. Questions and variations on questions break out and spread across the room like grassfires and I am continually saying, "I just don't know!"

Everyone understands my unwillingness to make direct inquiries of Glenna herself. Besides Brent, many men in Ragged Point have lost wives permanently or temporarily in this way. Intuitively, we all understand that this is an age of adventure for women. We are learning to respect their privacy while, at the same time, they are learning the special pain that goes with being a free and responsible person. It is not easy – it is like watching some great and beautiful creature being born.

The facts are these: two years ago, almost to the day, Glenna slipped out of the house at dawn and walked over to Moody's Fish Restaurant to catch the morning Greyhound for Biloxi. She wore a cotton print dress with a white belt and carried, according to Darrell Moody who sold her the ticket, an alligator-skin purse I had given her for Christmas and a Land's End canvas briefcase we shared for business purposes. She had seemed, Darrell recalls now, especially cheerful, and, with her coral lipstick and a faint trail of eyeliner, "so pretty she hurt your eyes."

From Biloxi, she went to Tennessee – Sheriff Buck and I interrogated a Biloxi ticket agent who swore she had paid for as far as Nashville. Lois Motherwell, Andy Motherwell's mother and a Grand Ol' Opry fan, claimed to have spotted her at a Merle Haggard concert that night, though Sheriff Buck tends to discount her story on the grounds that she did not think of it until three or four months later.

But we do not know where she went after Nashville (we know she left because the sheriff and I turned that city upside down searching for her). And except for a Tennessee state trooper who thought he could recall "a pretty lady with a briefcase hitchhiking, heading north," we had no other clue.

By 11:30 we have reached a consensus plan of action – I am to use my insider position, with as much circumspection as possible, to add whatever snippets I can glean to this precious store of information, using my eyes and ears but not my mouth ("like a fly on the wall," someone says, I forget who).

Bubba swears he will tell me anything Effie lets drop though we agree he must not appear to "pump" her. Sheriff Buck advises getting a look at that United Airlines bag for baggage tickets. Sand caught in the seams might indicate that she has been to the seashore. Brent Wardlow suggests checking her clothing when I do the laundry (the suggestion is greeted with guffaws of laughter and Brent turns a little red with irritation) – for store tags or dry-cleaning stubs.

Above all, I must not arouse her suspicion. Everyone agrees that Glenna must be the first to speak. I must not appear upset or condescending. Brent says I ought to act "as normal as possible."

As Bubba and I stroll along the breakwater toward Gulf Haven, my spirits begin to rise. I am full of the brotherhood of men and the good wishes of my neighbours; I feel a sudden rush of belonging, of being one with a community of people who know me and like me. Then suddenly I have the thought, "Glenna's back."

She's back, but she could leave again. It hits me like a blow. I grasp Bubba by the shoulder and make him stop. Though he is coloured, he is about the best friend I have, next to Glenna. When he looks into my face, he understands.

"Sure 'nough," he says, clapping his pink palms with glee. "Sure 'nough," he hoots.

He takes my hand and leads me for a step to two in a little tango dance. The noon sun catches us there, freezes us in its opaque whiteness, two men dancing under the cabbage palms. She's back.

At Gulf Haven a scene awaits us which brings my heart to my mouth. The Firbanks' Satellite is parked across the gravel drive next to the neon sign, forming a roadblock. Someone has tried to run my utility van past the Satellite and got stuck half-in, half-out of the azaleas. The driver's door is open and the engine running.

A Datsun station wagon belonging to the young couple in Cabin Six has nosed up to the Satellite and the young couple are standing next to it, waiting to drive out. The Firbanks are standing at the bottom of the step, watching Mama and Effie who are grappling together at the door. Mama has a death grip on the handle latch; Effie is trying to peel her fingers off.

"You leave her alone, Mizz Toby," says Effie, as Bubba and I run up. "You leave Glenna alone."

"Let go of'n my hand," gasps Mama, who has bad lungs and is turning blue from the exercise. Seeing me, she suddenly abandons the struggle.

"Never mind," she says, her eyes savage with triumph. "E.A.'s here. E.A., she's locked the door from the inside. She's locked us out. She tried to leave in your van but Ted foxed her."

Glenna is not in sight though her presence is as palpable as the odour of peach blossoms. I know she is just inside the door and can hear every word we say.

"I believe it's *our* van, Mama," I begin. "Just as much hers as mine. That's the way the ownership reads anyway."

"E.A. Toby, you can't be serious. She was going to steal it and run off again. She just came back for more of your money."

Now I do not know why Mama hates Glenna so much (maybe it is only that my wife is still young and has all her hopes before her), or why she is so down on life. But there have been times in the past – maybe once a day, in fact, since I was ten – when I have considered murdering her for the benefit of mankind. And it takes all my powers of self-restraint at this moment to keep from committing a crime against a person I love, for which the state now gives "lethal injections."

"Ted," I say, turning to the Firbanks, "you think you could move your car out of the way now? I appreciate the help and all, but the other guests here want to get out."

Then I quickly slip around by the rock path to the side door, hurrying to get inside before Mama catches her breath and tries to follow me.

A shadow slips down the hall into the guest bedroom as I step through the kitchen door and lock it. The house is silent except that I am almost sure I can hear Glenna's heart beating, shut away from me. Then I notice a note on the kitchen table. Trembling, I begin to read.

"E.A. I wasn't stealing the van. I just wanted – "

The letters slope off drunkenly as though she lost heart with her explanation, as though she realized how futile and humiliating it was to make any explanation at all. But it is still a note, a message addressed to me. It is something. And I suddenly forget myself and stride down the hall. I pause at the guest bedroom door. Listen. She is crying again, but muffling it. I can hardly stand the pain she is in.

I take a ballpoint from the plastic penholder in my breastpocket and scribble beneath her words: "G. You don't have to tell me." I add the phrase "Welcome home," but black it out. Then "I love you," and black that out too. My pen slips in my sweaty fingers and skips as I try to write against the door. I end the note with "Love, E.A." and leave it at that. Then I knock softly and push through.

Glenna is sitting on the edge of the bed, hunched over with a pillow cradled in her arms. When she sees me coming through the door, she makes a little gasp and drops something from her hand into the open United Airlines bag. Then she straightens up, pushes her hair back defiantly and rubs the heel of her hand across her upper lip to wipe away the moisture. I hand her the note.

She stares at it for three or five minutes. Maybe she is trying to make out the blacked-out phrases. Maybe this is just an excuse not to look at me. Anyway, I know it doesn't take three or five minutes to read a six-word message.

Despite my anguish, I take advantage of the moments to look around the room. There are some female things, combs, hair dryer, Tampax, conditioners, and shampoos on the bathroom counter. But beyond that she doesn't seem to have unpacked anything. I stare at the airline bag, pondering its secrets. In fact, there are a couple of baggage tickets and I memorize the codes to give to Sheriff Buck.

Glenna begins to rummage in her pocketbook. I offer her a tissue from the box on the dresser, but she shakes her head no without looking at me. Then I hold out one of my pens which she takes. She turns the note over and begins to write.

"E.A.," I read, standing next to her, then she stops to think.

Inadvertently, my hand brushes her shoulder. A wisp of her hair trails across my knuckles. Nothing more. And it wasn't anything I meant to do, not a caress or a liberty I was taking. But she twists away.

She writes in a burst, "E.A. Don't touch me. Don't come in this room again. Don't expect anything from me."

I reel backward toward the door, wounded, sweaty, feeling like a fool. My eyes sting. But I glance back once before I leave and she is staring at me, not at me (when I think about it), but through me, as though I weren't there. She presses a tear from her cheek with a forefinger and I see the tan line where her wedding ring used to be. She sees that I see and, pressing the hand into her lap, covers it with the other.

Her eyes stare back at me, neither angry nor apologetic. Suddenly I see how she has changed. Though she trembles and tears spring to her eyes, she carries herself with a new and unaccountable dignity as though she has learned some secret about sorrow and tragedy.

Later, in the office, after I have recovered, and checked in two new sets of guests, I call Sheriff Buck with the baggage codes. At first, he's boyishly excited, but then he catches the grave, neutral tone in my voice and senses that I have begun to stop caring about the rabbit hunt into Glenna's past. In ten minutes, he telephones back.

"Shit, E.A.," he says, in a tone of disbelief, "she went to the North Pole. She went clear up into Canada. Way up, E.A. One of those tickets was for Montreal. But the other was for some diddly little place in Indian country. I can't even find it on the road atlas. There ain't nothing but ice and snow where Glenna's been."

I hang up, not wishing to hear more. Imagining my wife hitchhiking north from the summer heat of Nashville, away from everything she'd ever known, north into another country, to where the people and houses begin to thin out, north beyond where the trees stop, to a desert of ice and rock. I take out the *National Geographic Atlas* I keep in the office and look up the place Sheriff Buck has named. It is a dot on an otherwise empty island far above the Arctic Circle. Someone has drawn an X over it with red ink. It makes my backbone shiver to see it.

During the night I am afflicted with strange nightmares. As soon as my head hits the pillow, I find myself in a world of twisting, heaving ice. Everywhere I turn, leads of grey water open up with a fearful ripping sound. In the distance I make out a figure, steadily drifting away from me. A great white bear looms above her – I feel sure to take her in its ugly embrace and bite her head off. I scream, "Glenna, Glenna!"

When I awake, I am crying into my pillow and my wife stands in the doorway, her face set in an expression of stern and terrible pity. She says nothing but continues to stare at me as though trying to puzzle something out. I am all twisted up in sheets sodden with sweat and for a time I am uncertain whether this is still the dream or not. Glenna wears pale blue baby-doll pyjamas which I had given her on a birthday and which she must have retrieved from our dresser drawer earlier in the day. Poised in moonlight, dressed like that, she is all legs and eyes. The odours of her shampoo and baby powder are just pure pangs of nostalgia worse than any pain of loss I have felt since she left.

I want to cry out again. I want to pretend I am still asleep so that under the guise of unconsciousness I might tell her all my most secret fears, my nights of loneliness, my mute love. But presently, with Glenna standing there, I really do fall asleep and when I wake up again, solitary in our nuptial Posturpedic, it is to the sound of the van door slamming shut and the engine catching. The terrors of my dreams come back and for a while I cannot move, only listen as the van sound disappears in the distance.

When I finally stumble out through the office into the breezeway in my boxer shorts, the morning sun is like a drop of blood on the horizon and my mother is standing next to the Firbanks' banana yellow Satellite with a cigarette and her claw-hammer and a look of silent judgement on her face.

The men at the Dunkin' Donut are constrained and quiet-spoken. It is clear from Ben Wardlow's stricken eyes that he believes Ragged Point has lost another wife for good. Sheriff Buck is practically in tears. He had, he says, staked out Gulf Haven for most of the night half-expecting Glenna to make a break for it after the way Mama treated her. He had intended to flag her down on the coast road and remonstrate with her. But at the last moment something held him back.

"It just din't feel right, E.A., trailing her in the dark. Gawd, I hate it. It peels in my guts. But she's got her own life to live, you know what I mean? I'm sorry, bud."

I understand. I nod and sip my coffee, trying to pretend that the moisture in my eyes is because my tongue is burned. Even at a distance, Sheriff Buck has sensed Glenna's new, inviolable dignity. I tell them about the *National Geographic Atlas* and the tiny red "X" beside that place name.

"There'd be Eskimos," says Elder Ottman, the Baptist minister, "maybe a mission or a government store, maybe even one of those Royal Canadian Mounties." Eyebrows shoot up. "Eskimos – means 'eaters of raw meat,' " he adds.

"Gawd," says Bubba, spluttering into a napkin.

An uncomfortable silence follows. I have not mentioned my nightmares nor the vision of Glenna standing in the doorway in her pyjamas. Naturally the men suspect something of the like but they are sensitive enough not to press for intimate details. It is all so painful – every word, every silence is understood to be a message on many levels of commiseration, shared hopelessness, awe, and fear. There is a restlessness amongst the women of Ragged Point as there is amongst the women of the nation, as though they had all inhaled some passing interplanetary dust.

Elder Ottman's wife, for example, recently stopped watching soap operas and began to check books on easel painting out of the town library. Lois Motherwell, Andy's mother, has moved a typewriter into the boathouse, neglecting her duties in the dry-goods store, and claims – though many of us believe she is only trying to divert attention from her true object – to be writing a sex novel. Five young mothers (including two blacks) have hired a babysitter together and spend their afternoons hang-gliding off Rattler Peak.

To tell the truth, when their husbands relate these exploits mornings at the Dunkin' Donut, it's not difficult to detect a note of pride in their voices. As well as of fear. For who knows (this is the common feeling, never expressed in so many words) where it will end?

Our silent meditation is shattered suddenly by the arrival of Stu Bollis, the man who drives the fish delivery truck. Horn blaring, he nearly dents Sheriff Buck's municipal Plymouth in his rush to park. He climbs the steps three at a time and bursts through the door with a grin.

"She ain't gone, E.A.!" he exclaims. "She ain't gone. I knew you'd think she was gone t'minute I saw your van."

"Where is she, Stu?" I ask, trying to conceal my excitement, trying to shake loose the skin of ice congealing over my thoughts.

"Down at the point, parked in the pines. I seen her out on the rocks. She's got her pants rolled up to her knees and her shoes off and she's just looking out at the water. I reckon she is thinking, don't you?"

I squeeze his wrist for thanks and nod to Sheriff Buck. He grabs his Stetson as he and Bubba come after me. He squeals the tires getting out of the parking lot, lays rubber down Water Street, pops the siren once for the stoplight at Jefferson Davis, then hits sixty-five leaving town. At the Ragged Point turn-off, he pulls a U-turn and drops me on the gravel. He and Bubba give me the thumbs up as they head out. Bubba gives a little wave.

I walk nervously through the pines where the van is parked, past the log barrier, picnic tables, and wire trash baskets, and out onto the rocks. Tide is out. Pelicans and laughing gulls cruise a hair's breadth above the waves. Glenna is seated just as Stu described her, only there is a tiny pile of fresh sand dollars drying next to her hip and her feet are sandy and wet.

Hearing me scrambling over the rocks, she looks up and smiles. She doesn't say anything, mind you, but she smiles. And the smile says she is pleased to see me and that she understands the whole community effort it took to get me there. We both look toward town and see Sheriff Buck's Plymouth creeping along Water Street so that he and Bubba can keep us in sight as long as possible. Glenna shakes her head and giggles, then lays back on her elbows and preens in the sun. Her expression says, "Oh my, I had forgotten how much I loved the heat," a sentiment I can understand, considering where she has been.

But the look also fills me with sadness for what I have lost and in spite of my resolve to keep things upbeat I suddenly have to put my hand over my face to suppress a sob. It is purely natural to want things to stay the way they are. I love the new Glenna, maybe even more than the old, but she is different, grander, more mysterious, more separate. And it suddenly occurs to me that, though Glenna has gone north into the vast cold emptiness of Canada, I also have been on a trip, a voyage of loneliness on which all the ports are familiar but the boat is empty.

But then I become aware of Glenna's hand touching my own on the tidal rock. It is an electric gesture that sends a thrill into my bones. She covers my hand with hers, then takes it up and laces her fingers between mine. I dare not look at her. I dare not say a word. I dare not even return pressure for pressure against her slim and fragile digits.

The warmth of her touch sends new terrors coursing through the veins and arteries of my body. It burns against me like some holy relic left by martyrs (though I am not a religious person I have read about this sort of thing in *Reader's Digest Condensed Classics*).

Presently, my wife stands and pulls me up, though I still have not looked into her face. I keep my eyes steadily fixed on the gulf, with its comforting emptiness festering under the sun. All is vanity the slapping waves tell us, all is flesh and the flesh abideth not. We collect the sand dollars in my baseball cap and walk back to the van. Somewhere between the water and the van she takes my hand again.

Gulf Haven is just as we left it except that the office door stands open and our house has the atmosphere of a desolate cave. It is also somewhat unusual not to see the Firbanks sitting in their lawn chairs next to the Satellite, drinking from highball glasses and casting sour and disapproving glances at everything through their aviator Ray-Bans. Glenna and I are setting the sand dollars on the stone porch to dry when we are disturbed, suddenly, by the sound of a chair scraping inside.

When I go there to check, I find Mama and the Firbanks seated at the kitchen table. There are drink glasses and bottles on the Lazy Susan and the air is choked with tobacco smoke. Worst of all, in the centre of the table, Glenna's airline bag has been turned inside out and there are a number of items on display. *Evidence* is the word that comes to mind as I see the look on Mama's face.

Three pairs of eyes bore in on slim, blonde Glenna, as she slips into the room behind me. The eyes are like steel nail heads. And my wife takes a position a little apart, making no effort to retake my hand. I feel like a judge, or that I am unwillingly about to have some terrible truth thrust upon me.

The objects on the table are foreign and add to my confusion. At first nothing is recognizable. Pieces of cloth-ing made out of animal skins with leather laces. An ivory box with tiny black figures etched on the cover. A pair of high fur boots. Things difficult to connect with Glenna in her Princess Di haircut and white sweatpants. They are about as alien as you can get in Ragged Point.

Clearing her throat, Mama advances an object toward the centre of the table with her claw-hammer, like a crou-pier sliding a pile of chips. It is the strangest thing I have ever seen – a tiny jet-black statue with ivory accessories, minutely carved and polished in such a way that the stone seems to billow and fold itself into whitened creases. I look more closely in spite of myself, knowing that Mama has engineered this moment, my discovery, my acquiescence in judgement, though I don't quite know what the judgement is yet.

I peer at the curious statue – there are two people, a couple, Eskimos I can tell. The man (I can make out a wispy moustache and his long lank hair) holds a barbed ivory spear with a piece of twine attached to the end of it. Next to him stands a woman and a dog.

My body gives an involuntary shiver and the hair begins to crawl up the back of my neck. There is something mutely, uncomfortably intimate about the statue, and familiar. The man clutches the woman's hand; the woman holds the dog on a twine leash. Their eyes are fixed on some icy horizon – they exude an aura of strength and primitiveness, as though they had just stepped out of the Stone Age, from a time when the human race was younger, freer and closer to the natural world from which it had sprung.

Then I see with a jolt that the woman is my wife, that the carver has etched her hair to make it seem blonde, that he has captured in some crudely perfect manner her look of hopeful dignity.

I begin to sweat – this is the secret of the secret, a story carved in stone. The statue is a thing of burning beauty, a piece of living rock, with warm polished surfaces that catch the light from the windows and send pulses of energy through the room. I cannot tear my eyes away from it, its implications for Glenna twisting and swirling in my mind like an ice-choked sea. Nothing holds. I have only a sense of her passion, her wonder, her strange unerring certitude, and the undeniable fact that she has come back, that she has torn herself away from this man, this frozen world, to return to Ragged Point.

Almost hypnotized by the force of this revelation, I am only half-aware of Mama as she stubs out her cigarette on a saucer and brandishes the claw-hammer. I have only time to form the words "No, Mama. No!" but the words die on my lips. With a hiss of rage, she smashes the hammer down, striking the statue squarely, shattering and pulverizing it. Dust and shards fly everywhere, onto the floor, the kitchen counter, the Firbanks' laps, clinking against bottle glass. Something strikes my chest and, dumbly, without thinking, I stoop to retrieve the tiny ivory spear.

In the morning, as we pack the van, an air of celebration, of dignified festivity settles over Gulf Haven. Bubba and Effie help carry loads to the van – I have hired them as permanent self-managing managers with salary, profit-sharing, and the house which they can live in. Needless to say Mama is against this, but since destroying Glenna's statue she has been unusually quiet. She and the Firbanks skulk in the pine shadows down by her cabin like a nest of timid viperish snakes.

Cars have been pulling up since first thing, disgorging well-wishers and helpers. Something is happening to Ragged Point, it is generally agreed. For once there is a feeling of hope, a feeling that things may turn out all right. And the forces of love and adventure, of passion and courage and virtue are in the ascendant.

Elder Ottman returned home the evening before to find his wife hunched over a stack of books as high as her waist on the desert regions of Australia. Sheriff Buck allows as that his wife Trudy wants to pay a visit up in Canada one of these days. Three of the five hang-gliding mothers are pregnant again and speaking of taking their unborn infants on a walking tour of Nepal before the season is out.

Glenna still does not talk much. In my arms last night she told me a little about the place where we were going. The Eskimos, she said, do not use that name for themselves. Instead, they are Inuit, which means the People. Some of the very old ones were alive before the first white men came. For centuries they thought they were the only human beings on earth.

"When they meet a stranger," she said, "they run forward holding their bare hands in the air, shouting, 'We are friends. See, we have no knives. We mean you no harm. We are friends.'"

She said they have eighty-nine words for snow, and that in the long summer day they will stand on the shore for hours staring out to sea. Sometimes they are watching for seals or walrus to hunt, but other times they are just staring, staring into the awesome emptiness. Itlulik, the man in the statue, also the man who carved it, is a hunter and an *anguloq*, a sort of medicine man.

"I loved him, E.A.," she said, holding me tight against her breast so I wouldn't turn away. "I wanted to tell you. I didn't want you to find out like that. I wanted to tell you, but I didn't know if you loved me enough to hear me out.

"I missed you the whole time. He's not kind like you. He's fierce. Even the other Inuit don't trust an *anguloq*. I told him I had to come back and find you again."

Before getting into the van for the last time, I embrace each of my friends from the Dunkin' Donut. We are brothers, fellow unravellers of the mysteries of existence. They wish me well. They tell me to send them back messages, so that the world will seem a little more clear to them. It is a sad yet happy moment. Bubba dances me a step or two; Effie crushes me against her enormous breasts and laughs.

I don't know where we are going really. I have to trust the luminous stranger beside me. For courage I press my shirt pocket, where amongst the pens I carry Itlulik's tiny ivory spear which my wife has let me keep. In my mind I practise the words of greeting which in my heart I have always known.

"I am a friend. See, I have no knife. I mean you no harm. I am a friend."

ABOUT THE AUTHORS

ANDRÉ ALEXIS was born in 1957. He has had fiction published in *Descant, Noovo Masheen,* and *Ambit* (UK). He is currently a member of Tarragon Theatre's Playwrights Unit (1989-1990). He has lived in Toronto since 1987.

GLEN ALLEN was born in Toronto. He completed high school there and worked for several years in the construction trades. Since 1966, he has been a newspaper reporter, magazine editor and correspondent and, briefly, a "Morningside" radio producer. He has worked in various parts of Canada, the U.S., Europe, and Latin America. Between 1979 and 1981 he taught English at a foreign language institute in southern China. His short stories have appeared in journals, including "*north*" and *Canadian Dimension.* He has had poetry published in *Fiddlehead.* He won the National Newspaper Award for Feature Writing in 1982 and a National Magazine Award in 1988. He is currently bureau chief for *Maclean's* magazine in the Atlantic provinces. He lives in Dartmouth, Nova Scotia.

MARUSIA BOCIURKIW was born in Edmonton, a first-generation Ukrainian-Canadian. She is a writer, video-filmmaker, and feminist activist, living in Toronto. Her articles and short stories have appeared in *Fuse* magazine, *Rites*, *Kinesis*, *Fireweed*, and an upcoming Women's Press fiction anthology. Her videos and films are screened at festivals across North America.

VIRGIL BURNETT was trained in the visual arts and has worked as an illustrator for many publishers in many places. His short fiction has appeared in *Harpers* and *Penthouse*, and he has published poetry in numerous magazines, including *Harpers*, *The Chicago Review*, *Descant*, *Canadian Fiction Magazine*, and *The Malahat Review*. His novel, *Towers at the Edge of a World*, was published in 1980. Since then, he has divided his time between drawing and writing. He has recently completed a play, *The Red Box*, and is presently at work on a suite of stories.

MARGARET DYMENT is a writer and teacher of creative writing, currently living in Ottawa but about to move to Victoria, B.C. Her stories and poems have appeared in a number of literary magazines and anthologies, including *Best Canadian Stories*. She is now completing a book of short stories with the help of a grant from the Ontario Arts Council.

CYNTHIA FLOOD'S short stories have appeared in a wide range of Canadian literary magazines, in five anthologies, on the CBC, and in film. Her first collection of short fiction, *The Animals in their Elements*, was published in 1987 by Talon Books of Vancouver. She is currently writing a linked sequence of stories with the working title of *The Small Colonial Girl*. Cynthia Flood lives in Vancouver.

DOUGLAS GLOVER was born and raised on a tobacco farm in southwestern Ontario. He is the author of two short story collections, *The Mad River* and *Dog Attempts to Drown Man in*

Saskatoon, and two novels, *Precious* and *The South Will Rise at Noon*. His stories have appeared in *Best Canadian Stories* (1985, 1987, 1988) and *Best American Short Stories* (1989). "Story Carved in Stone" will appear in a new collection, *I, a Young Man Called Early to the Wars*, to be published by Viking in January 1991. Douglas Glover divides his time between Waterford, Ontario, and Saratoga Springs, New York.

TERRY GRIGGS was born in Little Current, Manitoulin Island in 1951 and lived there until 1968. She has published short stories in a number of periodicals and anthologies, including *The Canadian Forum, The Malahat Review, Room of One's Own, The New Quarterly, The New Press Anthology #1, The Macmillan Anthology* 1 and 3, and *Street Songs 1: New Voices in Fiction*. A collection of her work is to be published in the fall by The Porcupine's Quill. She lives in London, Ontario.

RICK HILLIS's book of poems *The Blue Machines of Night* was a finalist for the 1989 Gerald Lampert Award. His short story collection *Limbo River* was recently awarded the prestigious Drue Heinz Literature Prize in the U.S. The title story, "Limbo River," which appears in this anthology, was nominated for the Pushcart prize in the U.S. Currently a Stegner Fellow at Stanford University, Rick normally resides in Saskatoon.

THOMAS KING is a Native writer of Cherokee, Greek, and German descent. He is a member of the Native Studies department at the University of Lethbridge and is currently teaching in American Studies at the University of Minnesota. His short stories and poems have appeared in journals in Canada and the U.S. He has co-edited a volume of critical essays on the Native in literature and has edited an anthology of short fiction by Native writers in Canada. His first novel,

Medicine River, appeared earlier this year, and he is the editor of the recently published *All My Relations: An Anthology of Contemporary Canadian Native Fiction*. He is currently working on a second novel and a screenplay.

K.D. MILLER was born in Hamilton, Ontario, and educated at the University of Guelph and the University of British Columbia. Her short fiction has appeared in *The Capilano Review* and *Writ Magazine*. In 1981 she won first prize in the *Flare* Magazine Fiction Competition with the story "Now Voyager." This year, "Inchworm" was awarded third prize in the CBC Literary Competition. K.D. Miller lives in Toronto.

JENNIFER MITTON received her M.F.A. in Creative Writing from the University of British Columbia, where she held a graduate fellowship as well as a number of scholarships. While at UBC she was fiction editor of *Prism international*, an editor of *f.(lip)*, and taught creative writing at Vancouver high schools. From 1984 to 1986 she held a CUSO posting in Nigeria. Jennifer Mitton's stories have been widely published in literary magazines, including *Matrix, Moosehead Anthology, Room of One's Own, The New Quarterly, Canadian Author and Bookman, Prairie Fire, The Malahat Review*, and *Fiddlehead*, and have won several awards. One of her stories is included in the anthology *Engaged Elsewhere: Short Stories by Canadians Abroad*. She received a Canada Council Explorations Grant to research a novel, *Fadimatu*, which she has now completed. Jennifer Mitton lives in Vancouver.

LAWRENCE O'TOOLE was born in Renews, Newfoundland in 1951. "Goin' to Town with Katie Ann" is his second published story, the first, "Mrs. Edstrom Will Be Eighty," appeared in the twentieth-anniversary issue of *Confrontation*. His journalism has appeared in the *New York Times*, the *London Times, New*

York Woman, *Destinations*, *Interview*, and *Entertainment Weekly*, among other publications. He has recently completed a trilogy of novels under the title of *Heart's Longing* set in Newfoundland from the Depression to the present.

KENNETH RADU'S first collection of stories, *The Cost of Living* (The Muses' Co./La Compagnie des Muses), was nominated for the 1988 Governor General's Award for Fiction. His first novel, *Distant Relations* (Oberon), received Quebec's QSPELL prize for best English-language fiction of 1989, and was also nominated for the 1989 W.H. Smith/*Books in Canada* First Novel Award. A second collection of stories, *A Private Performance*, will be published in the fall (1990) by Vehicule Press. Born in Windsor, Ontario, he now lives in Quebec, and has recently completed a draft of his second novel.

JENIFER SUTHERLAND is a writer and broadcaster. Her documentary on schizophrenia, "Family Circles," won three prizes for CBC Radio's "Ideas." "Table Talk" is her second published short story. Jenifer Sutherland lives in Toronto.

WAYNE TEFS was born in Winnipeg and raised in the northwest Ontario towns of Atikokan and Fort Frances. He attended Manitoba, Toronto, and McGill universities, and has taught at Regina, St John's College (Manitoba), and McGill. He has published two novels, *The Cartier Street Contract* and *Figures on a Wharf*, as well as short stories, reviews, and criticism. A novel, *The Canasta Players*, is forthcoming in the fall of 1990. He teaches at St John's-Ravenscourt School in Winnipeg.

ABOUT THE CONTRIBUTING JOURNALS

Border Crossings is a quarterly magazine about the arts, published in Winnipeg. Edited by Robert Enright and Meeka Walsh since its inception in 1983, it has been named "Magazine of the Year" at the Western Magazine Awards for three consecutive years. *Border Crossings* has also won six gold and silver awards at the National Magazine Awards for its fiction and poetry. Submissions and correspondence: 301 – 160 Princess Street, Winnipeg, Manitoba, R3B 1K9.

Canadian Fiction Magazine, founded by Geoff Hancock in 1971, is Canada's oldest literary magazine devoted exclusively to short fiction. Since its first issue it has fostered a national and international awareness of contemporary Canadian fiction in English, in French, and in translation from the unofficial languages of Canada. It has published entire issues devoted to single authors, an ongoing series of interviews with fiction writers, and a "future of fiction" series that encourages discussion about the aesthetics of contemporary innovative fiction. Editor: Geoff Hancock. Submissions and correspondence: Box 946, Station F, Toronto, Ontario, M4Y 2N9.

The Capilano Review is an interdisciplinary magazine which publishes poetry, fiction, drama, and work in the visual arts. From its beginnings over eighteen years ago, *TCR* has sought innovative and experimental work. 1989 was a transitional year, during which the editor's concern was to explore possible directions while sustaining the commitment to excellent new work. *TCR* continues to publish the work of artists and writers whose words and images add to the "fresh seeing" (in Emily Carr's words) through which art revitalizes the spheres of perception and engagement. Submissions and correspondence: 2055 Purcell Way, North Vancouver, B.C., V7J 3H5.

Descant has been committed, since it began in 1970, to presenting new work by both established and emerging writers and artists from Canada and around the world. Recent special-theme issues have focused on writing from Australia and New Zealand, and on the world of film. A wide variety of material is accepted for publication: essays, short fiction, poetry, scenarios, plays, film-scripts, visual essays. *Descant* regularly features work by visual artists and is itself printed by the award-winning printer, Porcupine's Quill. *Descant* has been a recipient of the Litho Awards for book design. Submissions and correspondence: P.O. Box 314, Station P, Toronto, Ontario, M5S 2S8.

Event is published three times a year by Douglas College in New Westminster, B.C. Each issue focuses on fiction, poetry, and reviews. *Event* has won awards for its writing and graphic design. Editor, Dale Zieroth, and Fiction Editor, Maurice Hodgson, say: "We make a distinction between competent craft and writing that inspires access to the reader's imagination." Open to both new and established writers. Submissions and correspondence: P.O. Box 2503, New Westminster, B.C., V3L 5B2.

Fireweed is a feminist quarterly committed to an editorial policy of cultural diversity. Existing for eleven years as a collective organization of women, *Fireweed* is determined to publish literary and cultural works from a feminist grass roots perspective. *Fireweed* accepts unsolicited submissions from all women and does not publish material considered racist, sexist, or homophobic. Guest collectives have produced some of *Fireweed*'s best issues, such as "Class is the Issue," "Lesbiantics," and "Asian Women." *Fireweed* welcomes ideas for future theme issues. For subscription information, or to send in submissions, write to *Fireweed*, P.O. Box 279, Station B, Toronto, Ontario, M5T 2W2, or call (416) 323-9512.

The Malahat Review publishes mainly short fiction and poetry, with some visual art, and essays in special issues. Editor: Constance Rooke; Assistant Editor: Marlene Cookshaw. *Malahat* is published at the University of Victoria, P.O. Box 1700, Victoria, B.C., V8W 2Y2.

The New Quarterly is a lively and unpretentious magazine which promotes new writers and new kinds of writing with a special interest in work which stretches the bounds of realism. We publish poetry, short fiction, and interviews, with occasional special issues on themes and genres in Canadian writing. These have included magic realism, family fictions, and Canadian writing in the Mennonite context. Submissions and correspondence: c/o ELPP, PAS 2082, The University of Waterloo, Waterloo, Ontario, N2L 3G1.

Prairie Fire is a quarterly magazine of contemporary Canadian writing, established in 1978. Regular features include stories, poems, essays, author-interviews, and book reviews. Every summer *Prairie Fire* publishes a fiction issue which contains the work of well-known authors as well as work by writers who are just beginning. Despite its name, *Prairie Fire* publishes work by writers from all regions of the country. General Editor: Andris Taskans; Fiction Editor: Ellen Smythe. Submissions and correspondence: 423 · 100 Arthur Street, Winnipeg, Manitoba, R3B 1H3.

For thirty years, *Prism international* has published work by writers both new and established, Canadian and international. Edited by graduate students of creative writing at the University of British Columbia, *Prism* looks for innovative fiction, poetry, drama, as well as creative non-fiction, in English or English translation. *Prism* also holds an annual fiction contest. Request guidelines or send submissions to: The Editors, *Prism international*, Department of Creative Writing, BUCH E462 – 1866 Main Mall, University of British Columbia, Vancouver, B.C., V6T 1W6.

Quarry Magazine was founded in 1952 on the Queen's University campus and began publishing quarterly in 1964 under the guidance of editors Tom Marshall and Tom Eadie. Other notable editors of *Quarry* have included David Helwig, Michael Ondaatje, Gail Fox, Robert Billings, Bill Barnes, Bronwen Wallace. The magazine is committed to discovering, developing, and publishing new Canadian poets, fiction writers, and playwrights, as well as essay writers and book reviewers. Publisher: Bob Hilderly; Editor: Steven Heighton. Submissions and correspondence: P.O. Box 1061, Kingston, Ontario, K7L 4Y5.

Zymergy, established in Montreal in 1987, is published twice a year and features the best in contemporary poetry and fiction, essays, book reviews, and translations. Editor and Publisher: Sonja A. Skarstedt. Submissions and correspondence: P.O. Box 1746, Place du Parc, Montreal, Quebec H2W 2R7.

Submissions were received from the following journals:

Antigonish Review
(Antigonish, N.S.)

Border Crossings
(Winnipeg, Man.)

Canadian Fiction Magazine
(Toronto, Ont.)

The Capilano Review
(North Vancouver, B.C.)

The Dalhousie Review
(Halifax, N.S.)

Descant
(Toronto, Ont.)

Event
(New Westminster, B.C.)

Exile
(Toronto, Ont.)

The Fiddlehead
(Fredericton, N.B.)

Fireweed
(Toronto, Ont.)

Grain
(Regina, Sask.)

Green's Magazine
(Regina, Sask.)

The Malahat Review
(Victoria, B.C.)

Matrix
(Ste-Anne-de-Bellevue, Que.)

New Quarterly
(Waterloo, Ont.)

NeWest Review
(Saskatoon, Sask.)

Other Voices
(Edmonton, Alta.)

The Pottersfield Portfolio
(Halifax, N.S.)

Prairie Fire
(Winnipeg, Man.)

Prairie Journal of Canadian Literature
(Calgary, Alta.)

Prism international
(Vancouver, B.C.

Quarry
(Kingston, Ont.)

Queen's Quarterly
(Kingston, Ont.)

TickleAce
(St. John's, Nfld.)

The Toronto South Asian Review
(Toronto, Ont.)

University of Windsor Review
(Windsor, Ont.)

Zymergy
(Montreal, Que.)